BABYMOUSE AND FRIENDS*

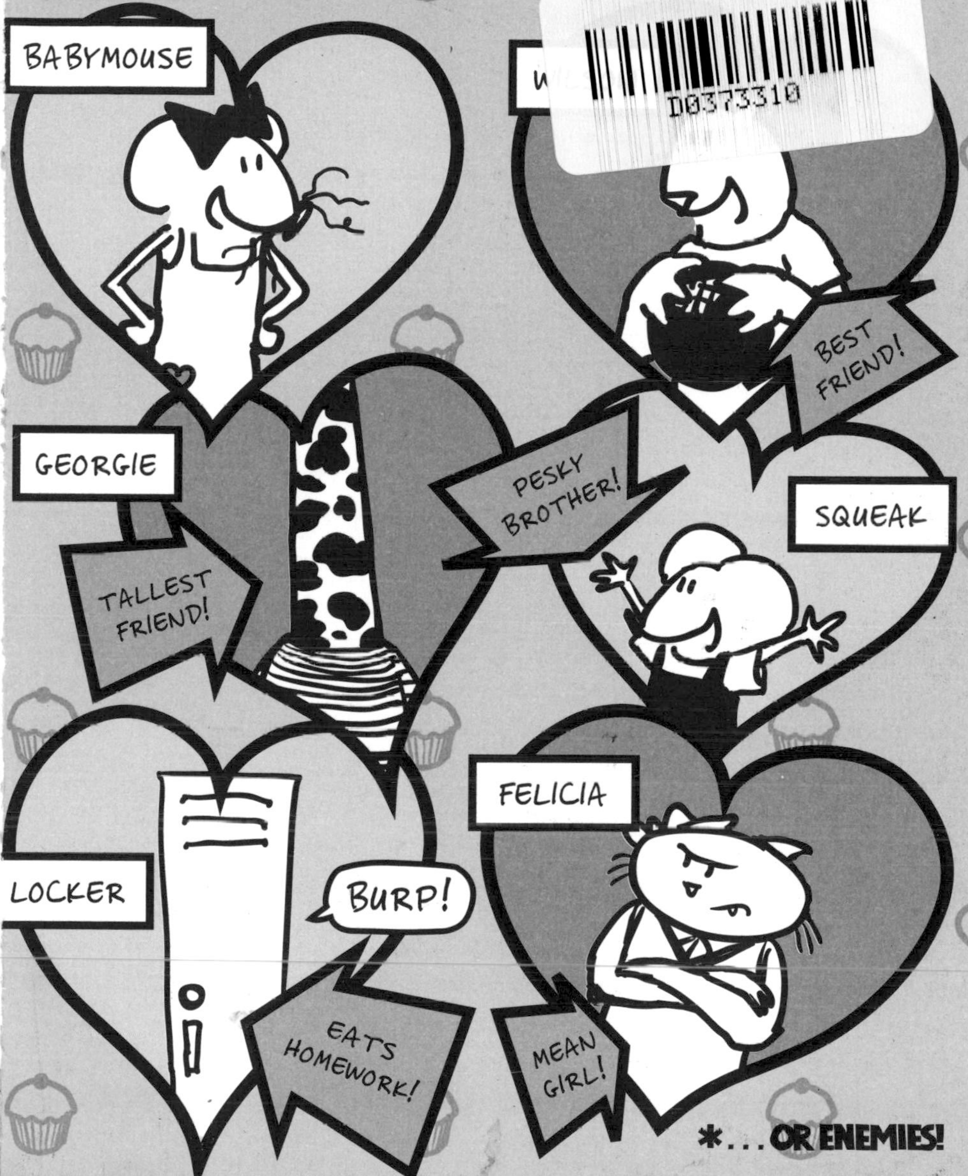
BABYMOUSE
BEST FRIEND!
GEORGIE
TALLEST FRIEND!
PESKY BROTHER!
SQUEAK
LOCKER
BURP!
EATS HOMEWORK!
FELICIA
MEAN GIRL!

*. . . OR ENEMIES!

NO ONE CAN READ JUST ONE!

Be sure to read **ALL** the **BABYMOUSE** books:

#1 BABYMOUSE: Queen of the World!
#2 BABYMOUSE: Our Hero
#3 BABYMOUSE: Beach Babe
#4 BABYMOUSE: Rock Star
#5 BABYMOUSE: Heartbreaker
#6 CAMP BABYMOUSE
#7 BABYMOUSE: Skater Girl
#8 BABYMOUSE: Puppy Love
#9 BABYMOUSE: Monster Mash
#10 BABYMOUSE: The Musical
#11 BABYMOUSE: Dragonslayer
#12 BABYMOUSE: Burns Rubber
#13 BABYMOUSE: Cupcake Tycoon
#14 BABYMOUSE: Mad Scientist
#15 A Very BABYMOUSE Christmas
#16 BABYMOUSE for President
#17 Extreme BABYMOUSE
#18 Happy Birthday, BABYMOUSE

BABYMOUSE
PUPPY LOVE

BY JENNIFER L. HOLM & MATTHEW HOLM

RANDOM HOUSE NEW YORK

EWWW! NOT ON THE COPYRIGHT PAGE!

Copyright © 2007 by Jennifer Holm and Matthew Holm.

Published in the United States by Random House Children's Books, a division of Random House LLC, a Penguin Random House Company, New York.

Random House and the colophon are registered trademarks of Random House LLC.

Visit us on the Web!
randomhouse.com/kids
Babymouse.com

Educators and librarians, for a variety of teaching tools, visit us at RHTeachersLibrarians.com

Library of Congress Cataloging-in-Publication Data
Holm, Jennifer L.
Babymouse : puppy love / by Jennifer & Matthew Holm.
  p. cm. — (Babymouse ; 8)
ISBN: 978-0-375-83990-0 (trade) — ISBN: 978-0-375-93990-7 (lib. bdg.)
l. Graphic novels. I. Holm, Matthew. II. Title. III. Title: Puppy love.
PN6727.H592B325 2007   741.5973—dc22   2007061012

MANUFACTURED IN MALAYSIA   25 24 23 22 21 20 19 18 17 16 15 14 13 12

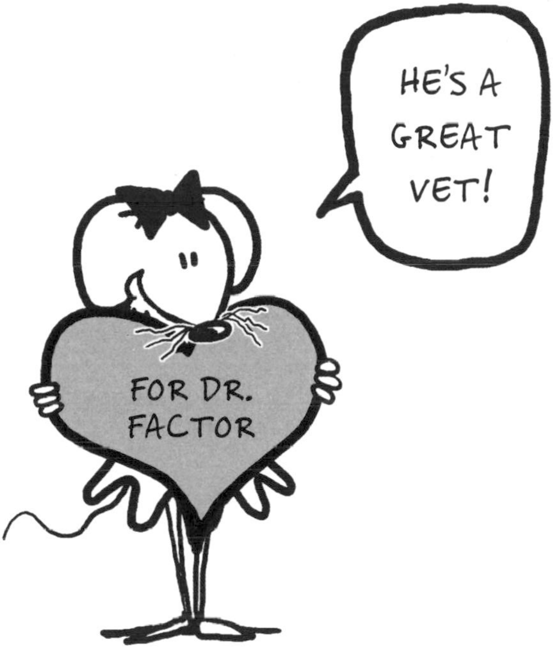
HE'S A GREAT VET!
FOR DR. FACTOR

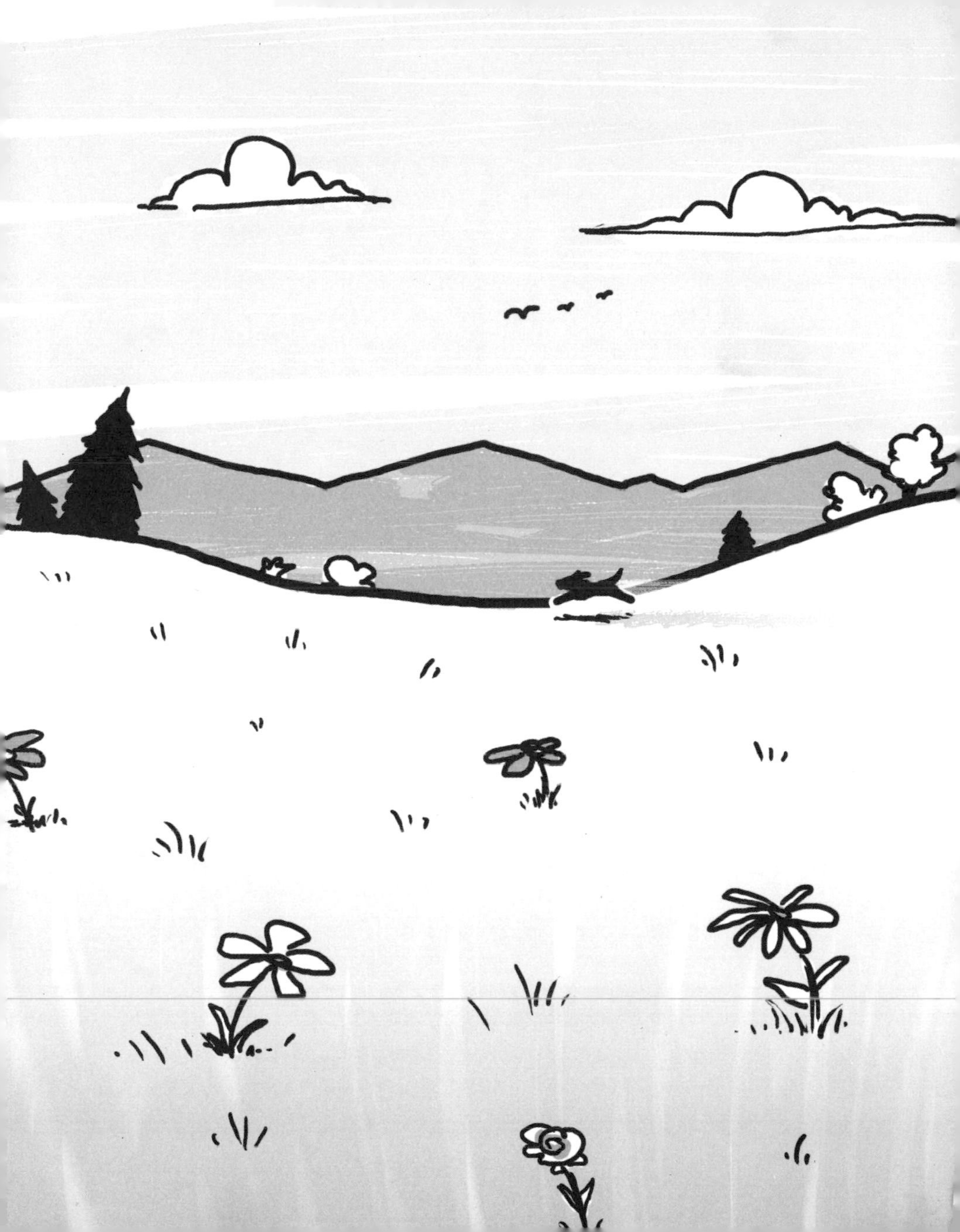

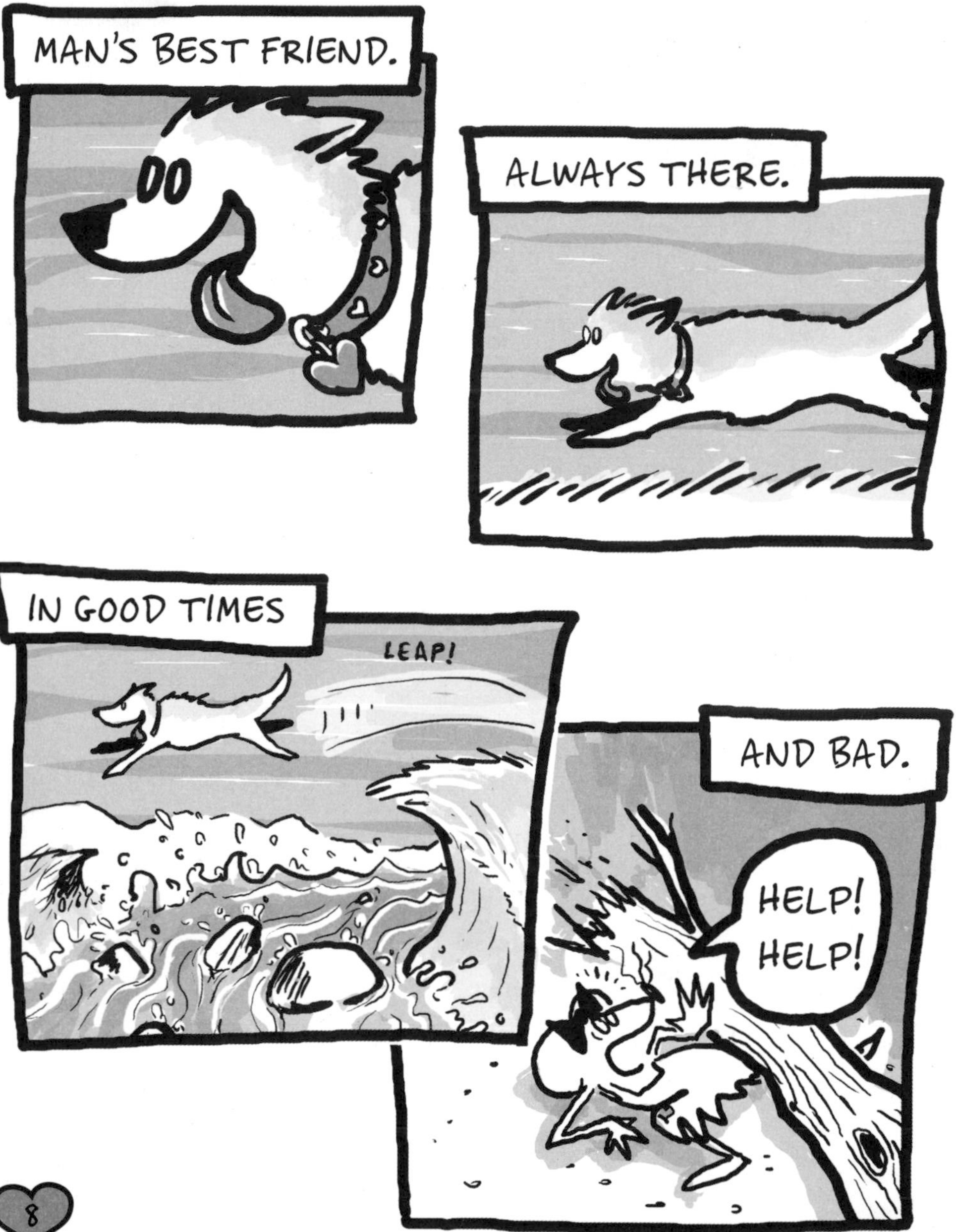
MAN'S BEST FRIEND.
ALWAYS THERE.
IN GOOD TIMES
LEAP!
AND BAD.
HELP! HELP!

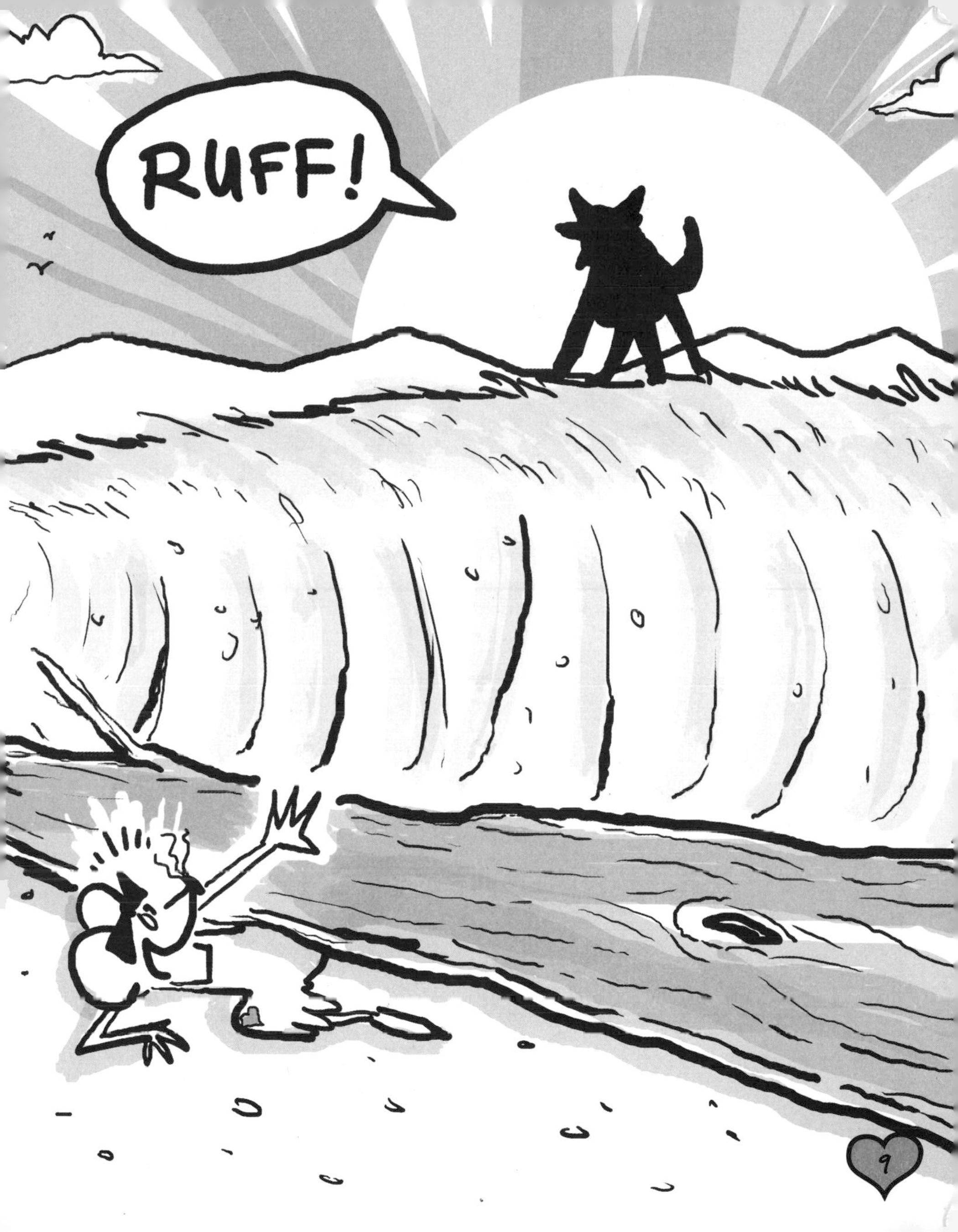
RUFF!

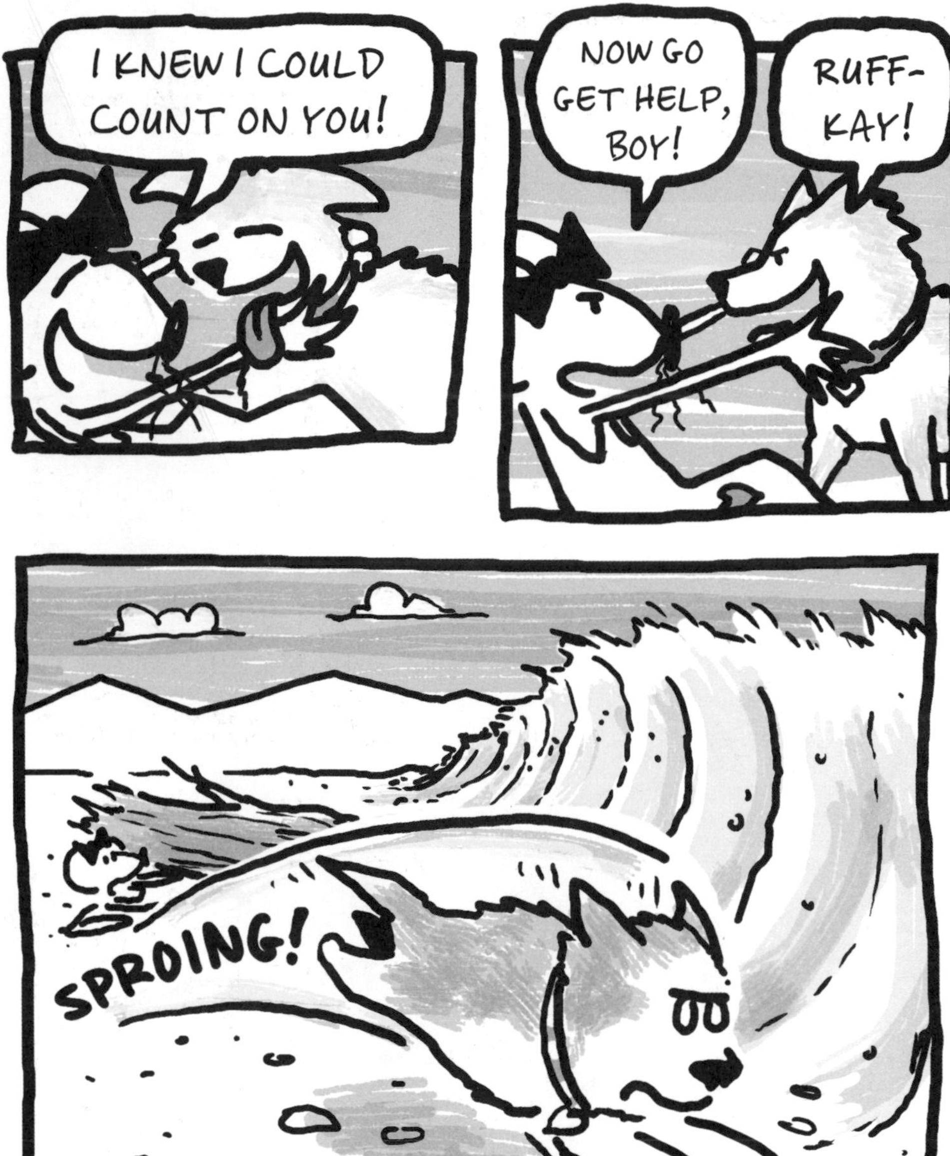
I KNEW I COULD COUNT ON YOU!
NOW GO GET HELP, BOY!
RUFF-KAY!
SPROING!

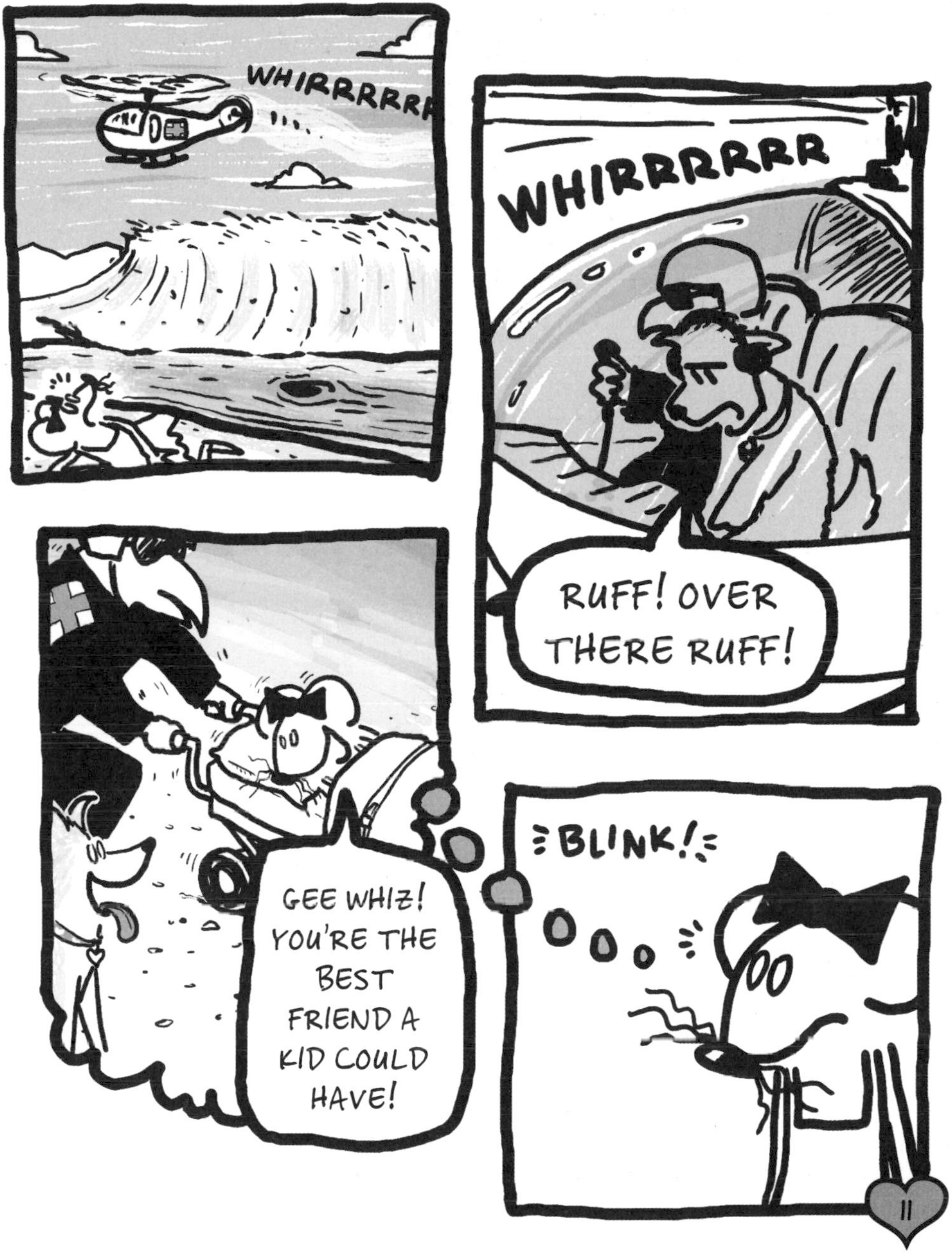
WHIRRRRRRR
WHIRRRRRRR
RUFF! OVER THERE RUFF!
GEE WHIZ! YOU'RE THE BEST FRIEND A KID COULD HAVE!
BLINK!

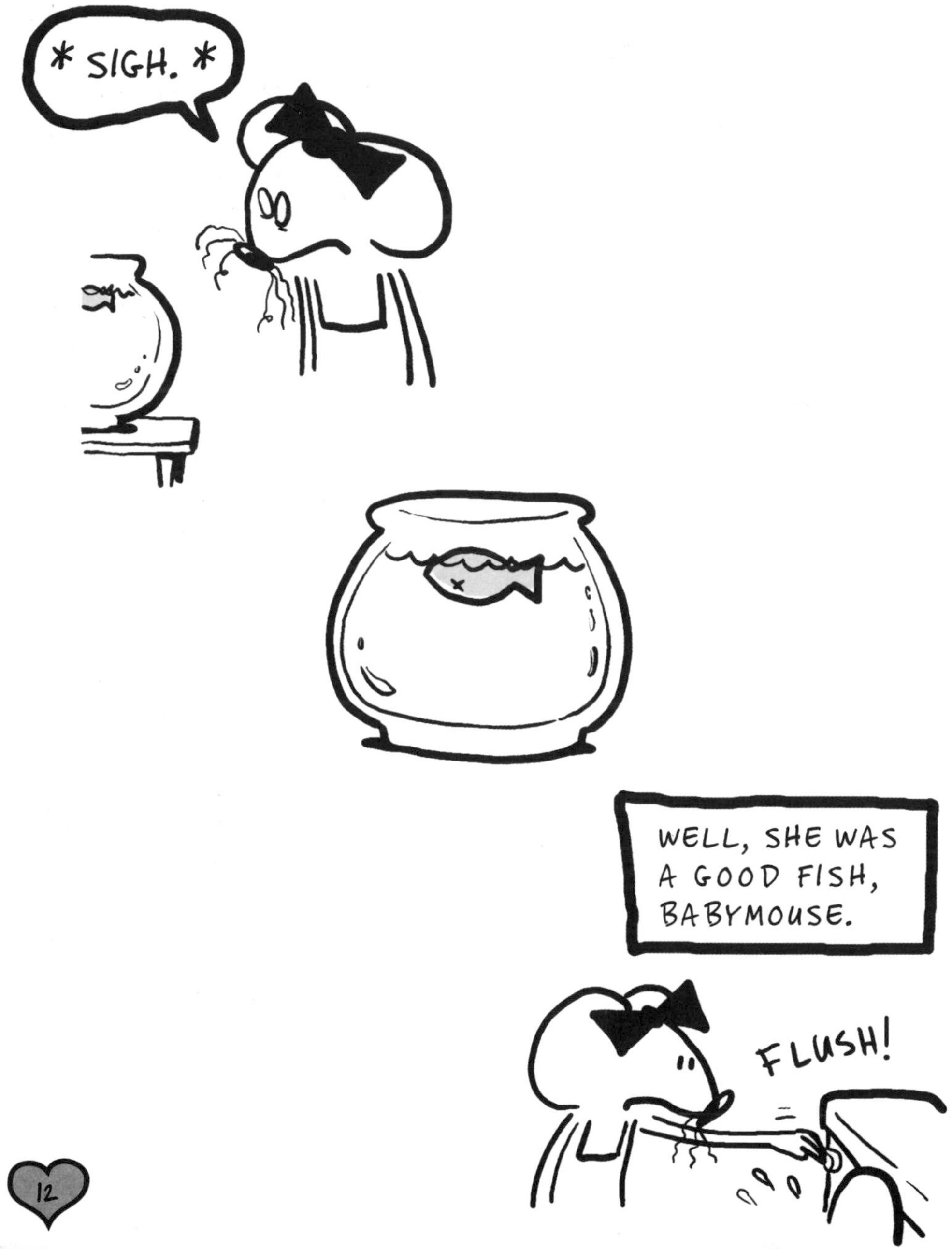
* SIGH. *
WELL, SHE WAS A GOOD FISH, BABYMOUSE.
FLUSH!

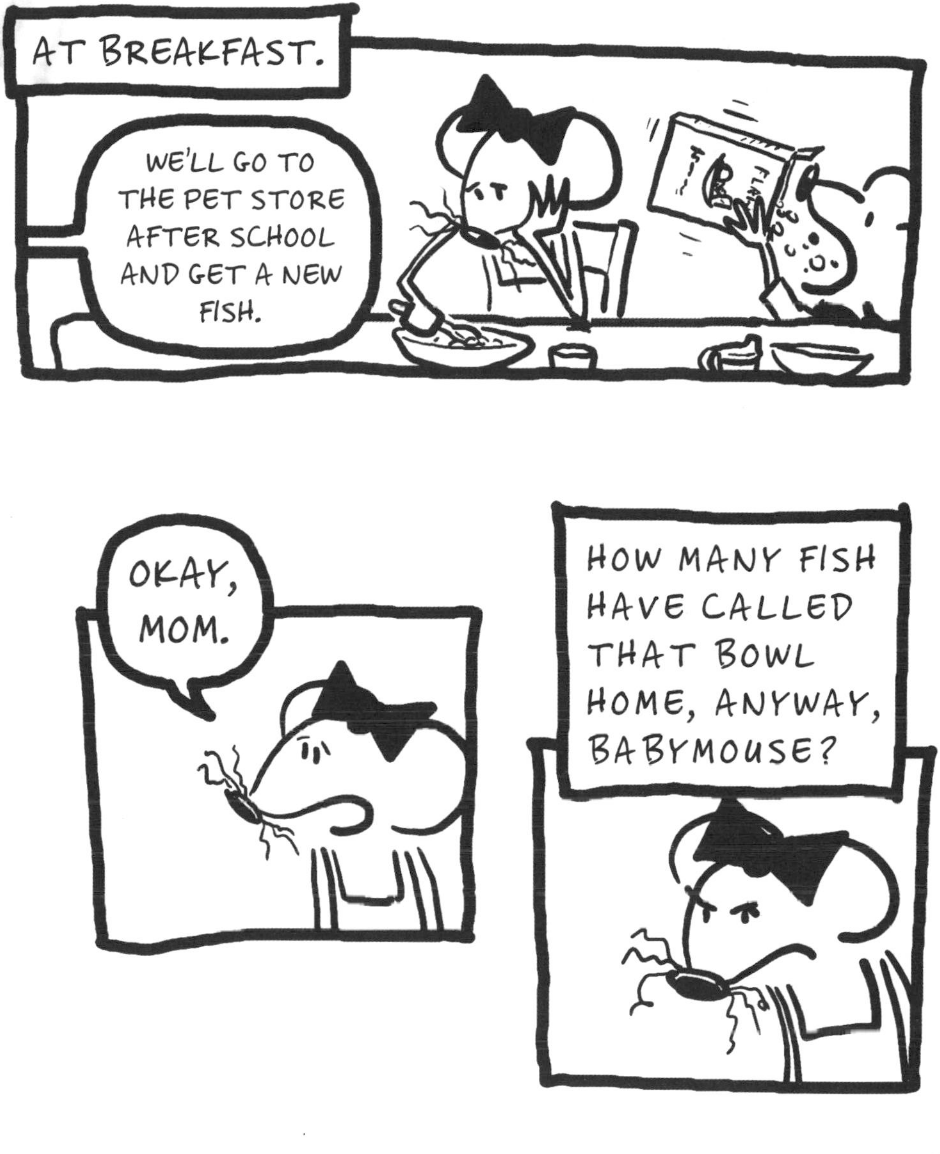
AT BREAKFAST.
WE'LL GO TO THE PET STORE AFTER SCHOOL AND GET A NEW FISH.
OKAY, MOM.
HOW MANY FISH HAVE CALLED THAT BOWL HOME, ANYWAY, BABYMOUSE?

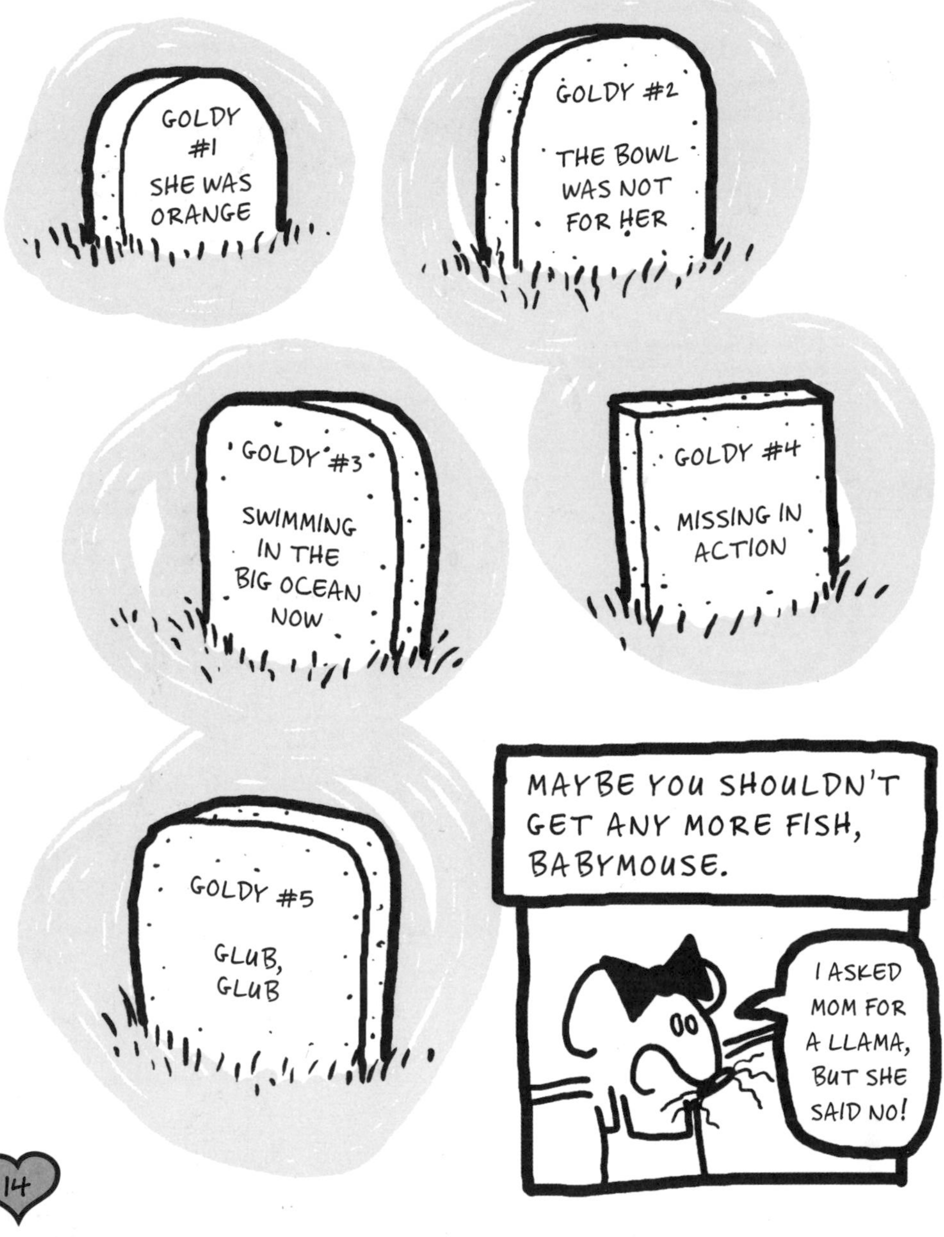
GOLDY #1 SHE WAS ORANGE
GOLDY #2 THE BOWL WAS NOT FOR HER
GOLDY #3 SWIMMING IN THE BIG OCEAN NOW
GOLDY #4 MISSING IN ACTION
GOLDY #5 GLUB, GLUB
MAYBE YOU SHOULDN'T GET ANY MORE FISH, BABYMOUSE.
I ASKED MOM FOR A LLAMA, BUT SHE SAID NO!

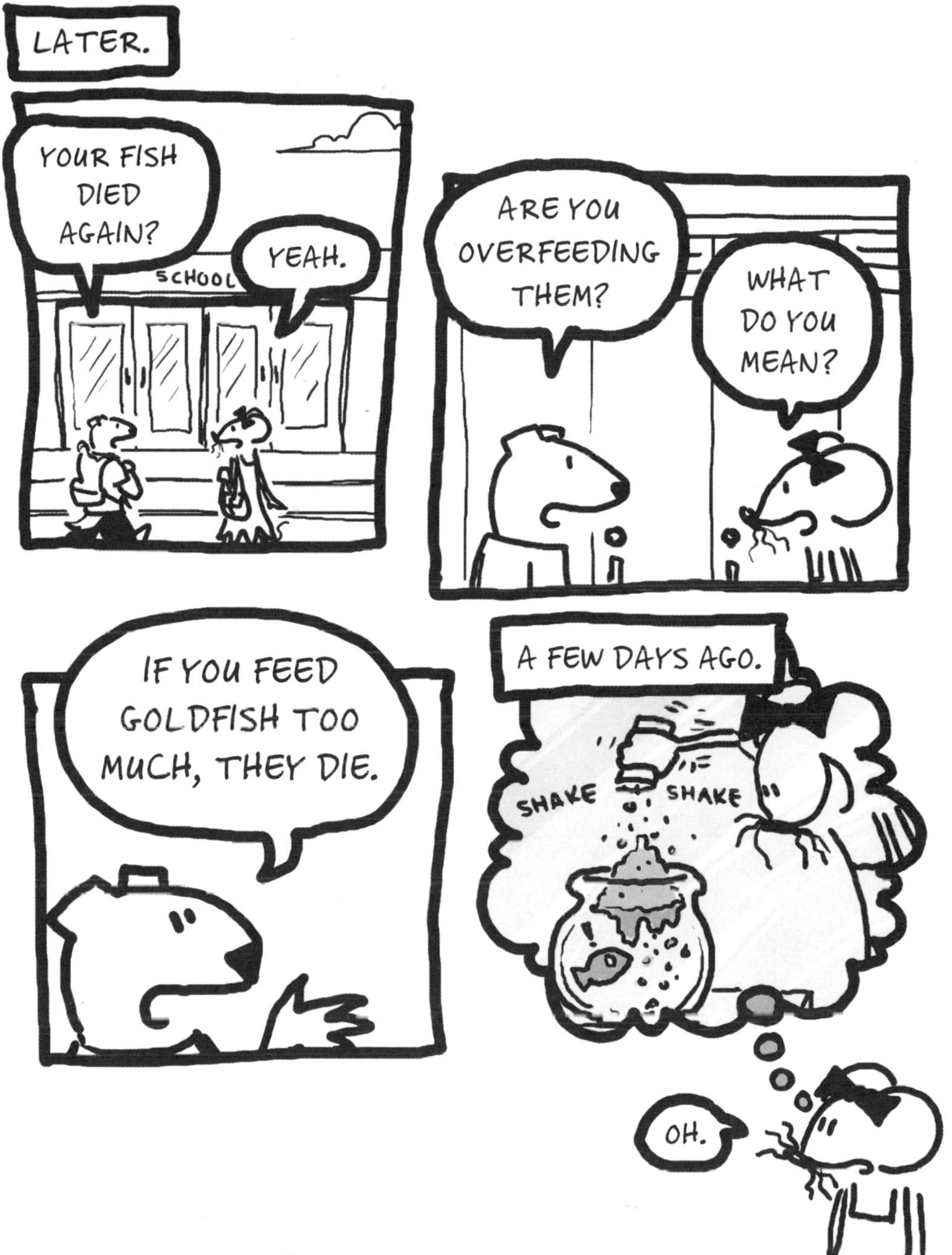
LATER.
YOUR FISH DIED AGAIN?
YEAH.
SCHOOL
ARE YOU OVERFEEDING THEM?
WHAT DO YOU MEAN?
IF YOU FEED GOLDFISH TOO MUCH, THEY DIE.
A FEW DAYS AGO.
SHAKE
SHAKE
OH.

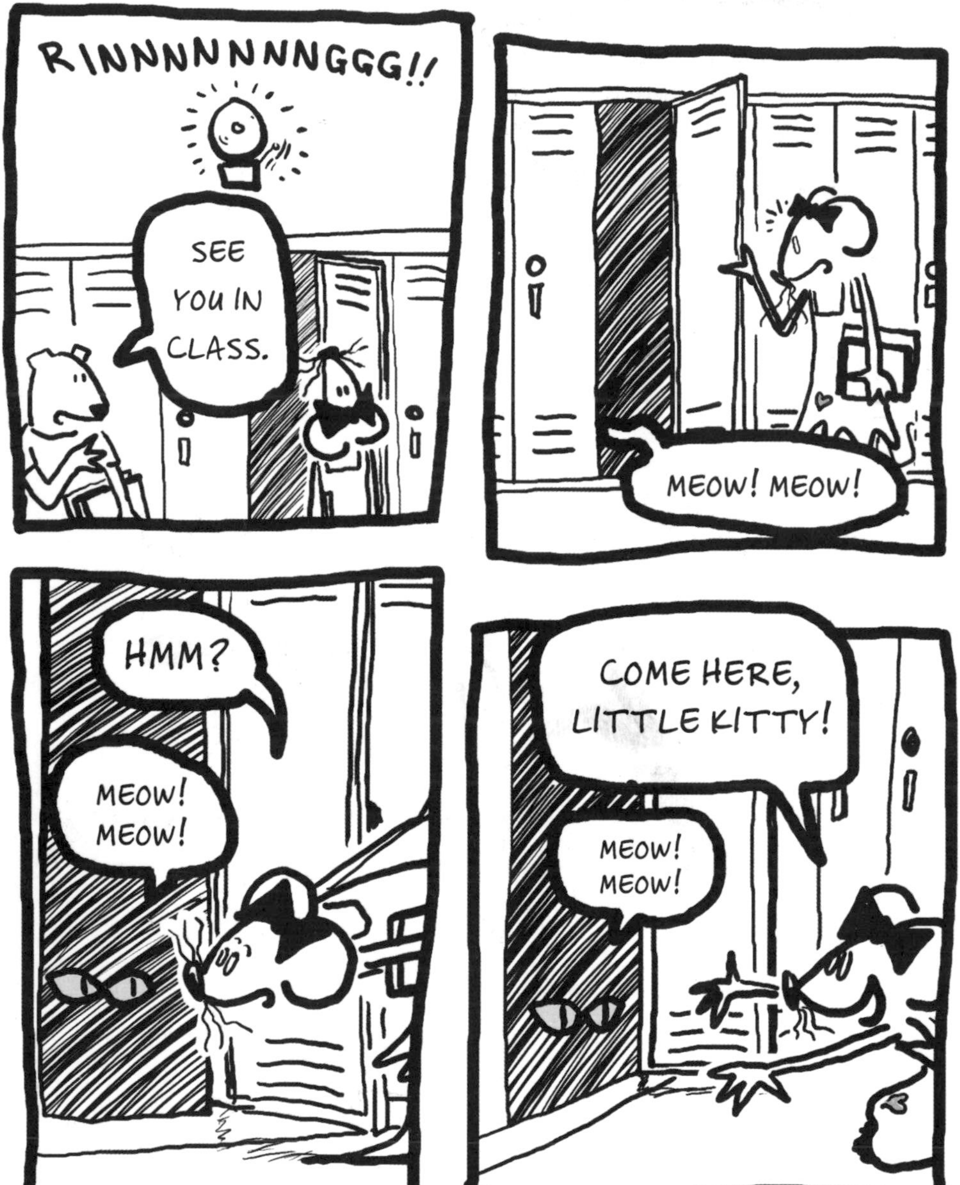
RINNNNNNNGGG!!
SEE YOU IN CLASS.
MEOW! MEOW!
HMM?
MEOW! MEOW!
COME HERE, LITTLE KITTY!
MEOW! MEOW!

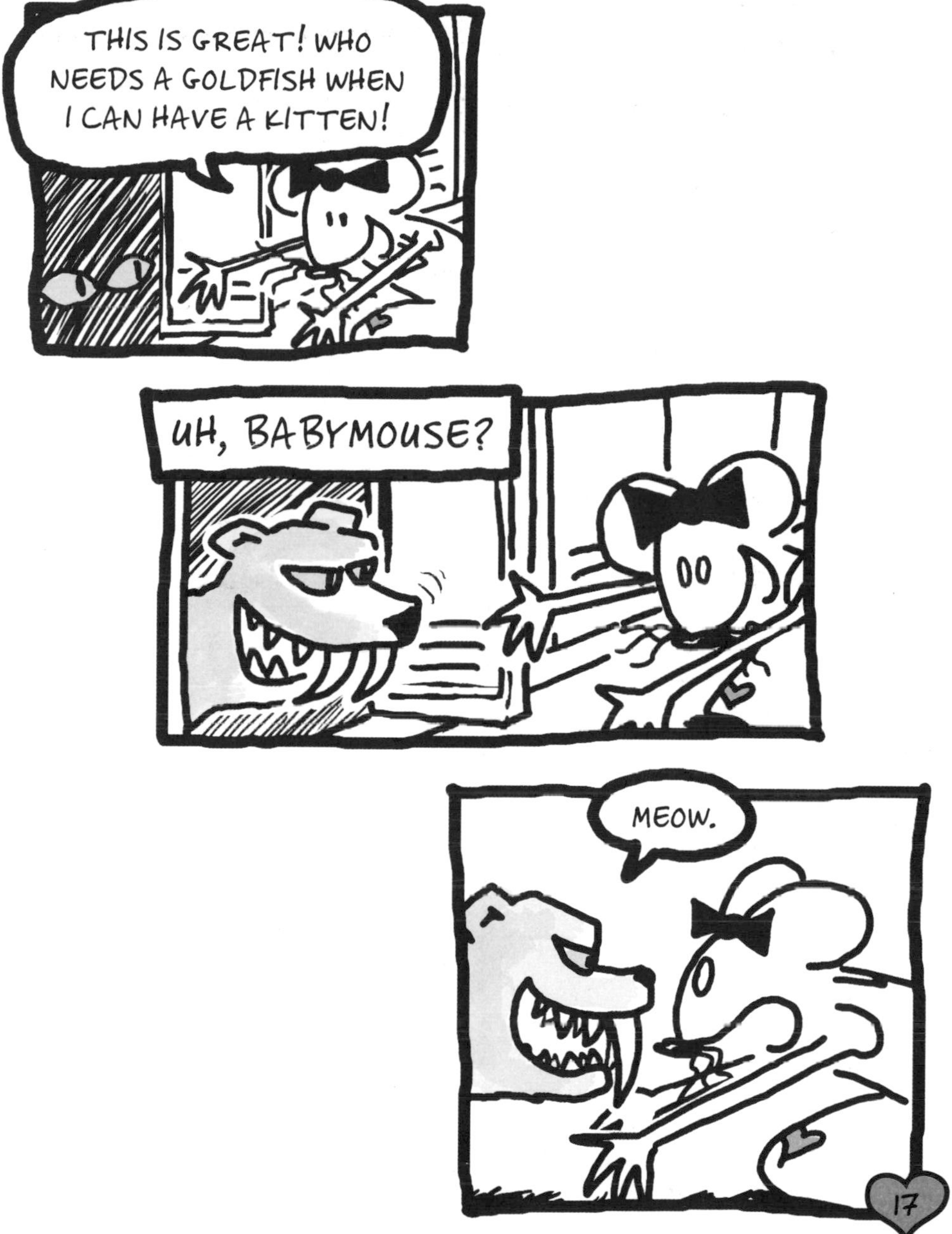
THIS IS GREAT! WHO NEEDS A GOLDFISH WHEN I CAN HAVE A KITTEN!
UH, BABYMOUSE?
MEOW.

AAAAAAAAAAAAGGHHHH!!
ZING!
GLAD TO SEE YOU'RE NOT LATE FOR ONCE, BABYMOUSE.

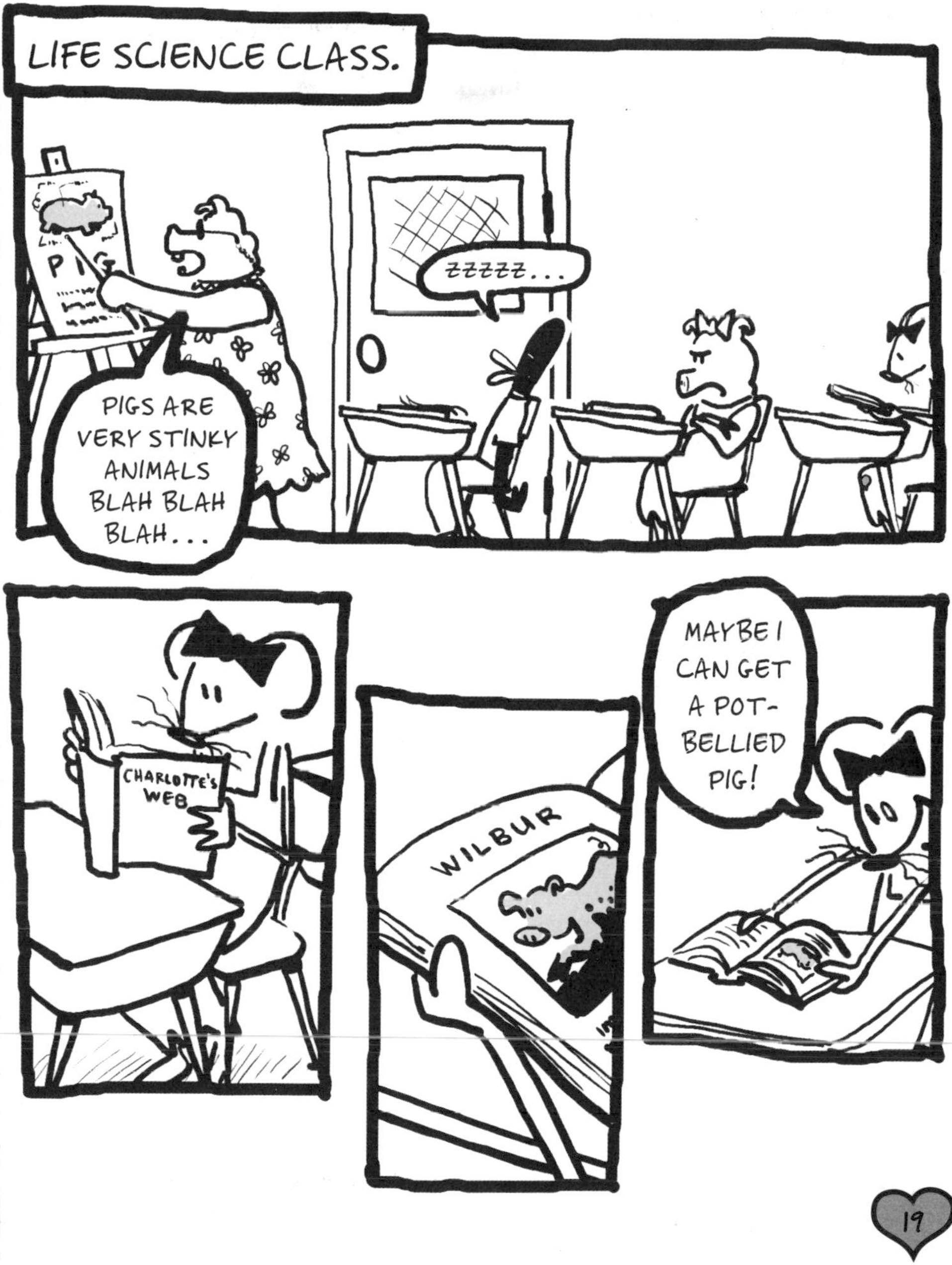
LIFE SCIENCE CLASS.
PIG
PIGS ARE VERY STINKY ANIMALS BLAH BLAH BLAH...
ZZZZZ...
CHARLOTTE'S WEB
WILBUR
MAYBE I CAN GET A POT-BELLIED PIG!

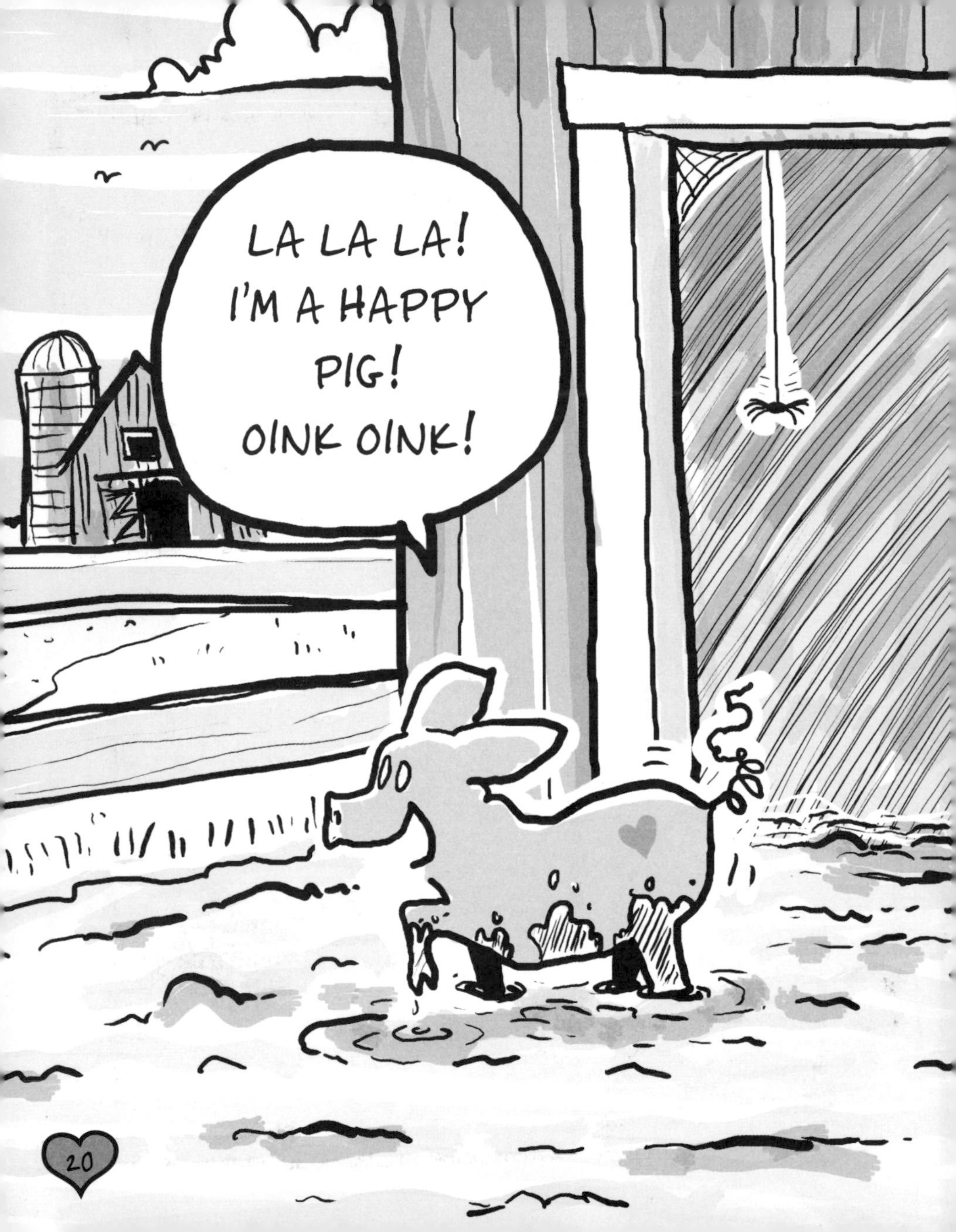
LA LA LA! I'M A HAPPY PIG! OINK OINK!

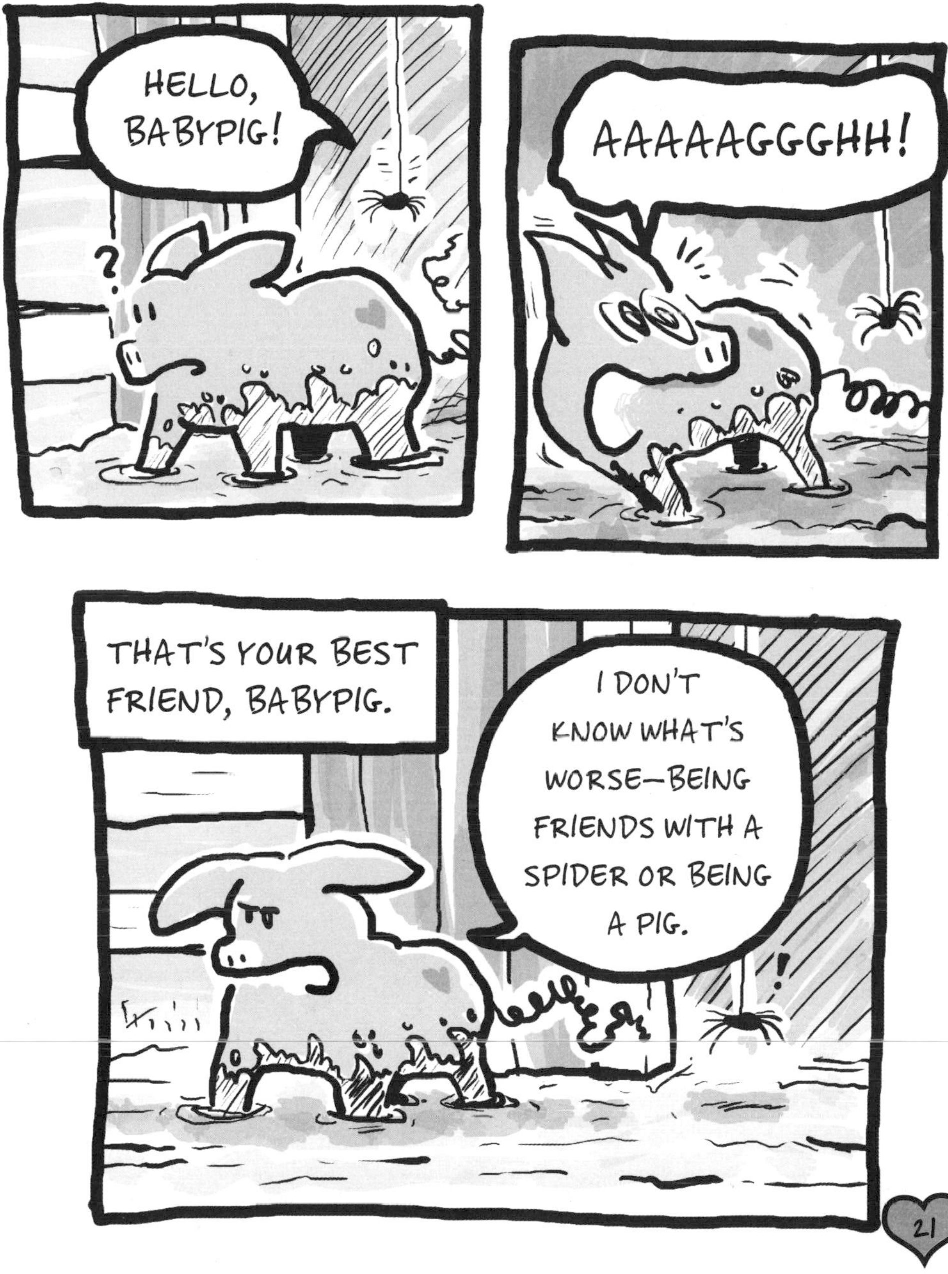
HELLO, BABYPIG!
?
AAAAAGGGHH!
THAT'S YOUR BEST FRIEND, BABYPIG.
I DON'T KNOW WHAT'S WORSE—BEING FRIENDS WITH A SPIDER OR BEING A PIG.
!

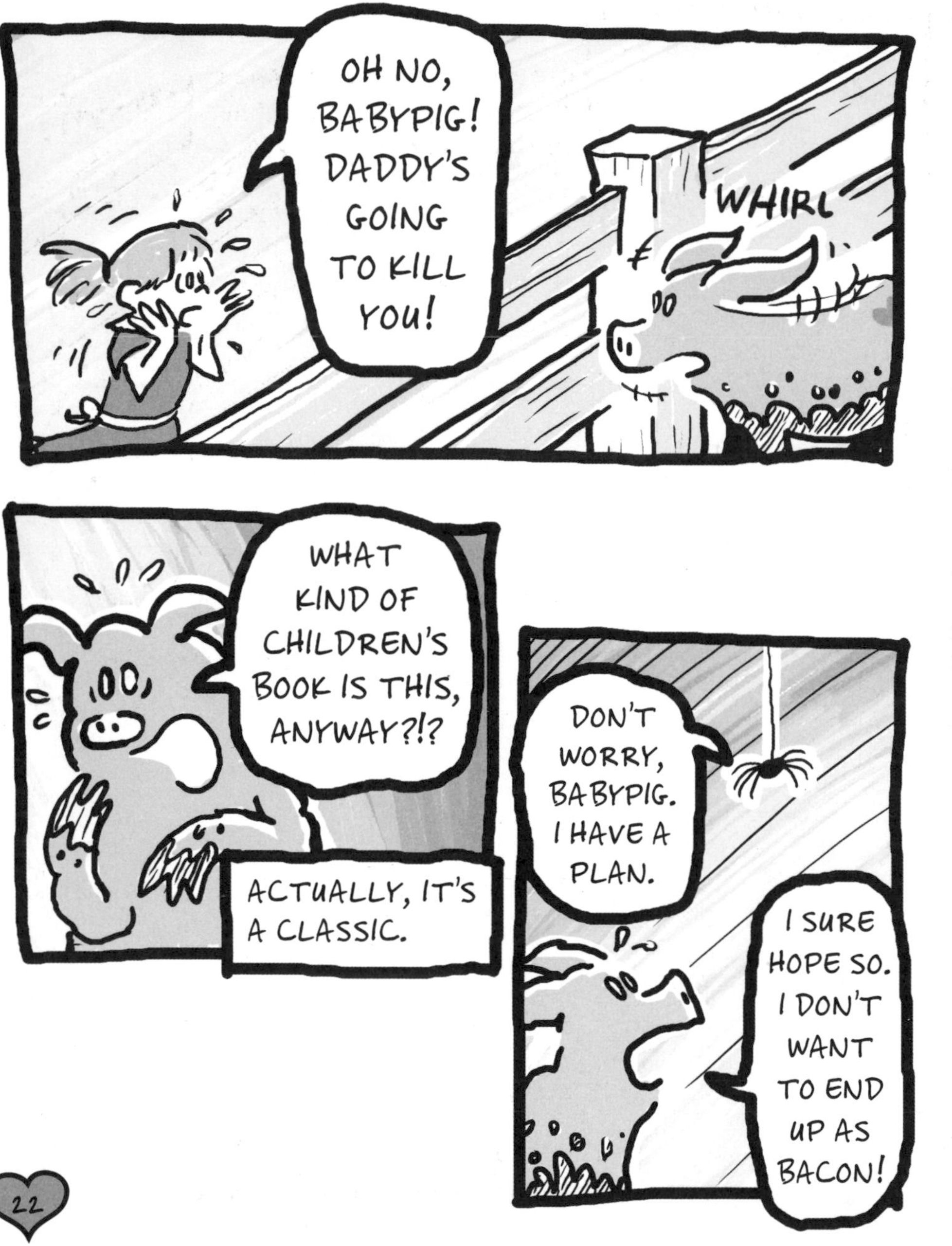
OH NO, BABYPIG! DADDY'S GOING TO KILL YOU!
WHIRL
WHAT KIND OF CHILDREN'S BOOK IS THIS, ANYWAY?!?
ACTUALLY, IT'S A CLASSIC.
DON'T WORRY, BABYPIG. I HAVE A PLAN.
I SURE HOPE SO. I DON'T WANT TO END UP AS BACON!

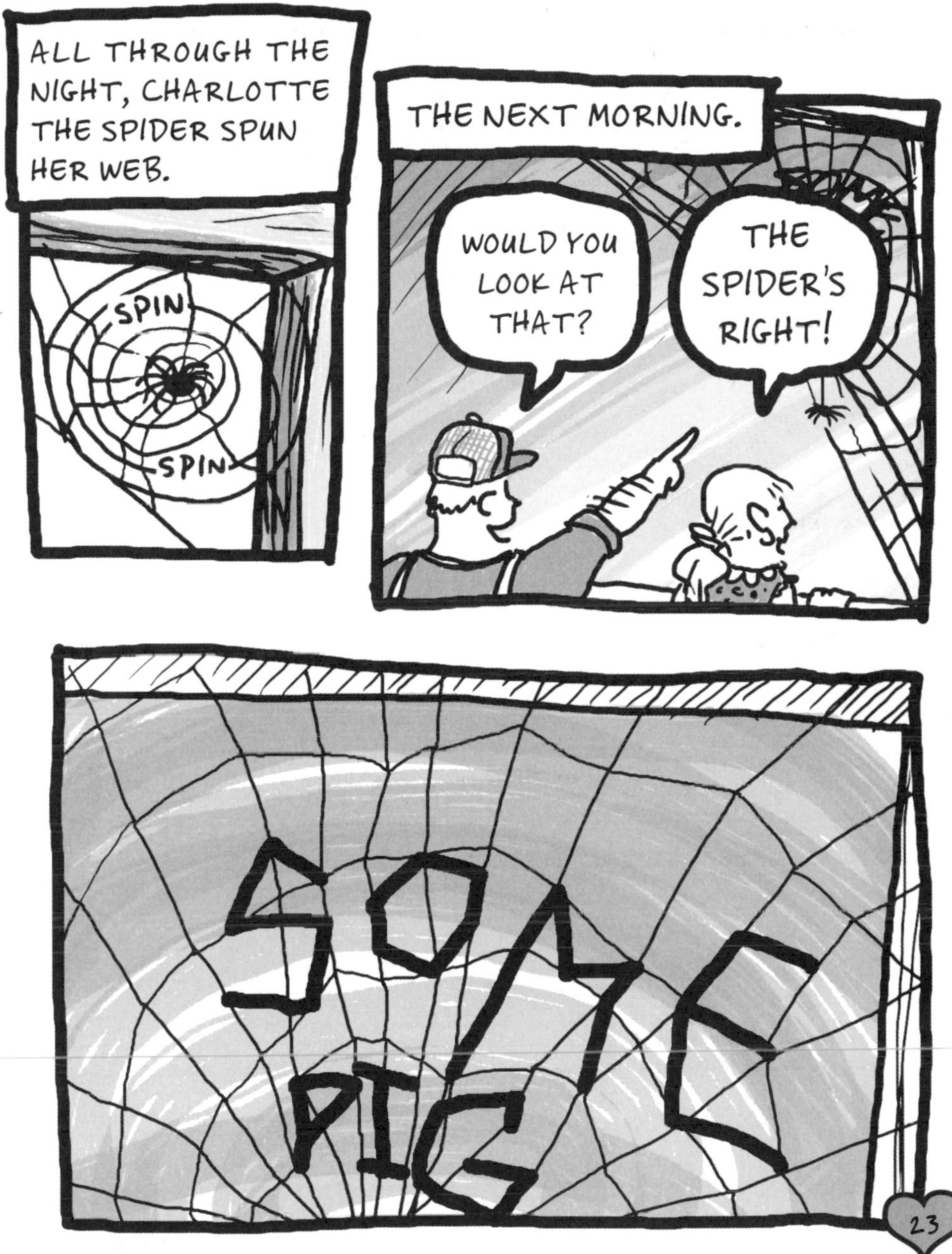
ALL THROUGH THE NIGHT, CHARLOTTE THE SPIDER SPUN HER WEB.
SPIN
SPIN
THE NEXT MORNING.
WOULD YOU LOOK AT THAT?
THE SPIDER'S RIGHT!
SOME PIG

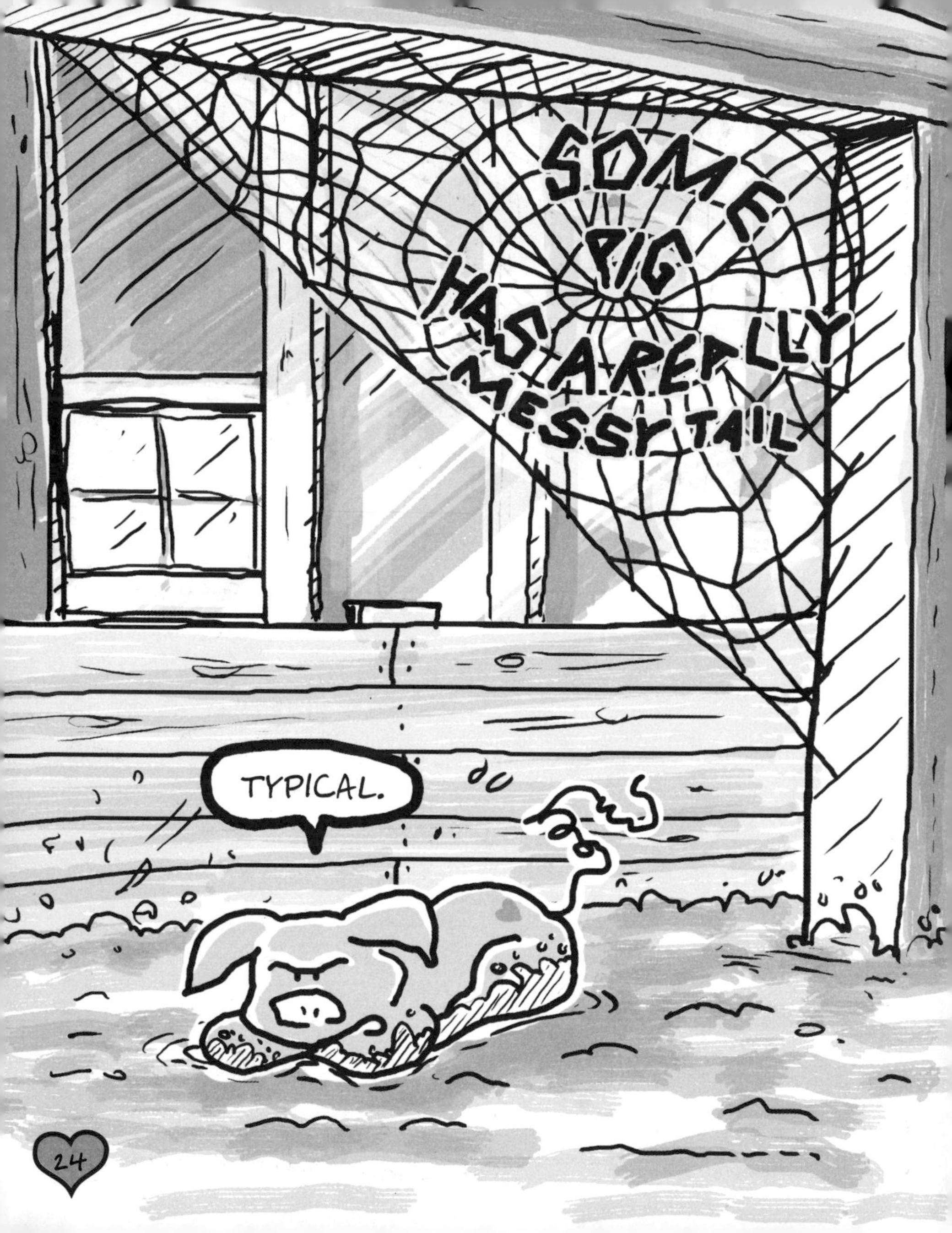
SOME PIG HAS A REALLY MESSY TAIL
TYPICAL.

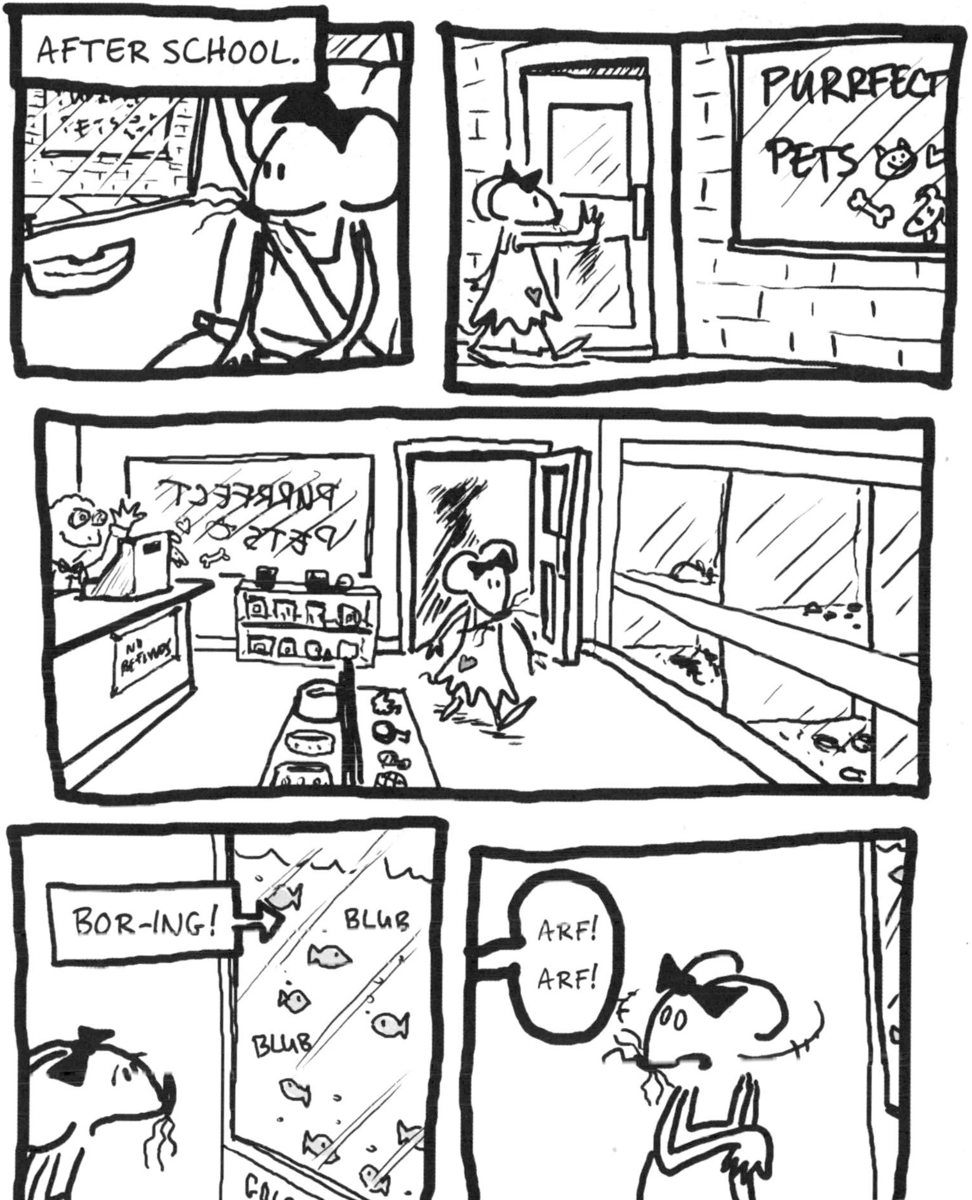
AFTER SCHOOL.
PURRFECT PETS
NO REFUNDS
BOR-ING!
BLUB
BLUB
ARF! ARF!

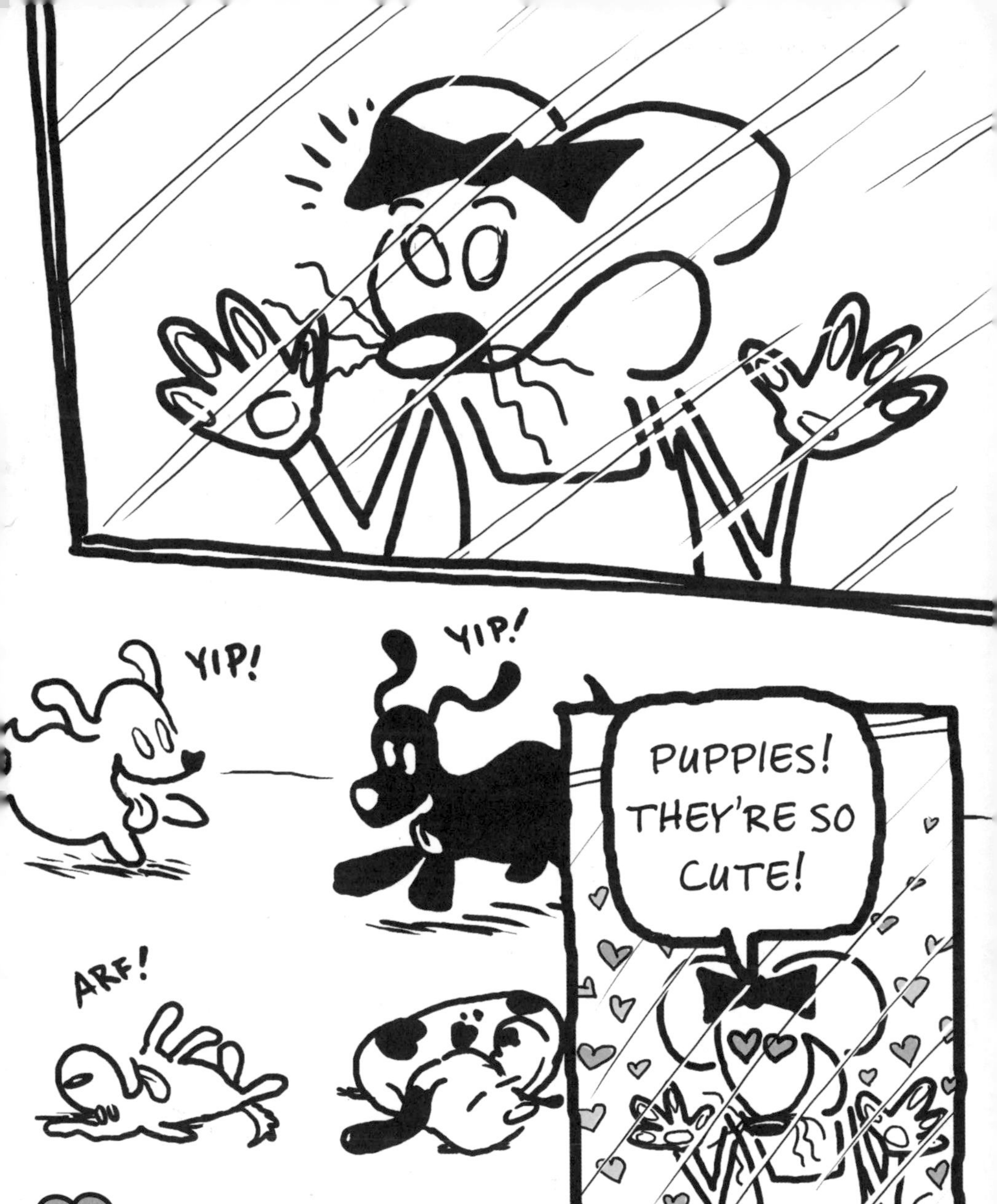
YIP!
YIP!
PUPPIES! THEY'RE SO CUTE!
ARF!

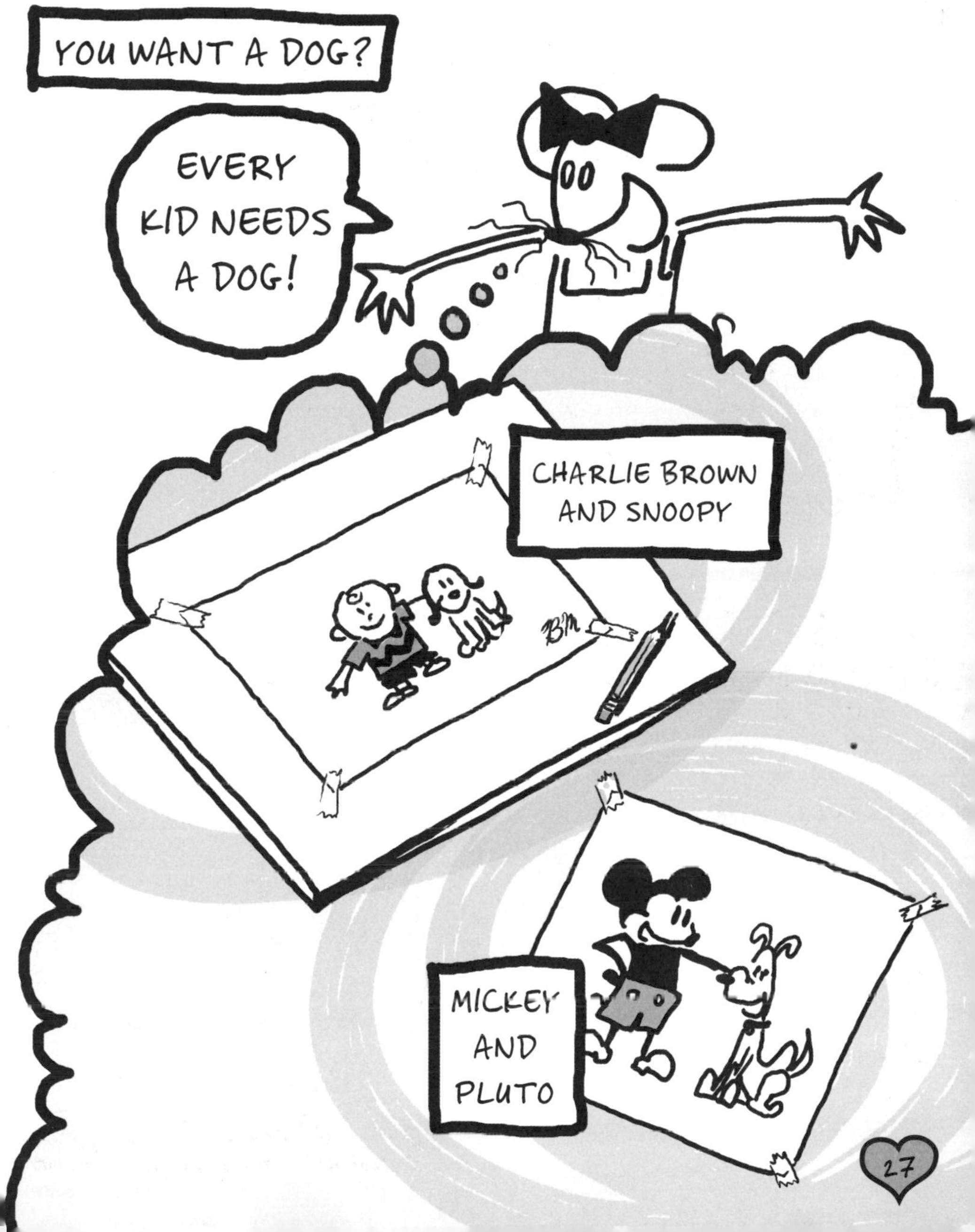
YOU WANT A DOG?
EVERY KID NEEDS A DOG!
CHARLIE BROWN AND SNOOPY
BM
MICKEY AND PLUTO

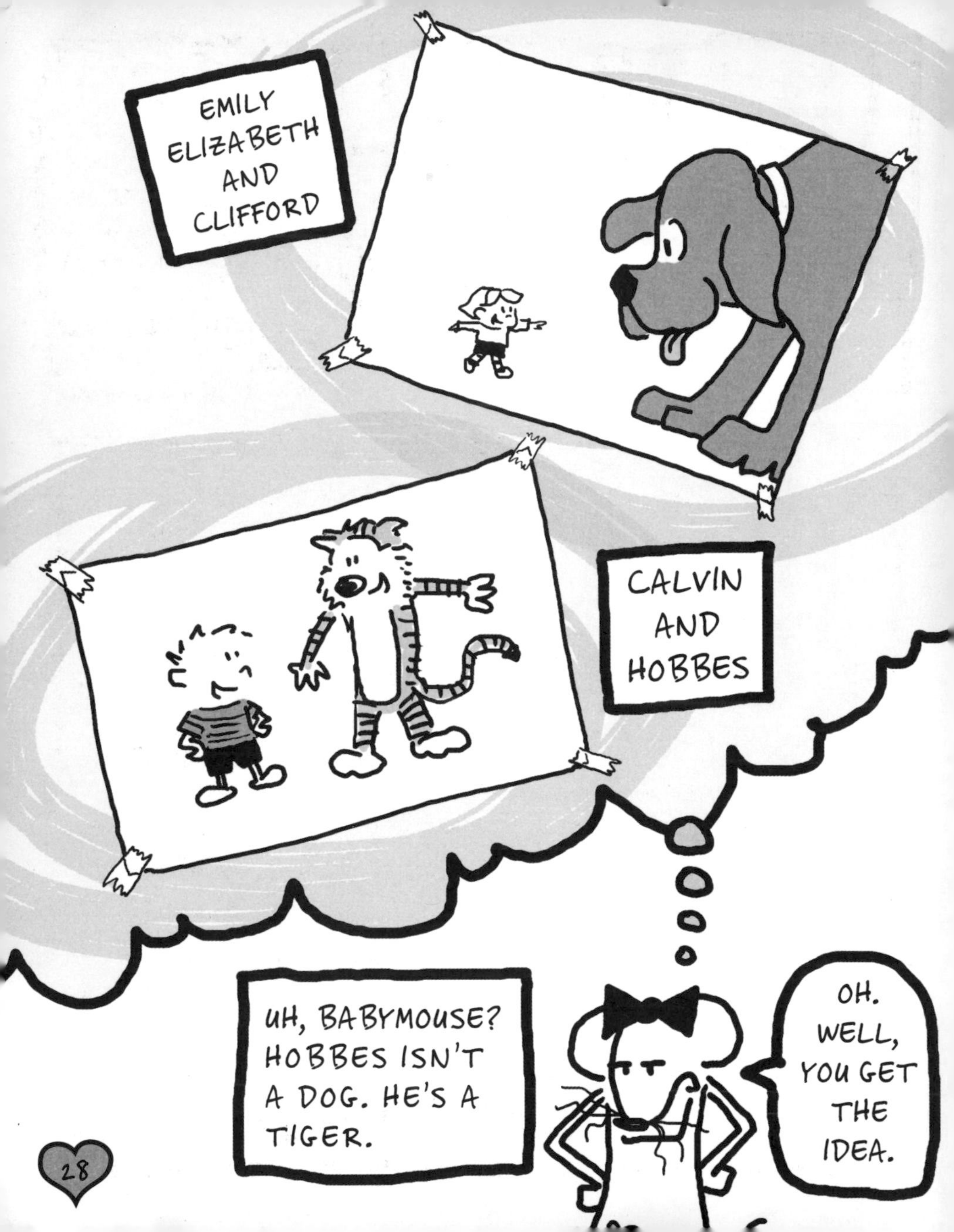
EMILY ELIZABETH AND CLIFFORD
CALVIN AND HOBBES
UH, BABYMOUSE? HOBBES ISN'T A DOG. HE'S A TIGER.
OH. WELL, YOU GET THE IDEA.

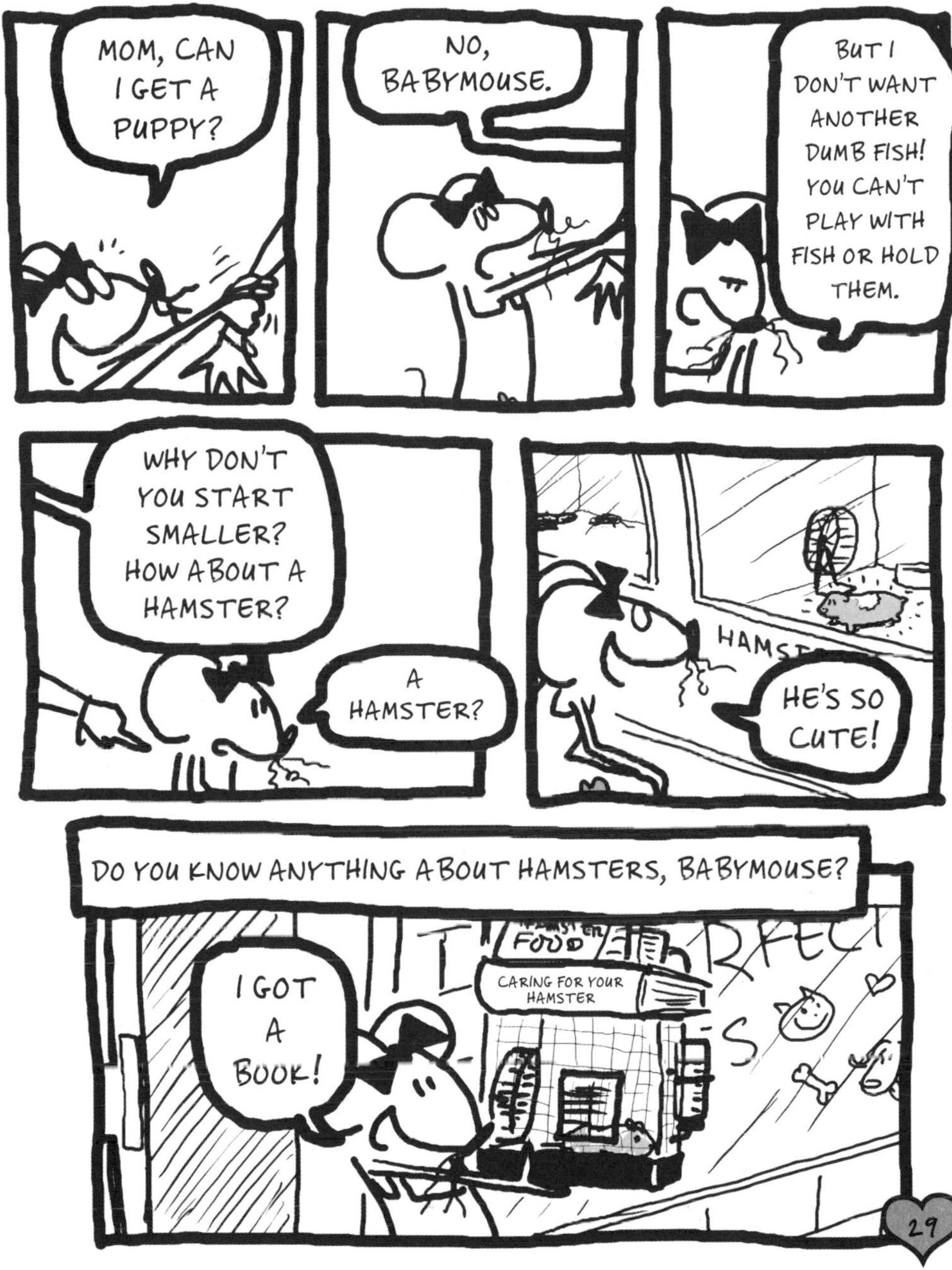
MOM, CAN I GET A PUPPY?
NO, BABYMOUSE.
BUT I DON'T WANT ANOTHER DUMB FISH! YOU CAN'T PLAY WITH FISH OR HOLD THEM.
WHY DON'T YOU START SMALLER? HOW ABOUT A HAMSTER?
A HAMSTER?
HE'S SO CUTE!
DO YOU KNOW ANYTHING ABOUT HAMSTERS, BABYMOUSE?
FOOD
CARING FOR YOUR HAMSTER
I GOT A BOOK!

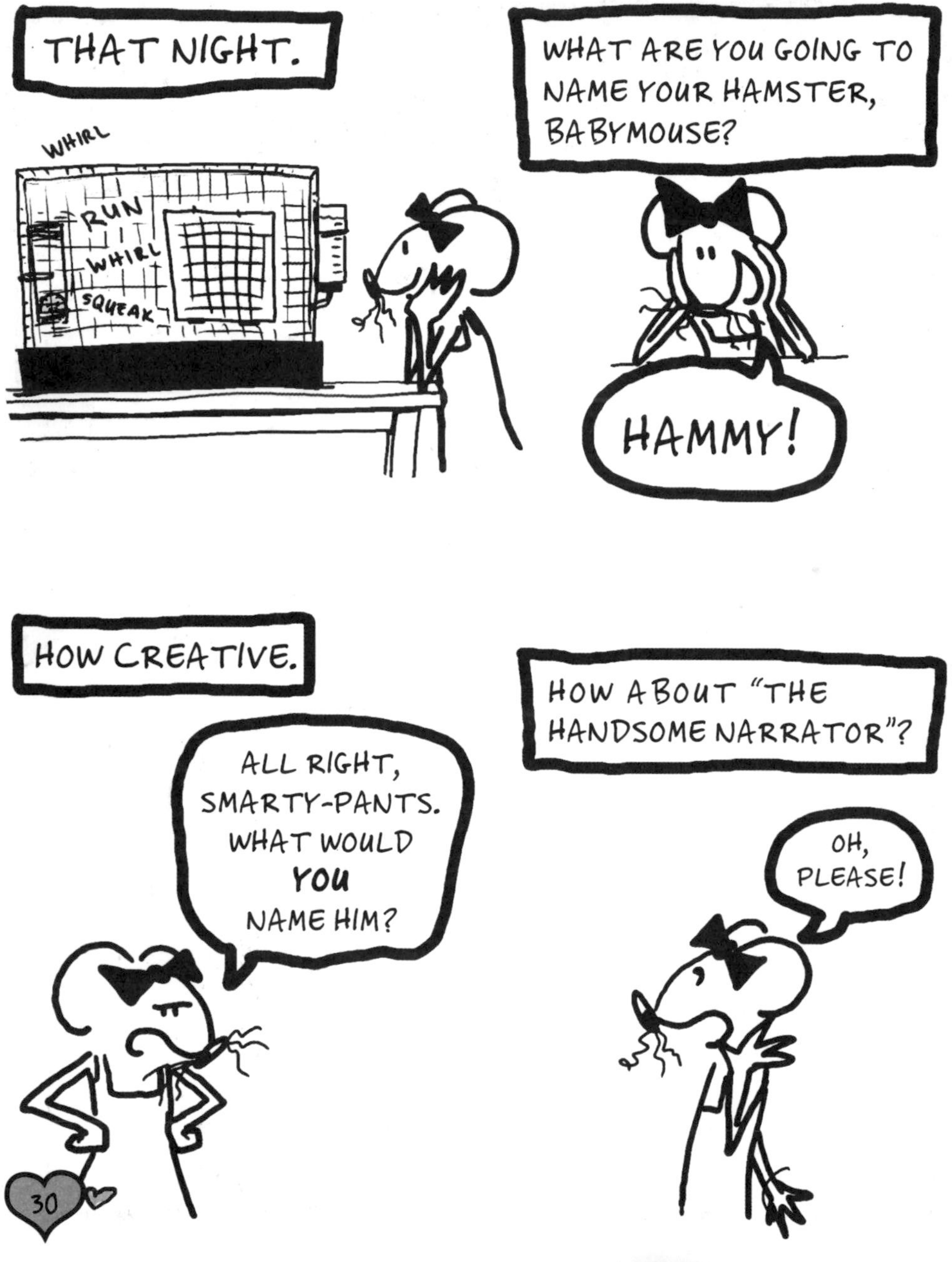
THAT NIGHT.
WHIRL
RUN
WHIRL
SQUEAK
WHAT ARE YOU GOING TO NAME YOUR HAMSTER, BABYMOUSE?
HAMMY!
HOW CREATIVE.
ALL RIGHT, SMARTY-PANTS. WHAT WOULD **YOU** NAME HIM?
HOW ABOUT "THE HANDSOME NARRATOR"?
OH, PLEASE!

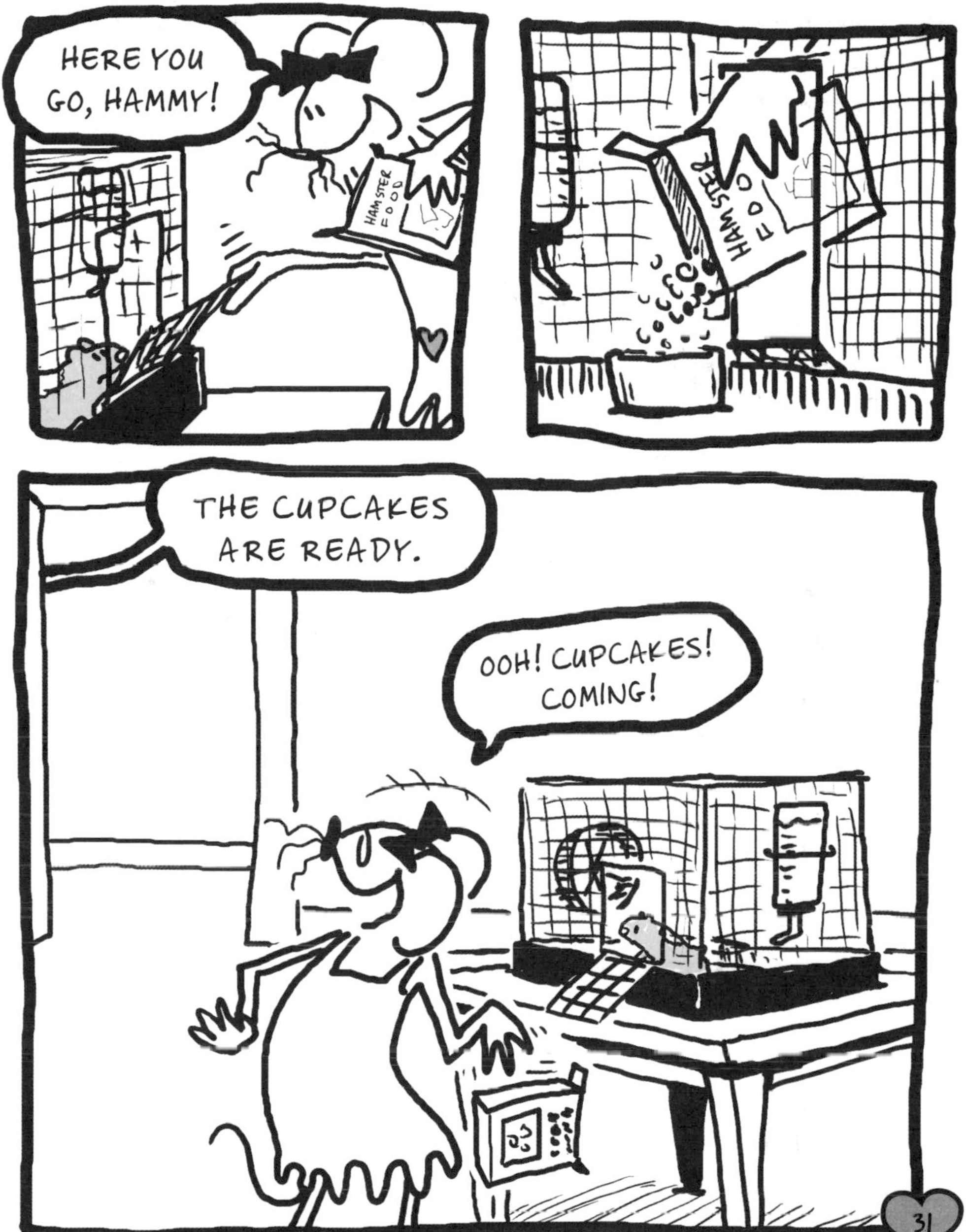
HERE YOU GO, HAMMY!
HAMSTER FOOD
HAMSTER FOOD
THE CUPCAKES ARE READY.
OOH! CUPCAKES! COMING!

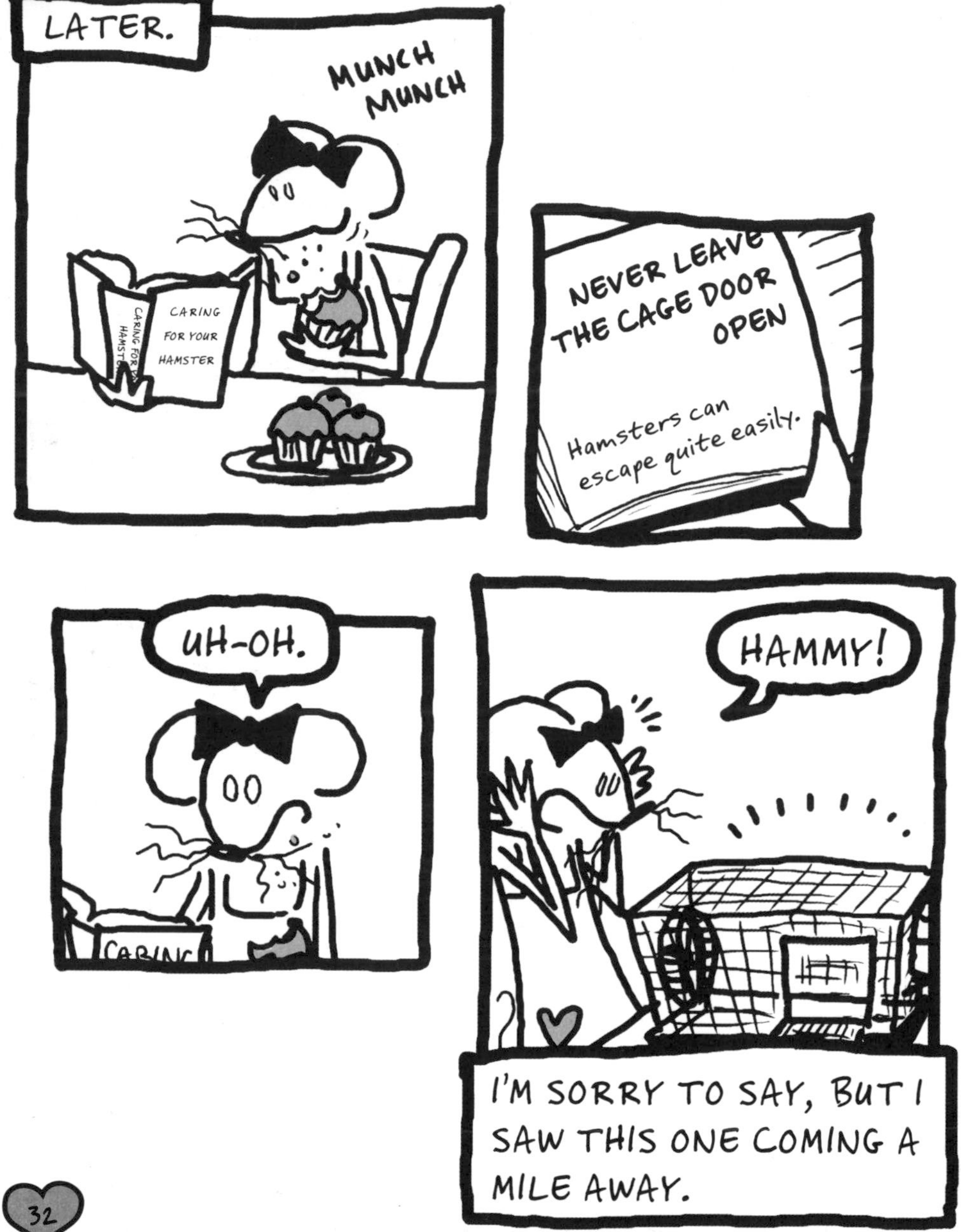
LATER.
MUNCH MUNCH
CARING FOR YOUR HAMSTER
NEVER LEAVE THE CAGE DOOR OPEN
Hamsters can escape quite easily.
UH-OH.
HAMMY!
I'M SORRY TO SAY, BUT I SAW THIS ONE COMING A MILE AWAY.

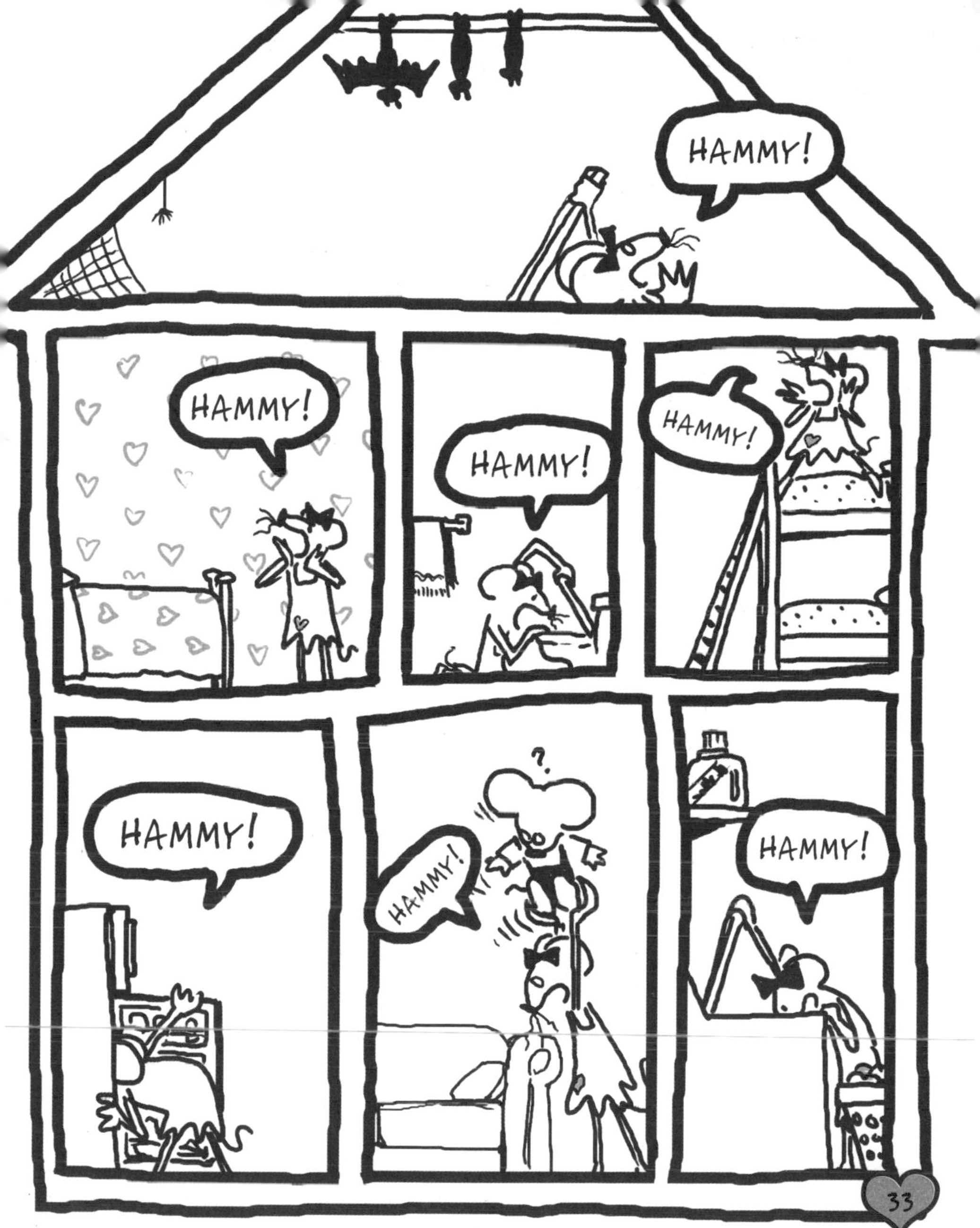
HAMMY!
HAMMY!
HAMMY!
HAMMY!
HAMMY!
HAMMY!
?
HAMMY!

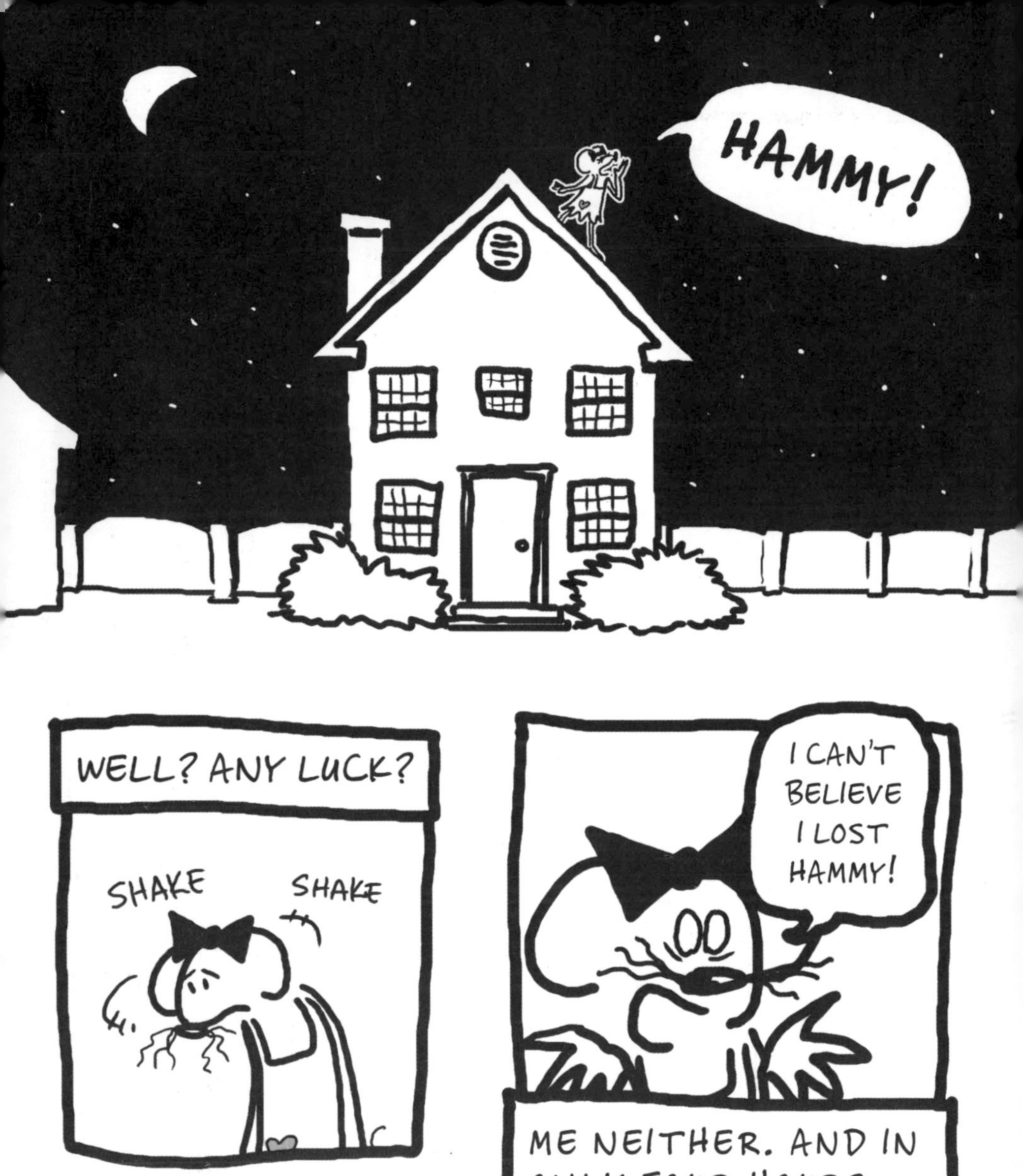
HAMMY!
WELL? ANY LUCK?
SHAKE
SHAKE
I CAN'T BELIEVE I LOST HAMMY!
ME NEITHER. AND IN ONLY FOUR HOURS. THAT'S A NEW RECORD.

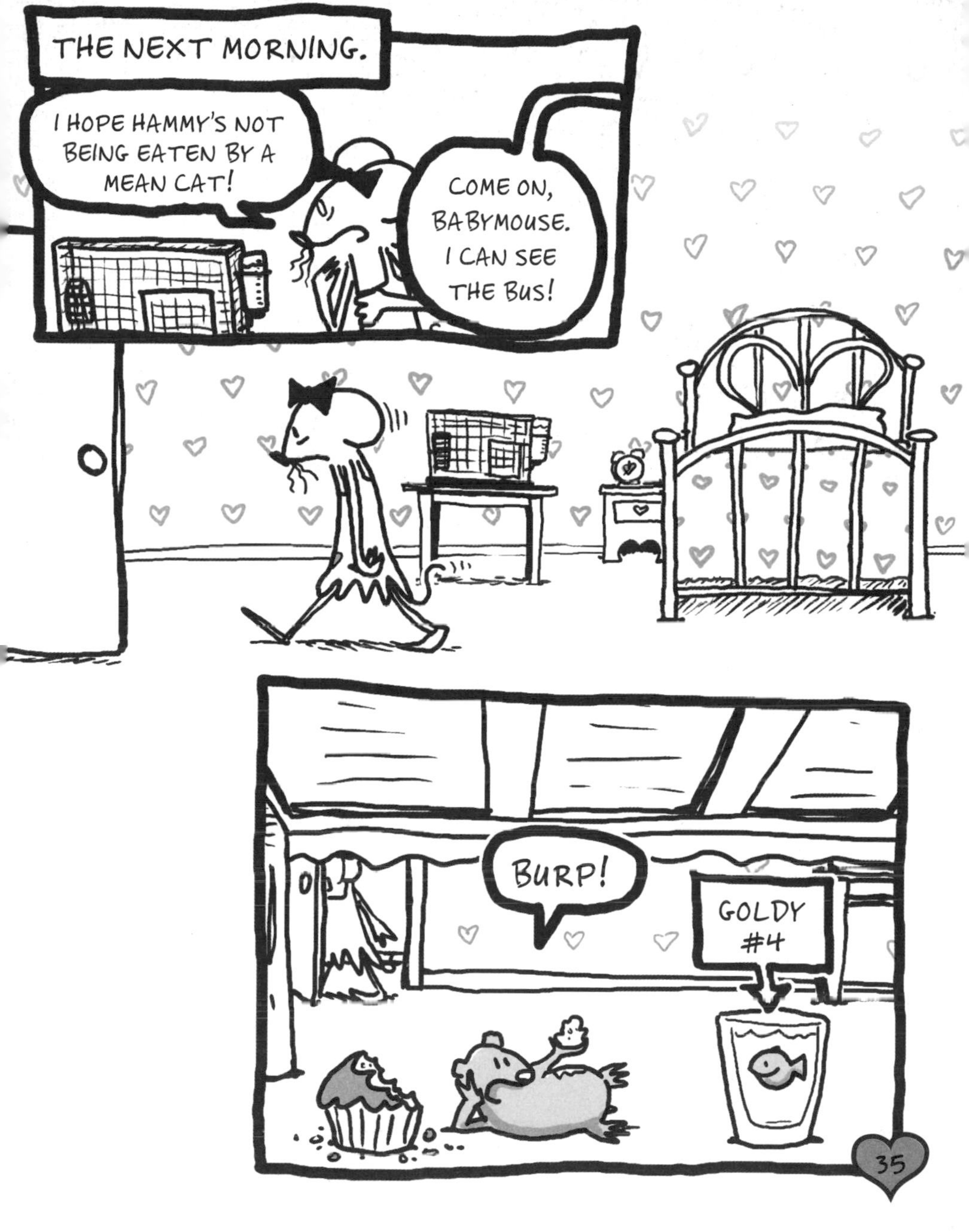
THE NEXT MORNING.
I HOPE HAMMY'S NOT BEING EATEN BY A MEAN CAT!
COME ON, BABYMOUSE. I CAN SEE THE BUS!
BURP!
GOLDY #4

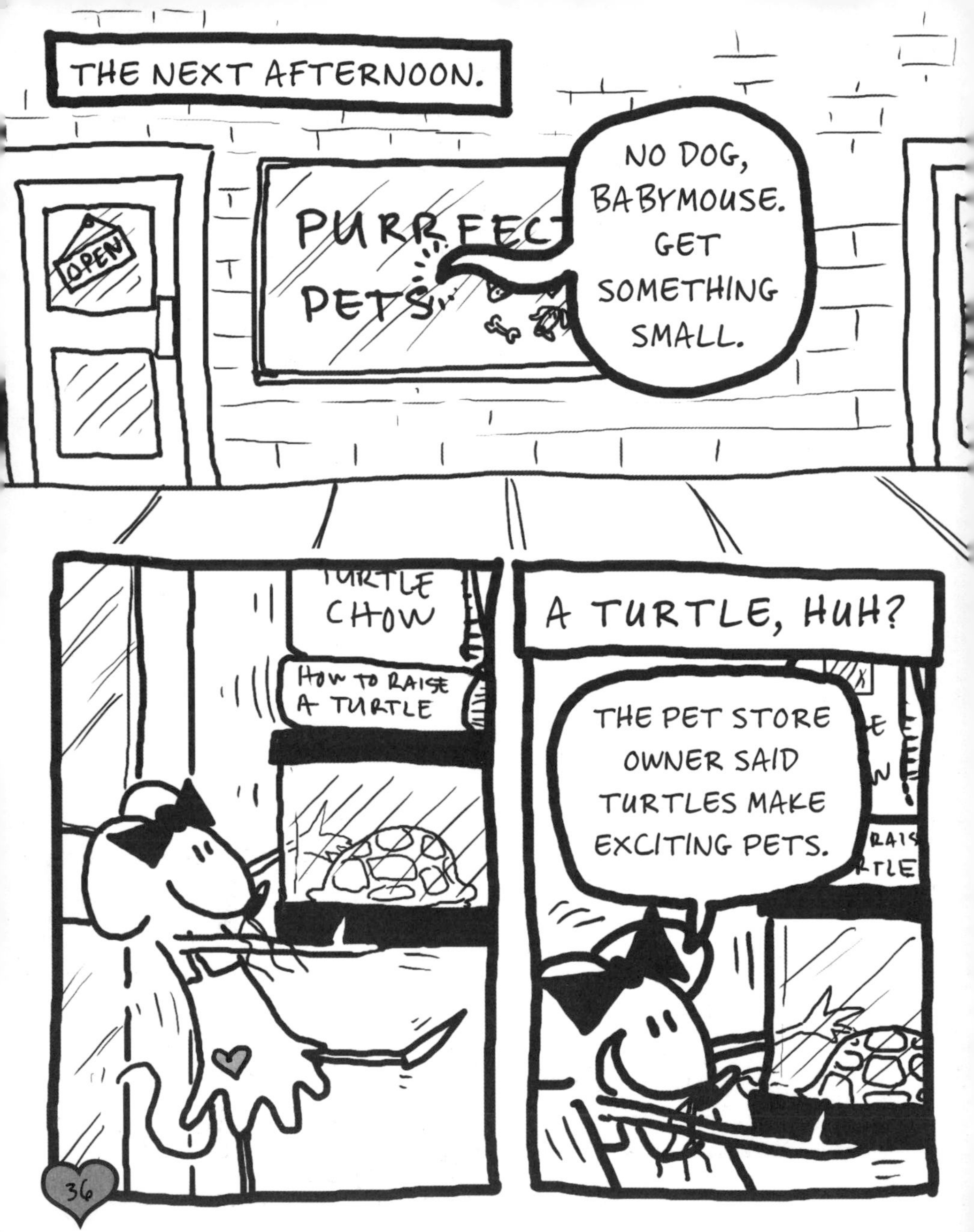
THE NEXT AFTERNOON.
OPEN
PURRFECT PETS
NO DOG, BABYMOUSE. GET SOMETHING SMALL.
TURTLE CHOW
HOW TO RAISE A TURTLE
A TURTLE, HUH?
THE PET STORE OWNER SAID TURTLES MAKE EXCITING PETS.

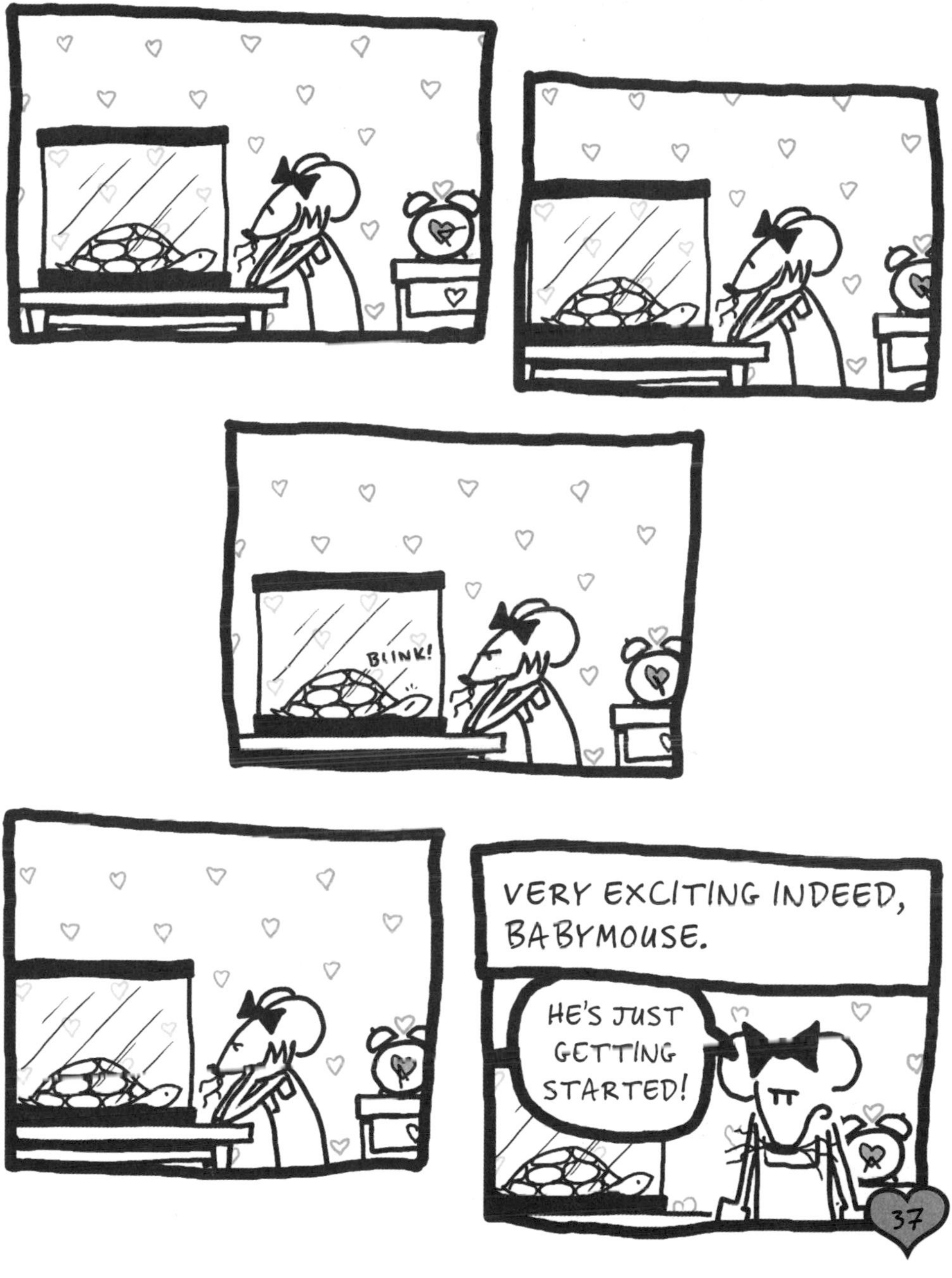
BLINK!
VERY EXCITING INDEED, BABYMOUSE.
HE'S JUST GETTING STARTED!

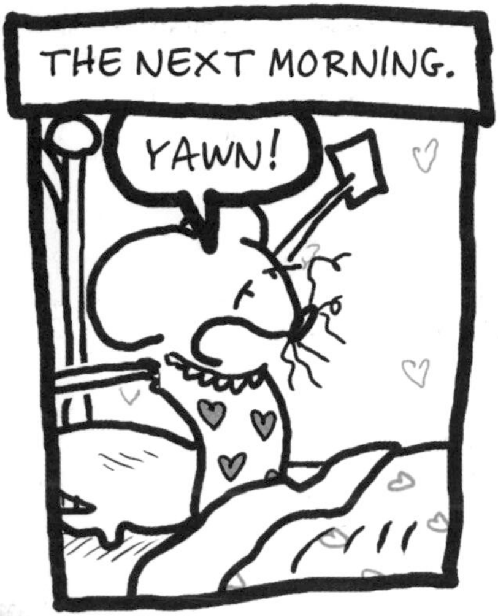
THE NEXT MORNING.
YAWN!

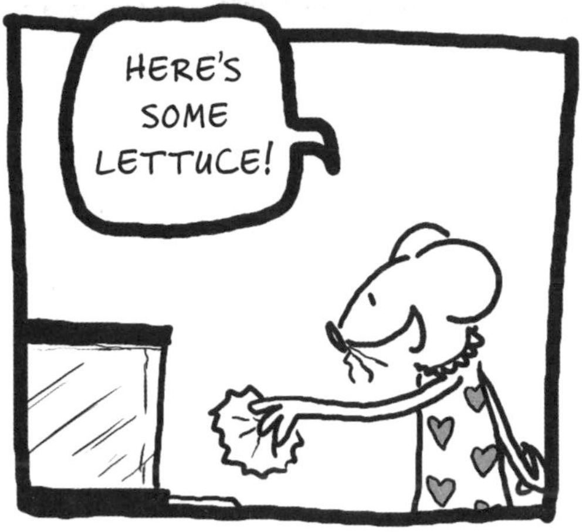
HERE'S SOME LETTUCE!

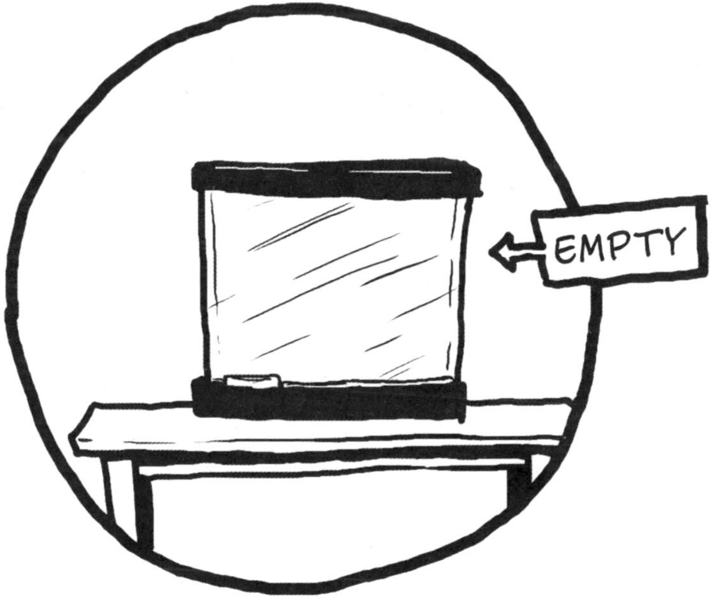
EMPTY

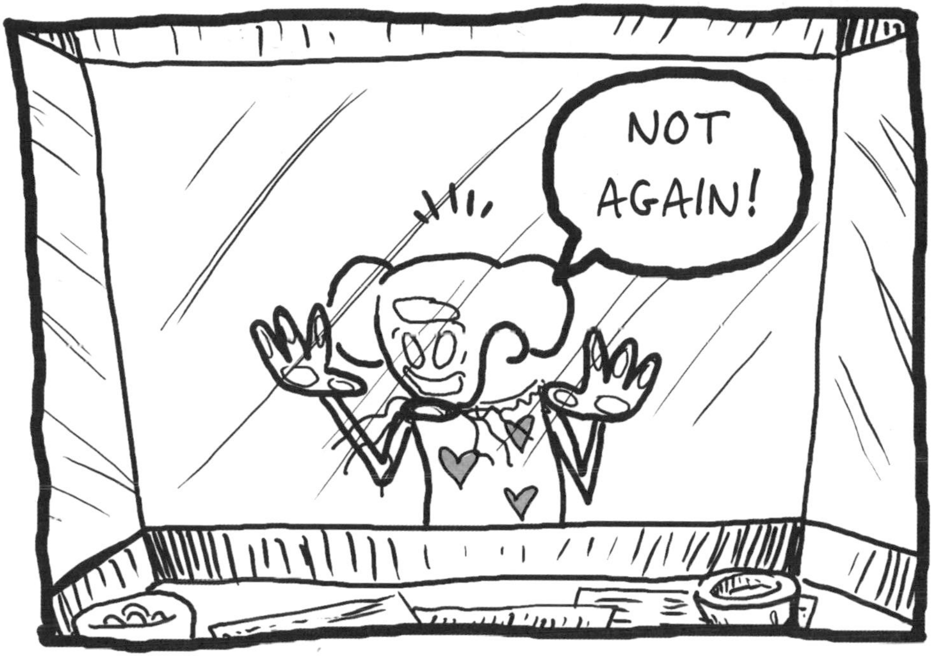
NOT AGAIN!

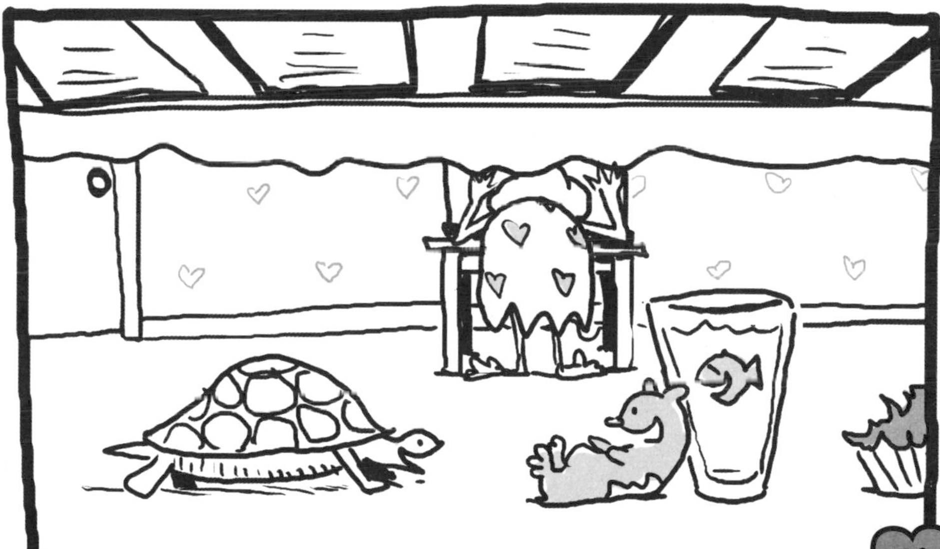

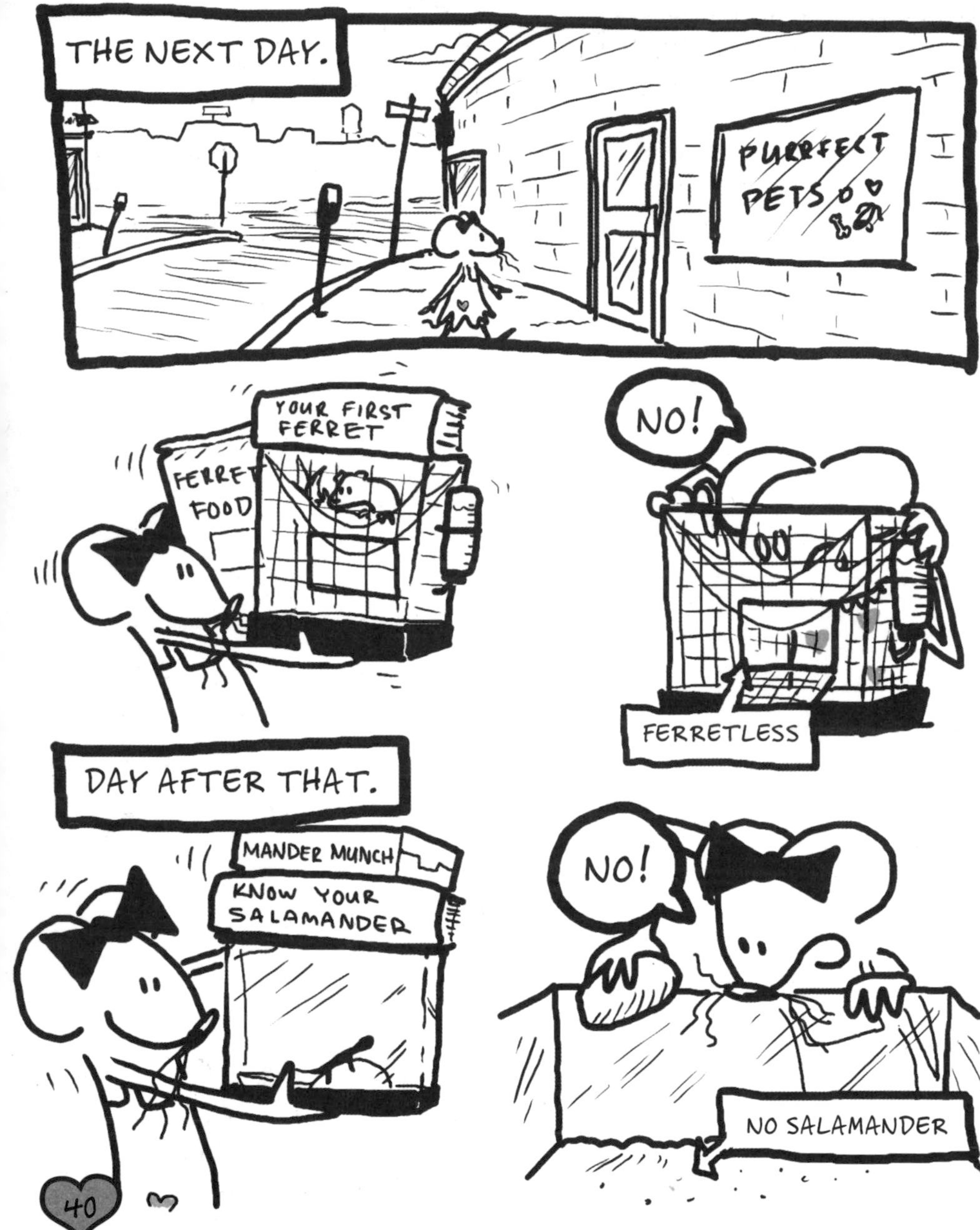
THE NEXT DAY.
PURRFECT PETS
YOUR FIRST FERRET
FERRET FOOD
NO!
FERRETLESS
DAY AFTER THAT.
MANDER MUNCH
KNOW YOUR SALAMANDER
NO!
NO SALAMANDER

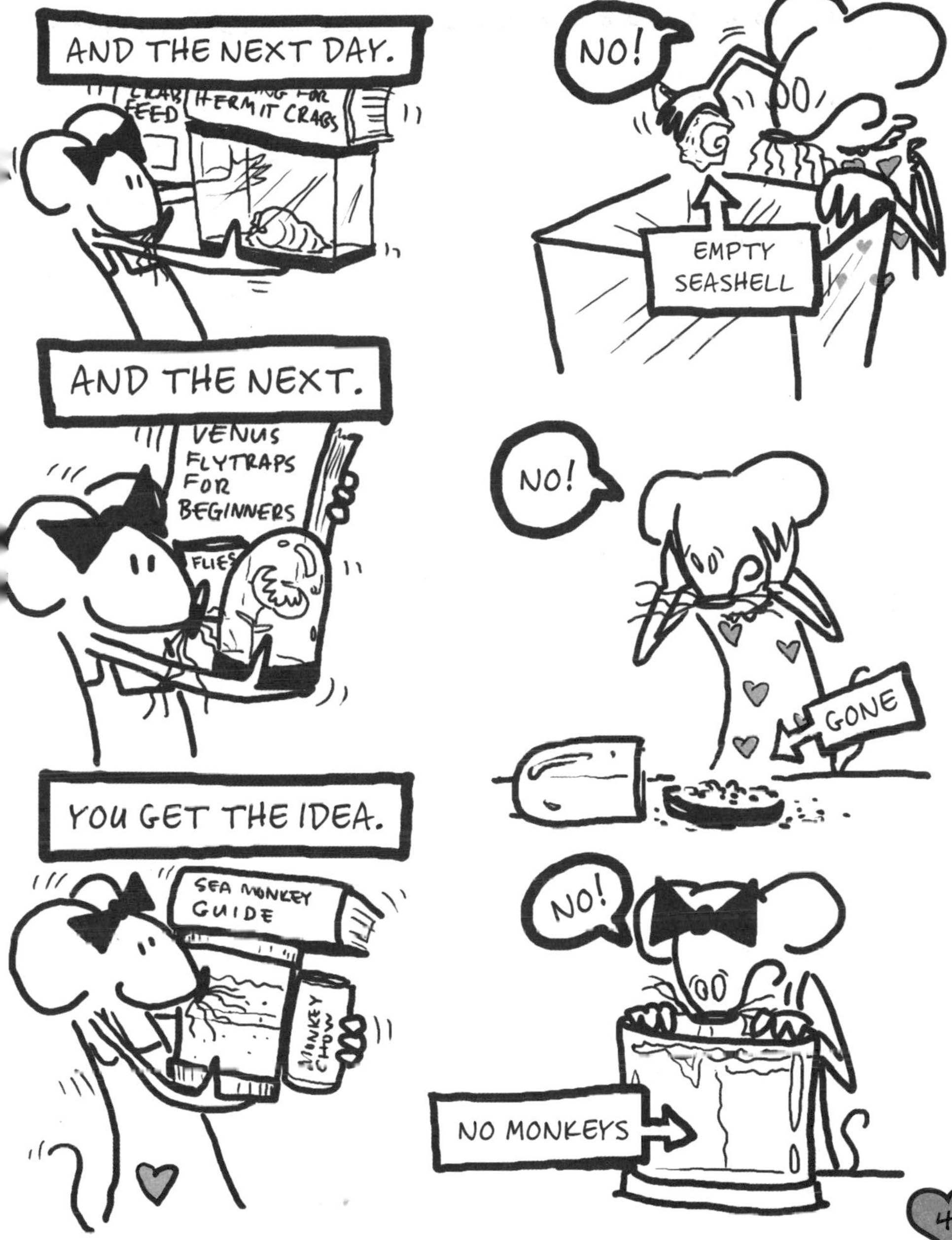
AND THE NEXT DAY.
FEED
HERMIT CRABS
NO!
EMPTY SEASHELL
AND THE NEXT.
VENUS FLYTRAPS FOR BEGINNERS
FLIES
NO!
GONE
YOU GET THE IDEA.
SEA MONKEY GUIDE
MONKEY CHOW
NO!
NO MONKEYS

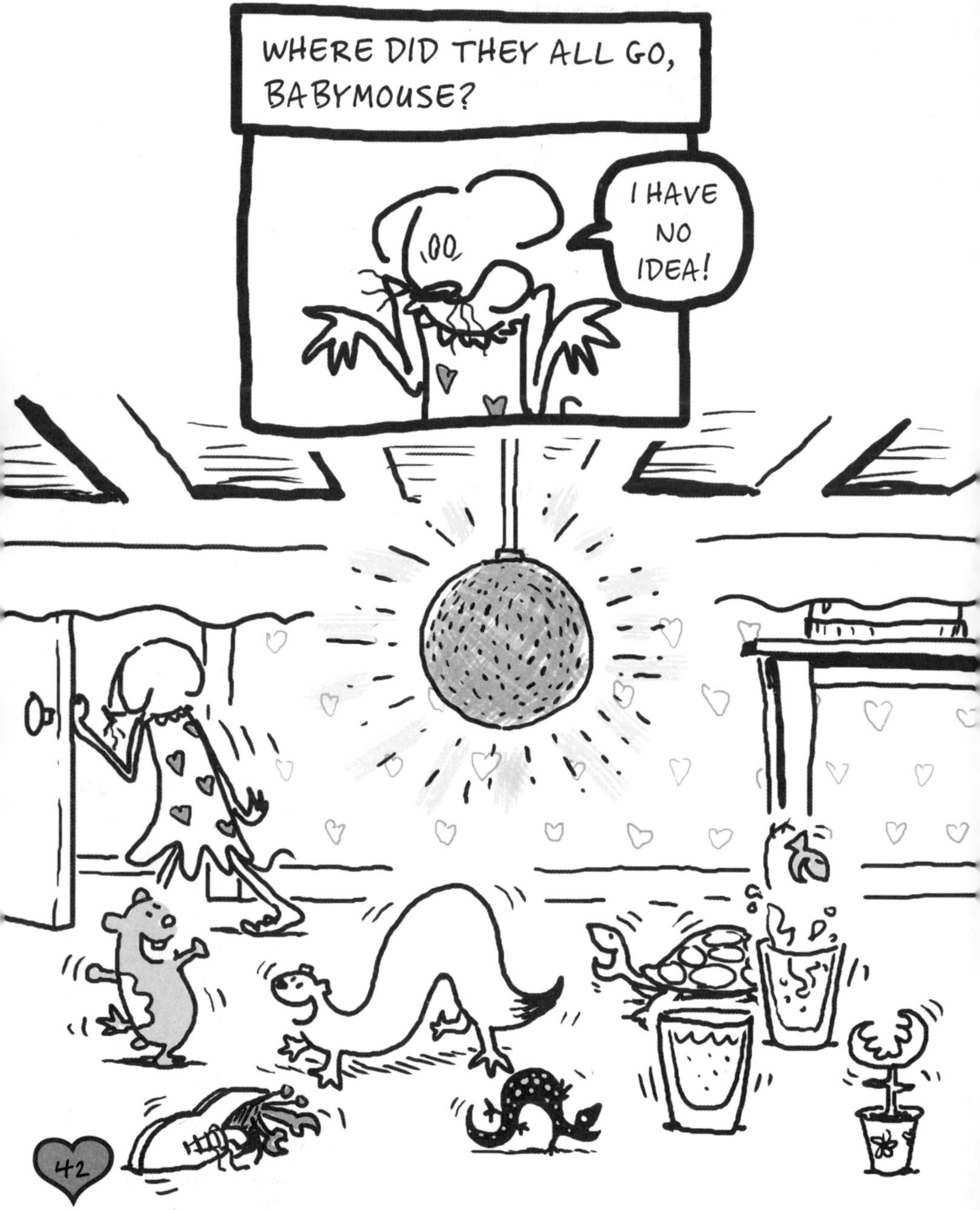
WHERE DID THEY ALL GO, BABYMOUSE?
I HAVE NO IDEA!

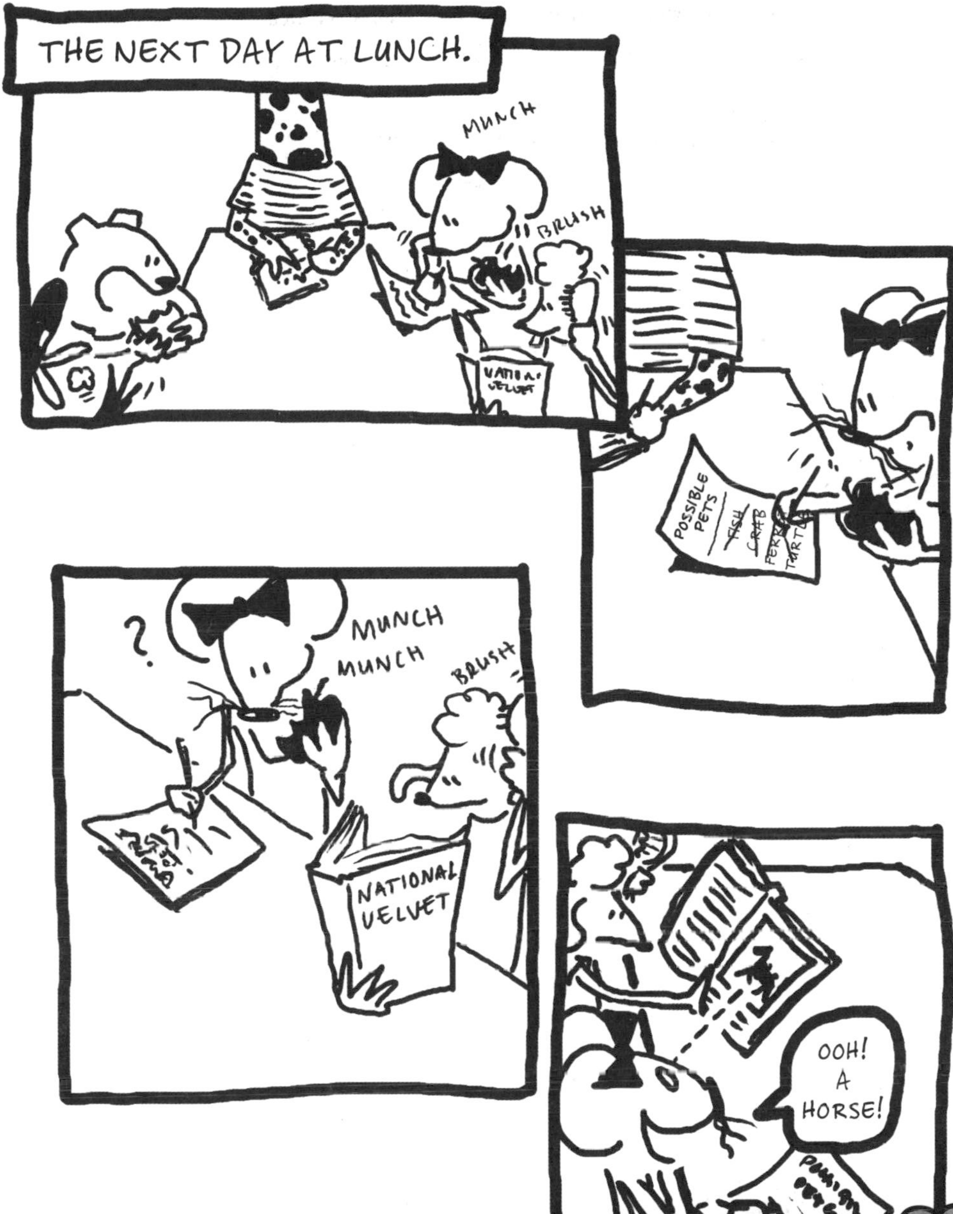
THE NEXT DAY AT LUNCH.
MUNCH
BRUSH
POSSIBLE PETS
FISH
CRAB
?
MUNCH
MUNCH
BRUSH
NATIONAL VELVET
OOH! A HORSE!

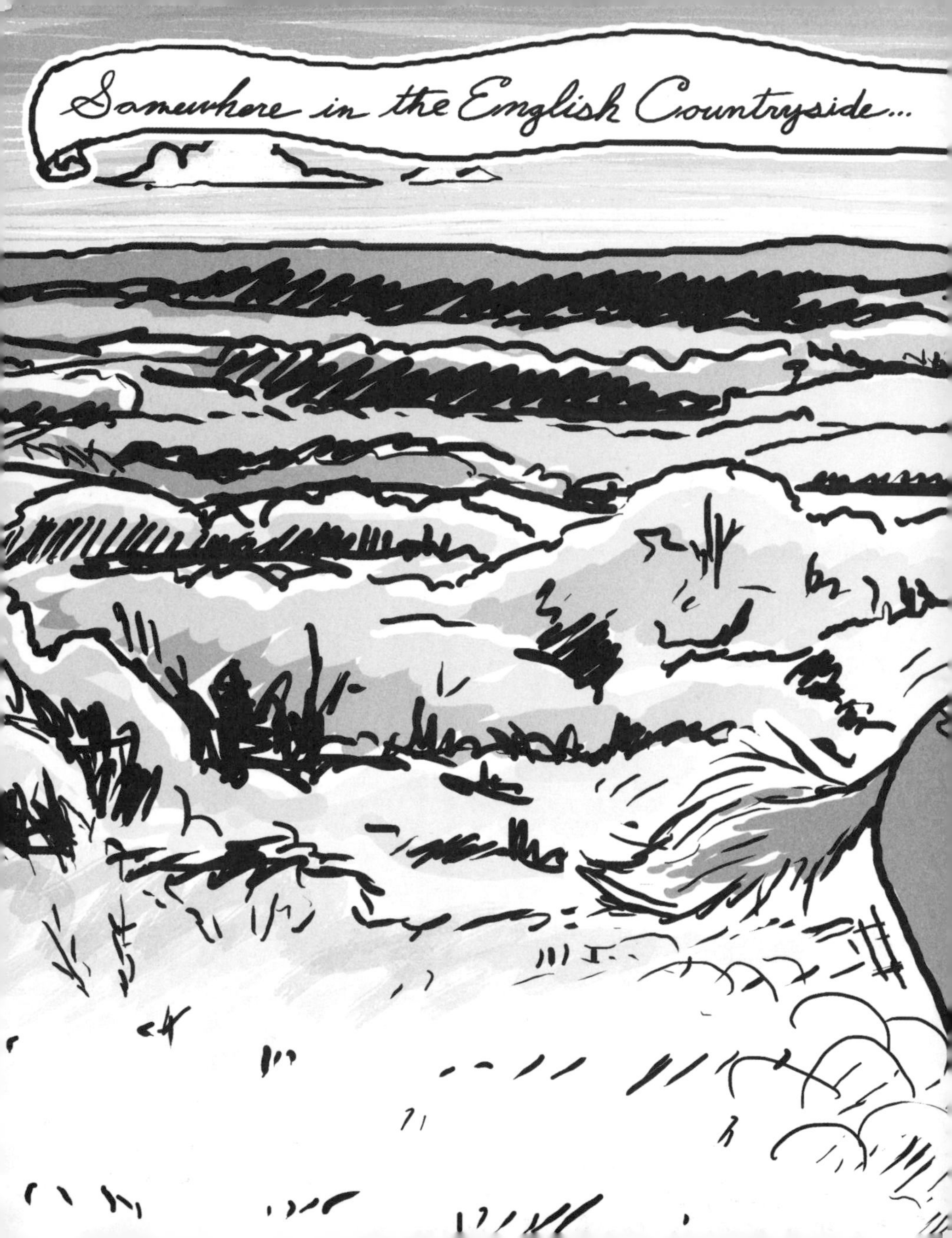
Somewhere in the English Countryside...

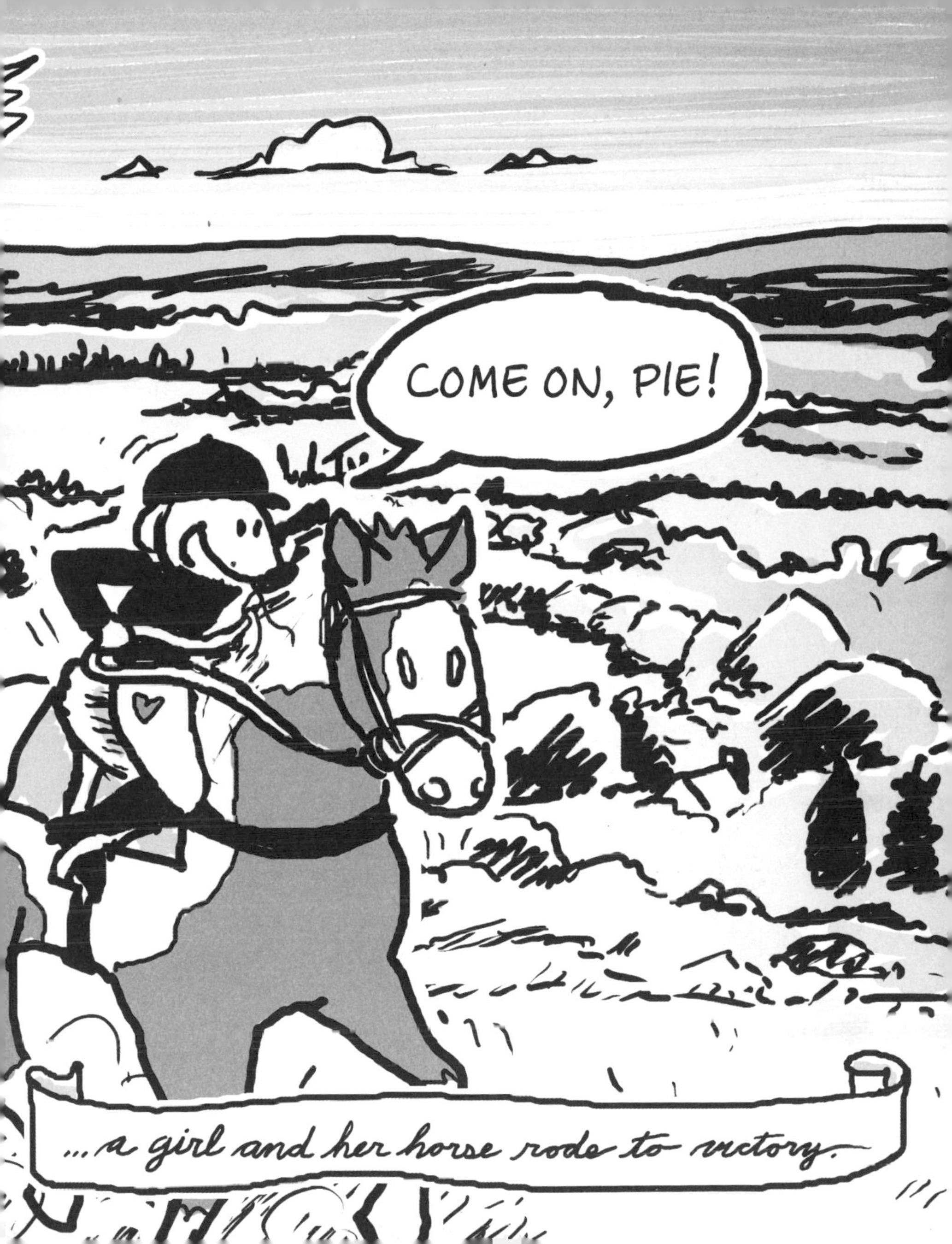
COME ON, PIE!
...a girl and her horse rode to victory.

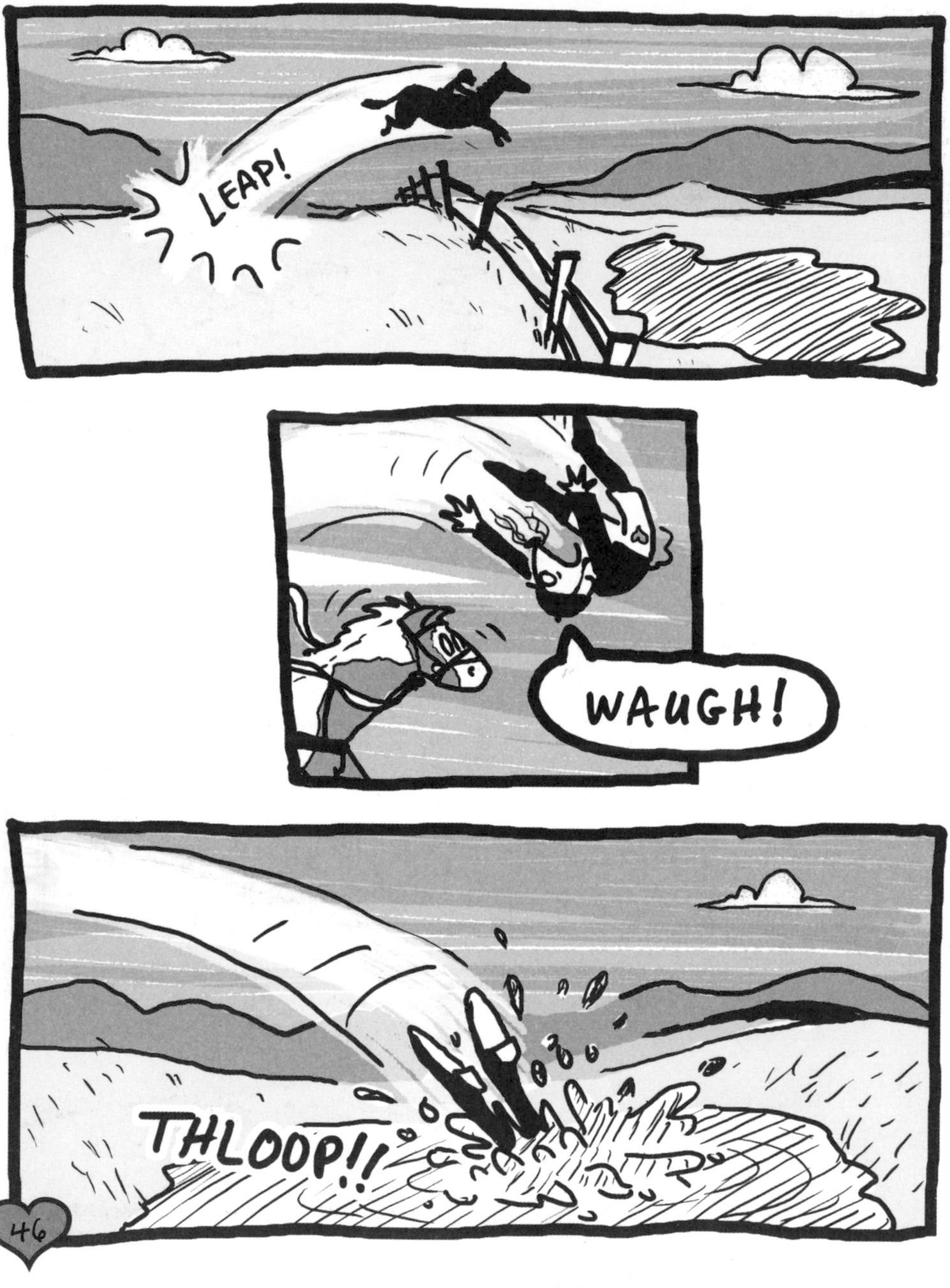
LEAP!
WAUGH!
THLOOP!!

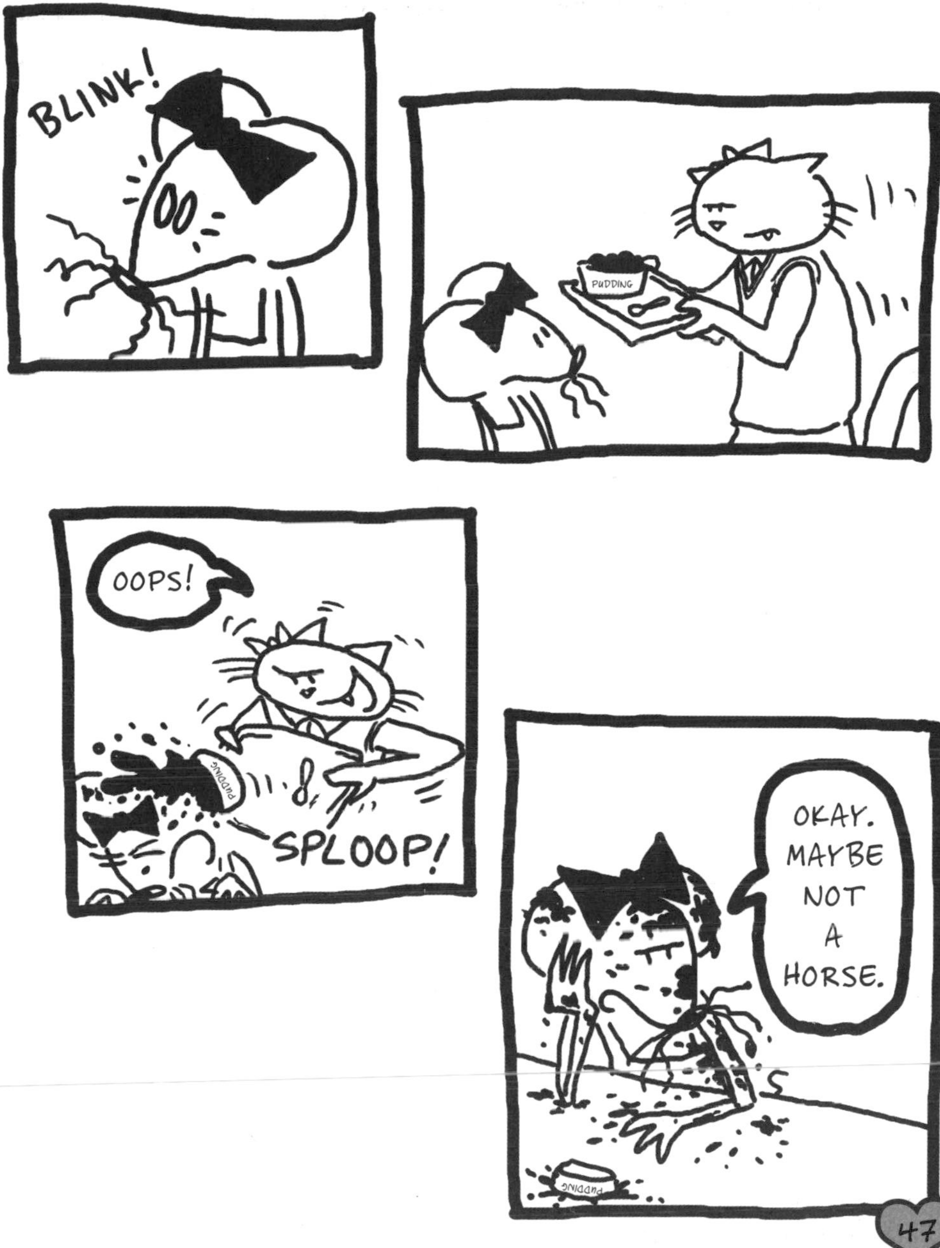
BLINK!
PUDDING
OOPS!
PUDDING
SPLOOP!
OKAY. MAYBE NOT A HORSE.
PUDDING

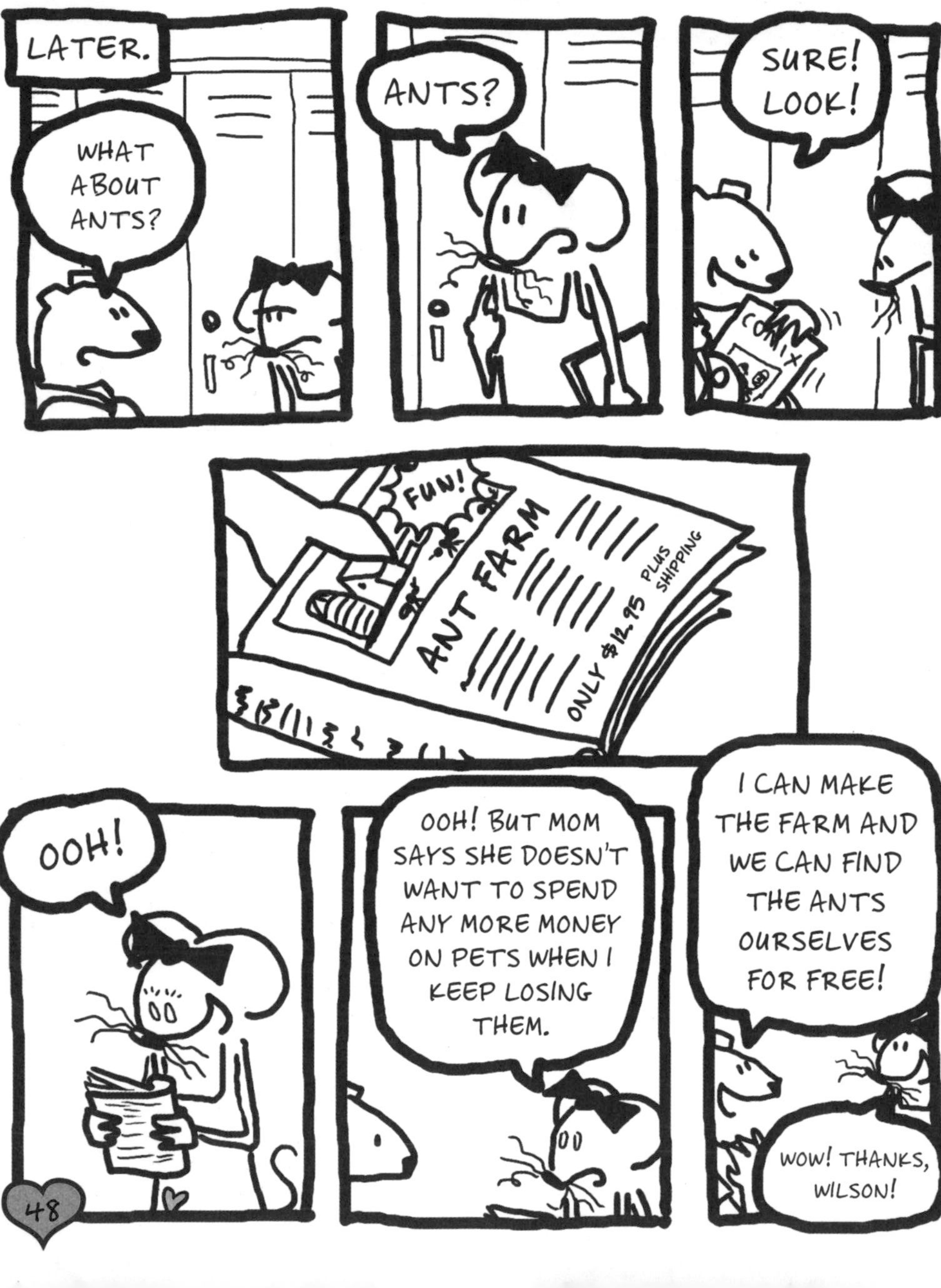
LATER.
WHAT ABOUT ANTS?
ANTS?
SURE! LOOK!
COMIX
FUN!
ANT FARM
ONLY $12.95
PLUS SHIPPING
OOH!
OOH! BUT MOM SAYS SHE DOESN'T WANT TO SPEND ANY MORE MONEY ON PETS WHEN I KEEP LOSING THEM.
I CAN MAKE THE FARM AND WE CAN FIND THE ANTS OURSELVES FOR FREE!
WOW! THANKS, WILSON!

AFTER SCHOOL.

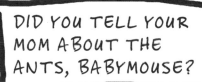

THAT NIGHT.

DID YOU TELL YOUR MOM ABOUT THE ANTS, BABYMOUSE?

NOT YET. BUT SHE WON'T MIND. MY PARENTS DIDN'T HAVE TO PAY FOR THESE PETS!

49

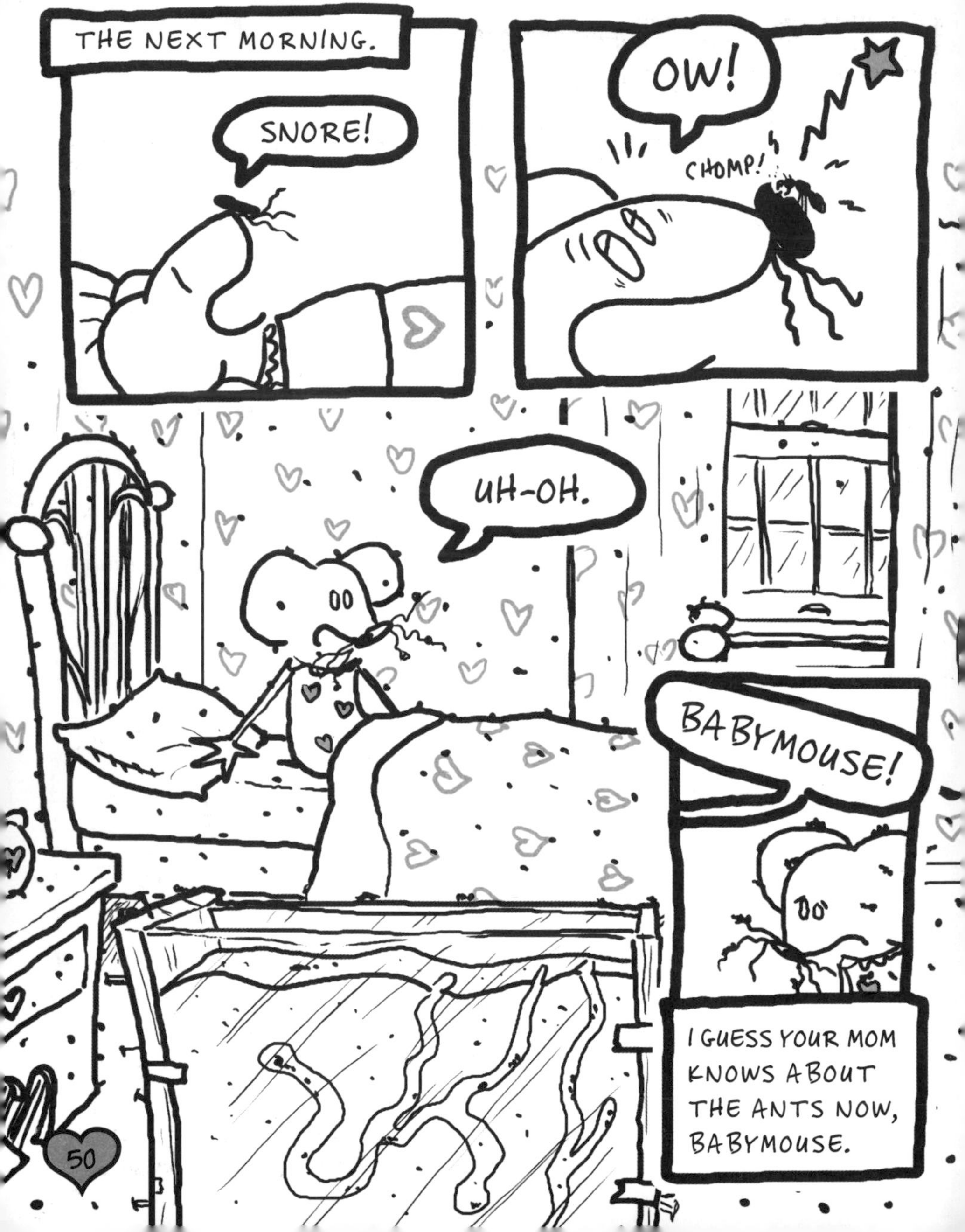
THE NEXT MORNING.
SNORE!
OW!
CHOMP!
UH-OH.
BABYMOUSE!
I GUESS YOUR MOM KNOWS ABOUT THE ANTS NOW, BABYMOUSE.

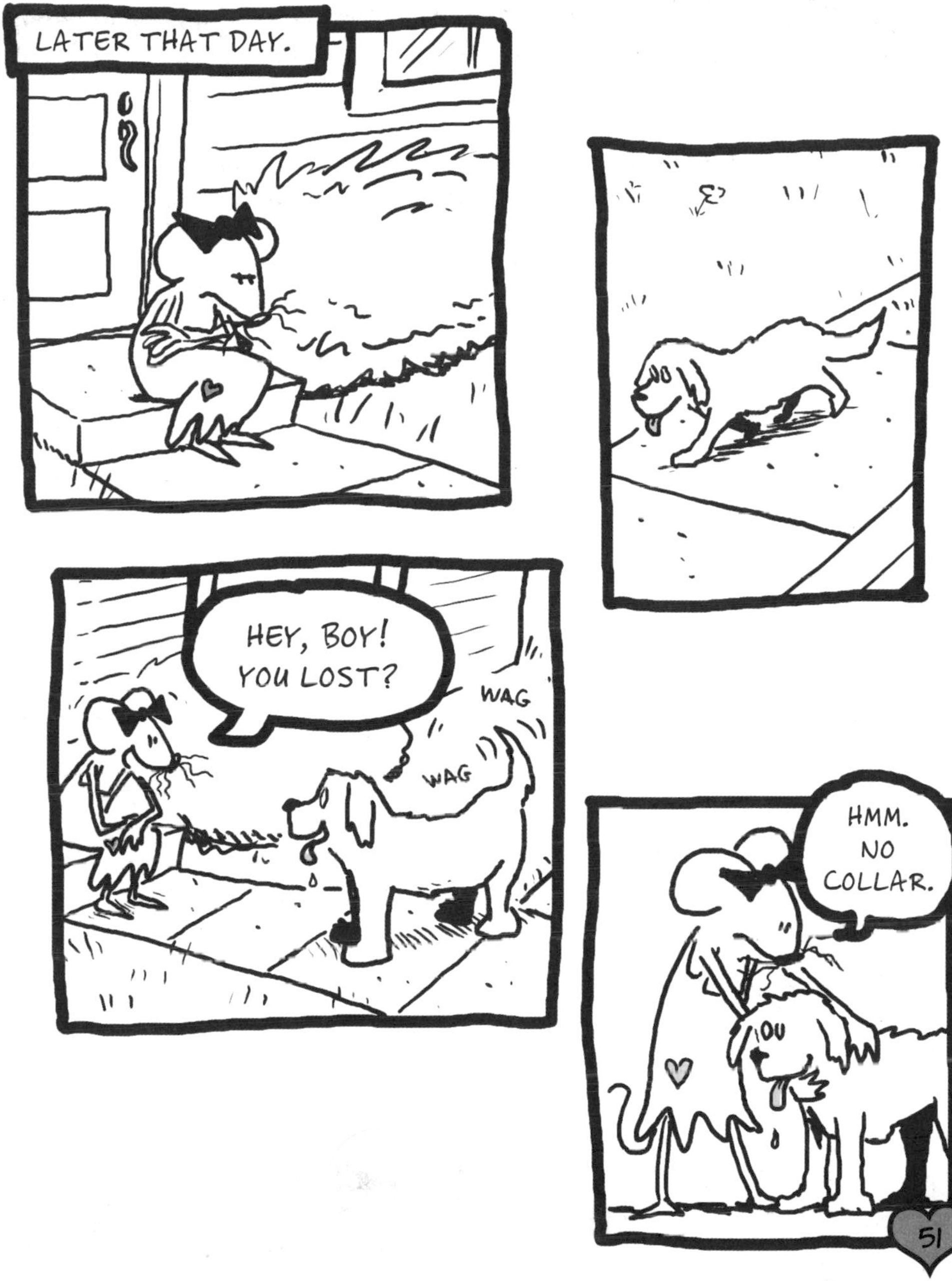
LATER THAT DAY.
HEY, BOY! YOU LOST?
WAG
WAG
HMM. NO COLLAR.

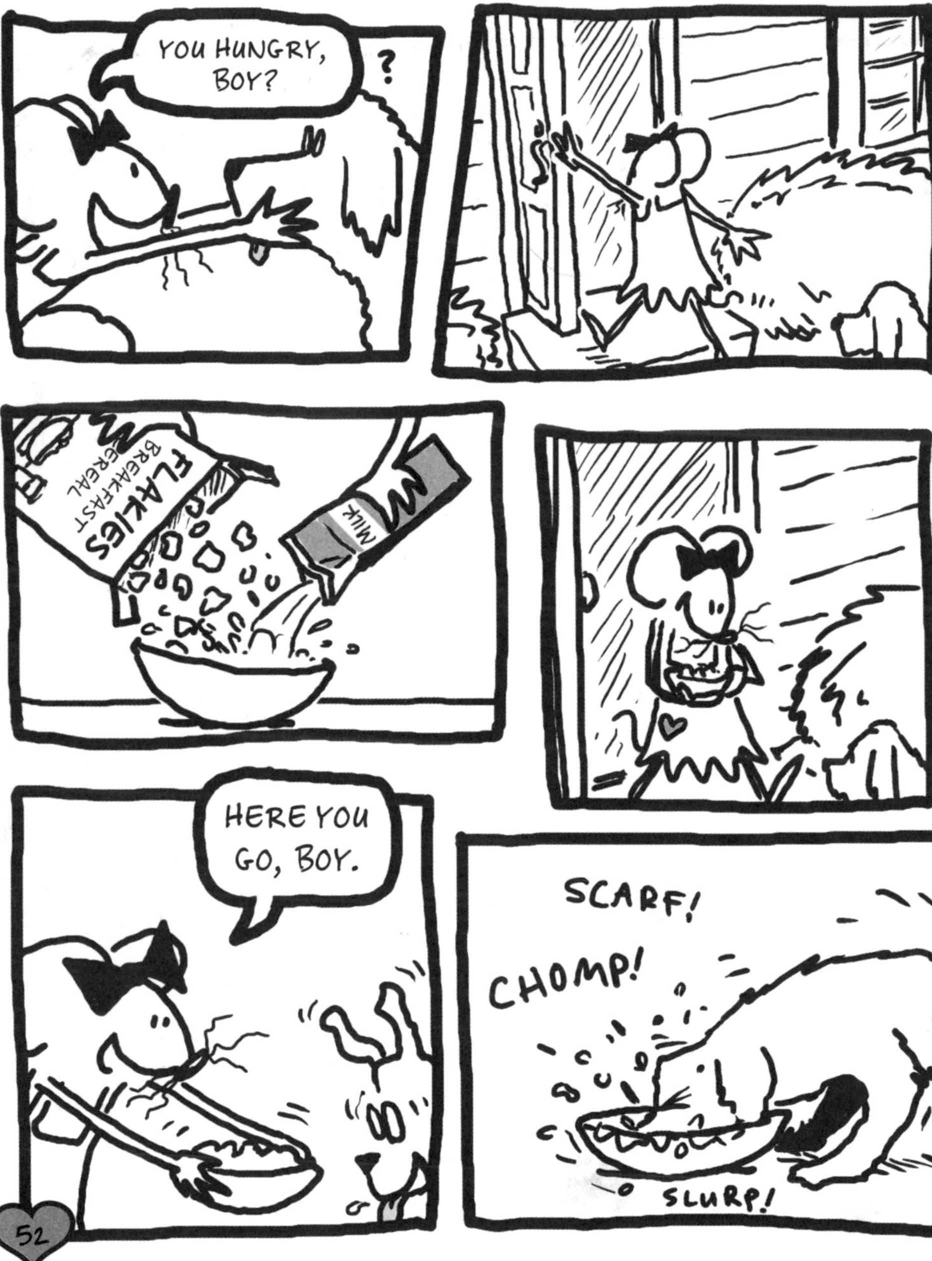
YOU HUNGRY, BOY?
?
FLAKKIES BREAKFAST BEREAL
MILK
HERE YOU GO, BOY.
SCARF!
CHOMP!
SLURP!

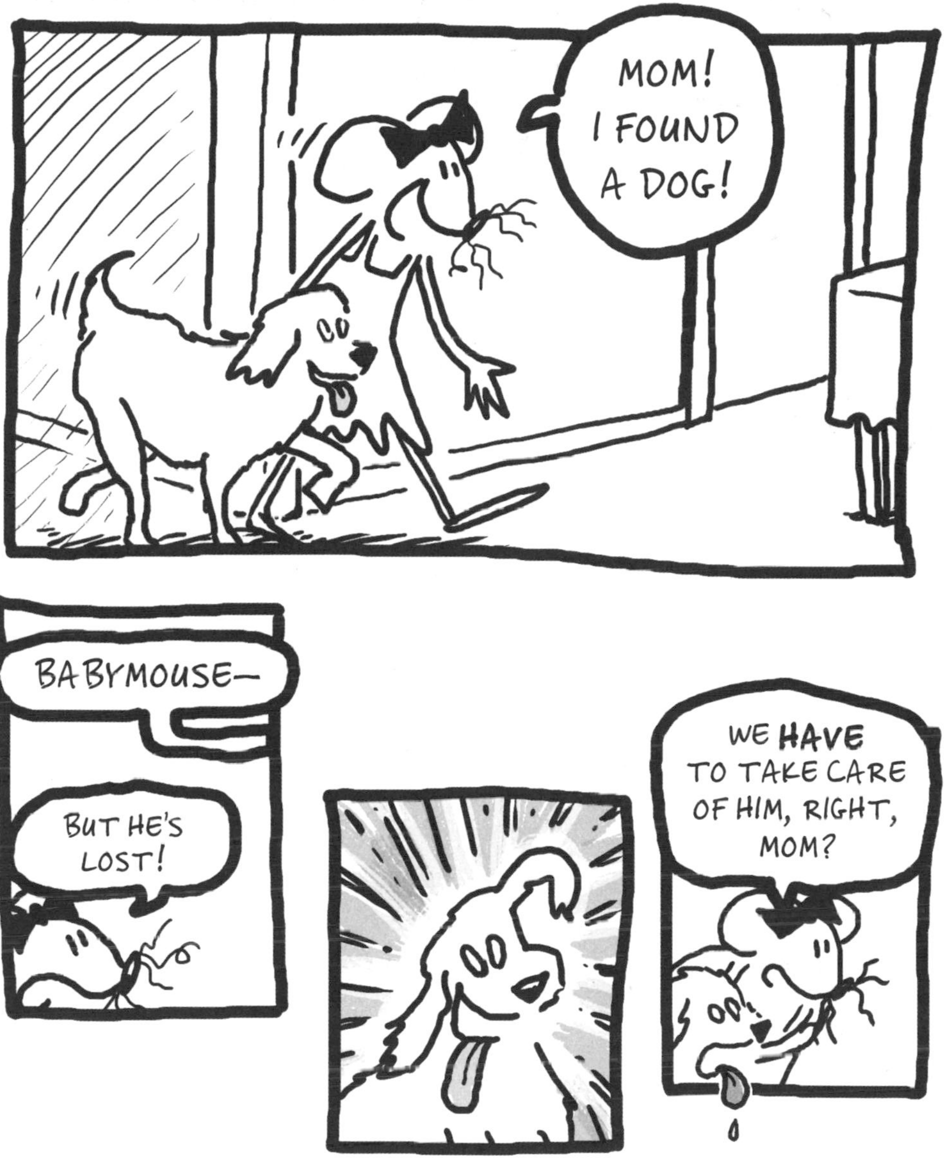
MOM! I FOUND A DOG!
BABYMOUSE—
BUT HE'S LOST!
WE **HAVE** TO TAKE CARE OF HIM, RIGHT, MOM?

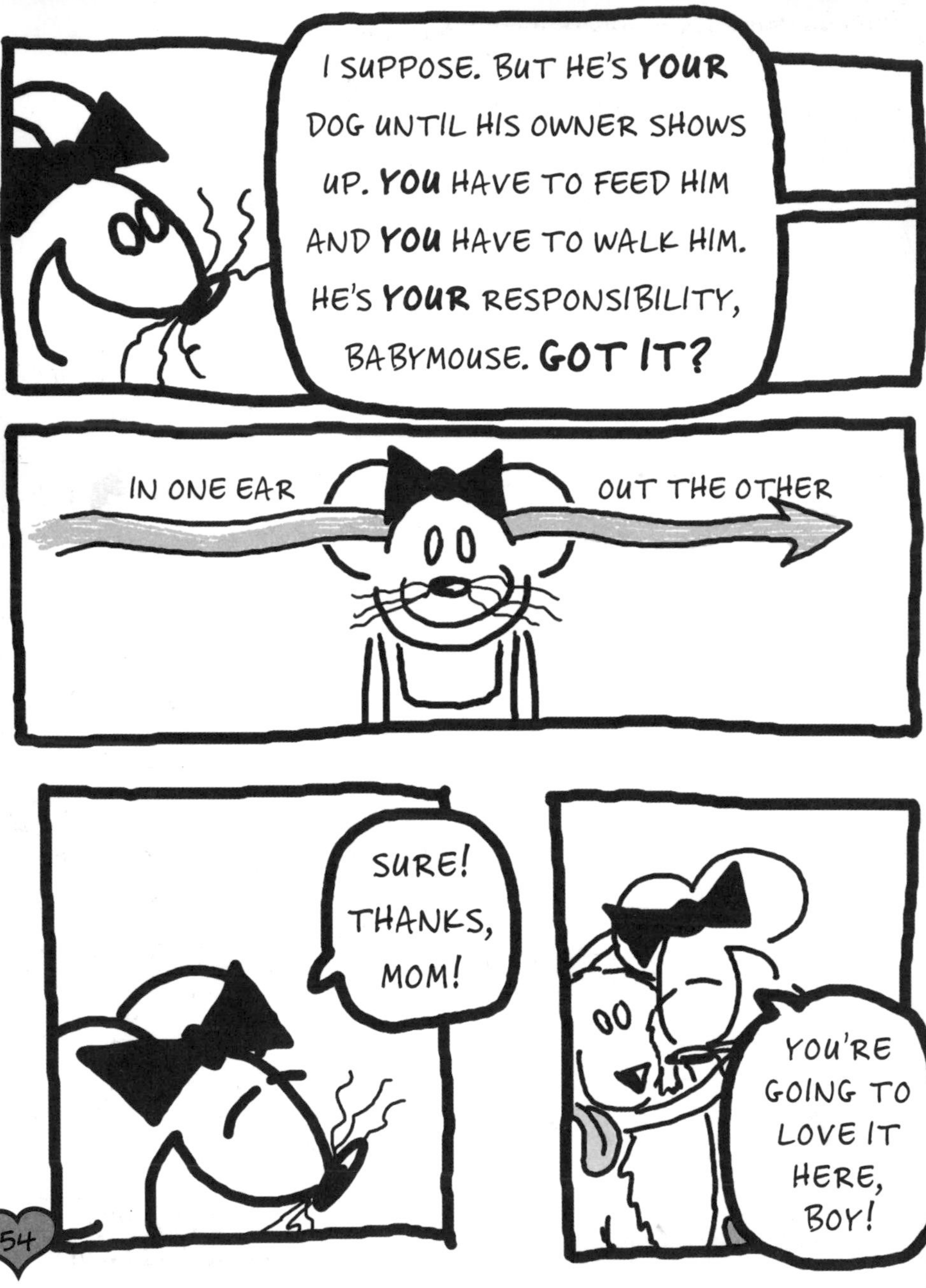
I SUPPOSE. BUT HE'S YOUR DOG UNTIL HIS OWNER SHOWS UP. YOU HAVE TO FEED HIM AND YOU HAVE TO WALK HIM. HE'S YOUR RESPONSIBILITY, BABYMOUSE. GOT IT?
IN ONE EAR
OUT THE OTHER
SURE! THANKS, MOM!
YOU'RE GOING TO LOVE IT HERE, BOY!

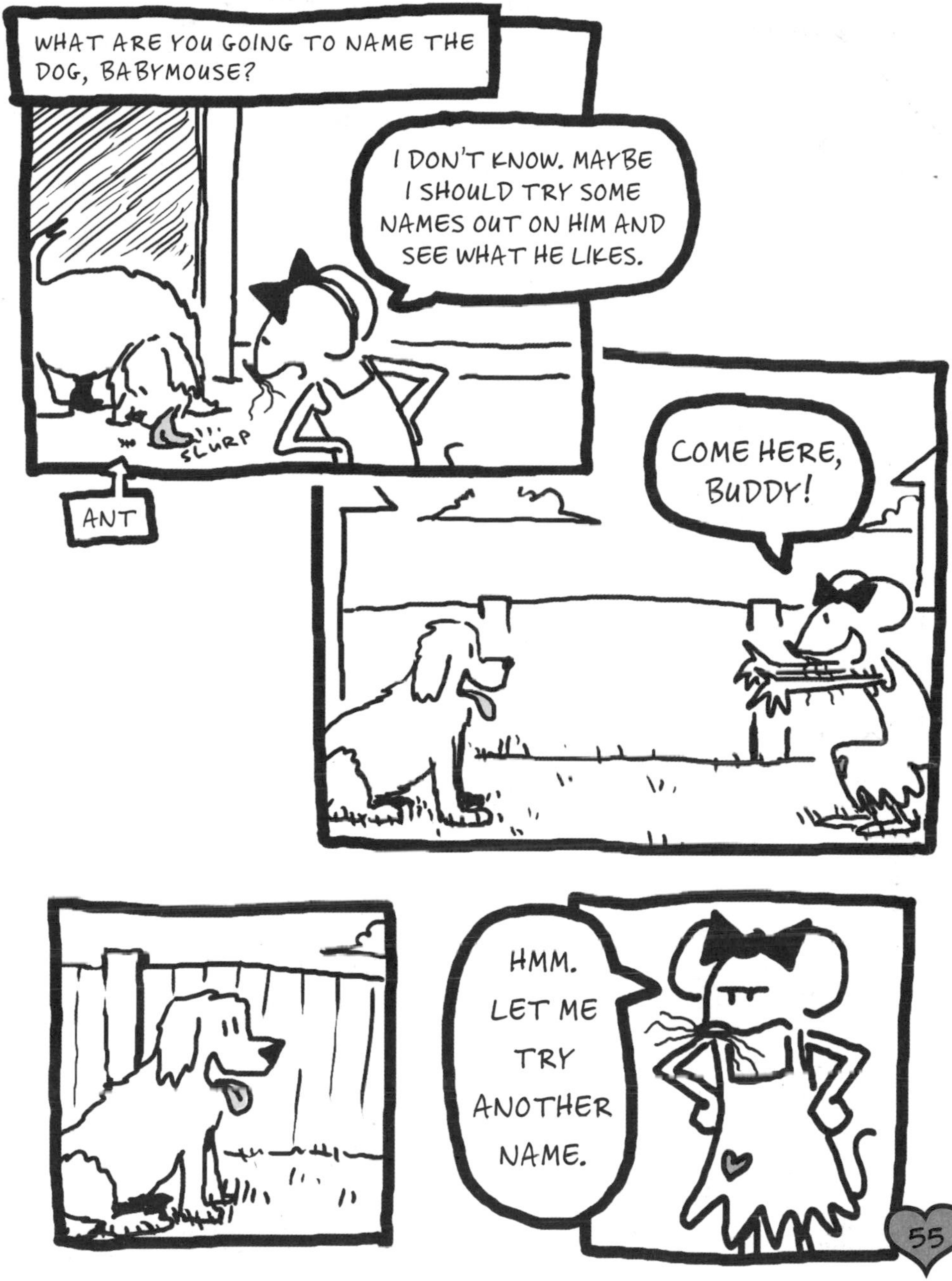
WHAT ARE YOU GOING TO NAME THE DOG, BABYMOUSE?
I DON'T KNOW. MAYBE I SHOULD TRY SOME NAMES OUT ON HIM AND SEE WHAT HE LIKES.
SLURP
ANT
COME HERE, BUDDY!
HMM. LET ME TRY ANOTHER NAME.

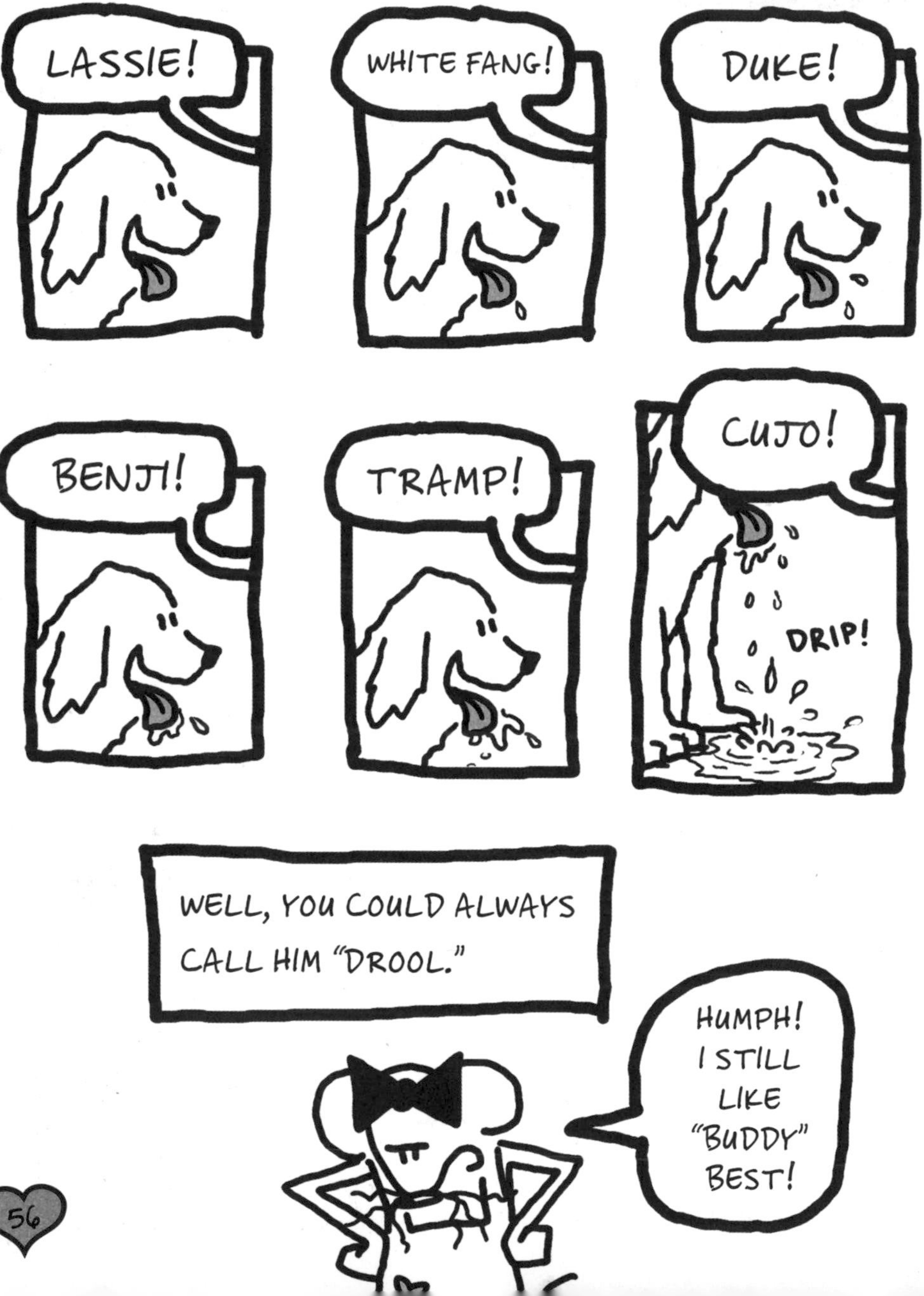
LASSIE!
WHITE FANG!
DUKE!
BENJI!
TRAMP!
CUJO!
DRIP!
WELL, YOU COULD ALWAYS CALL HIM "DROOL."
HUMPH! I STILL LIKE "BUDDY" BEST!

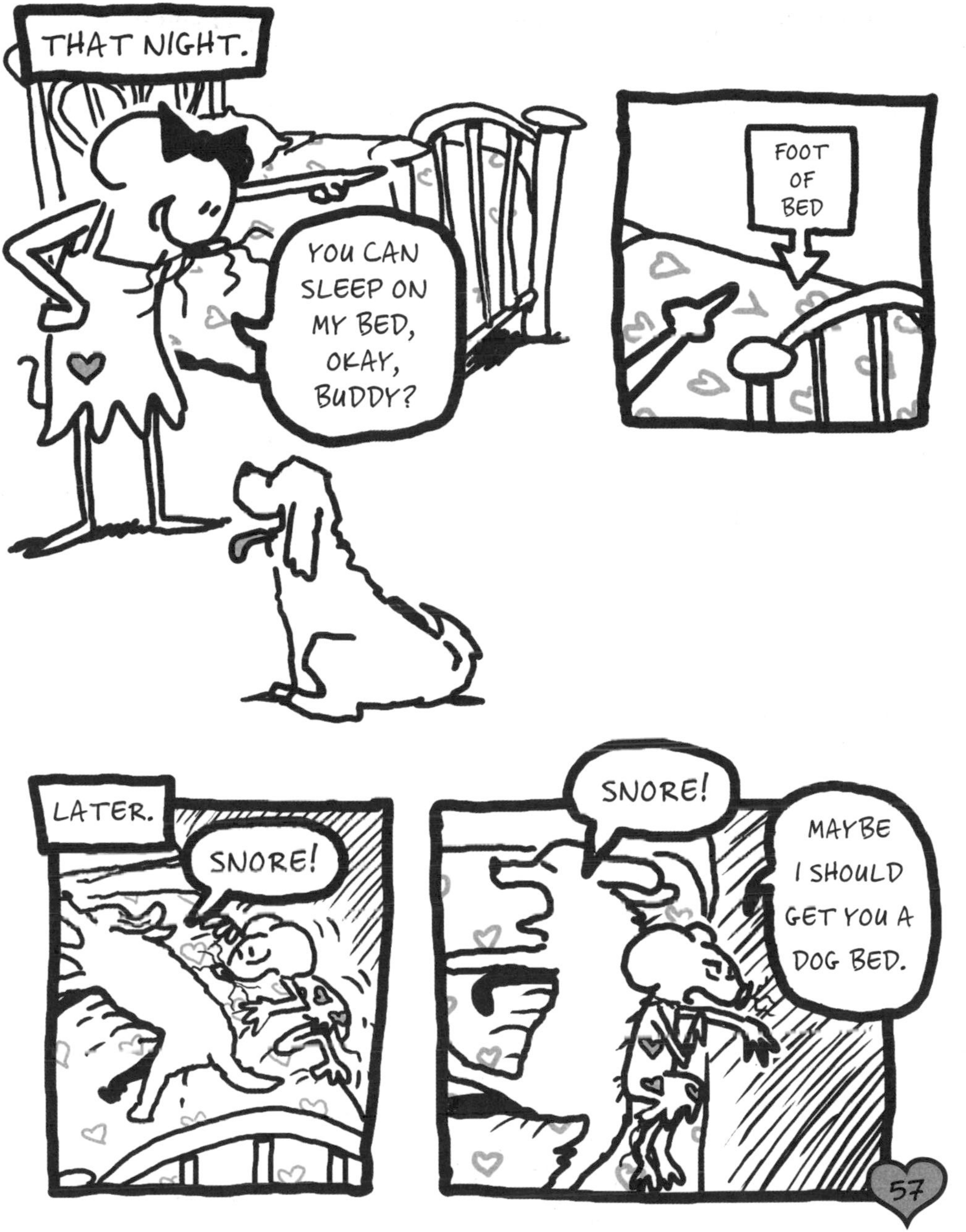
THAT NIGHT.
YOU CAN SLEEP ON MY BED, OKAY, BUDDY?
FOOT OF BED
LATER.
SNORE!
SNORE!
MAYBE I SHOULD GET YOU A DOG BED.

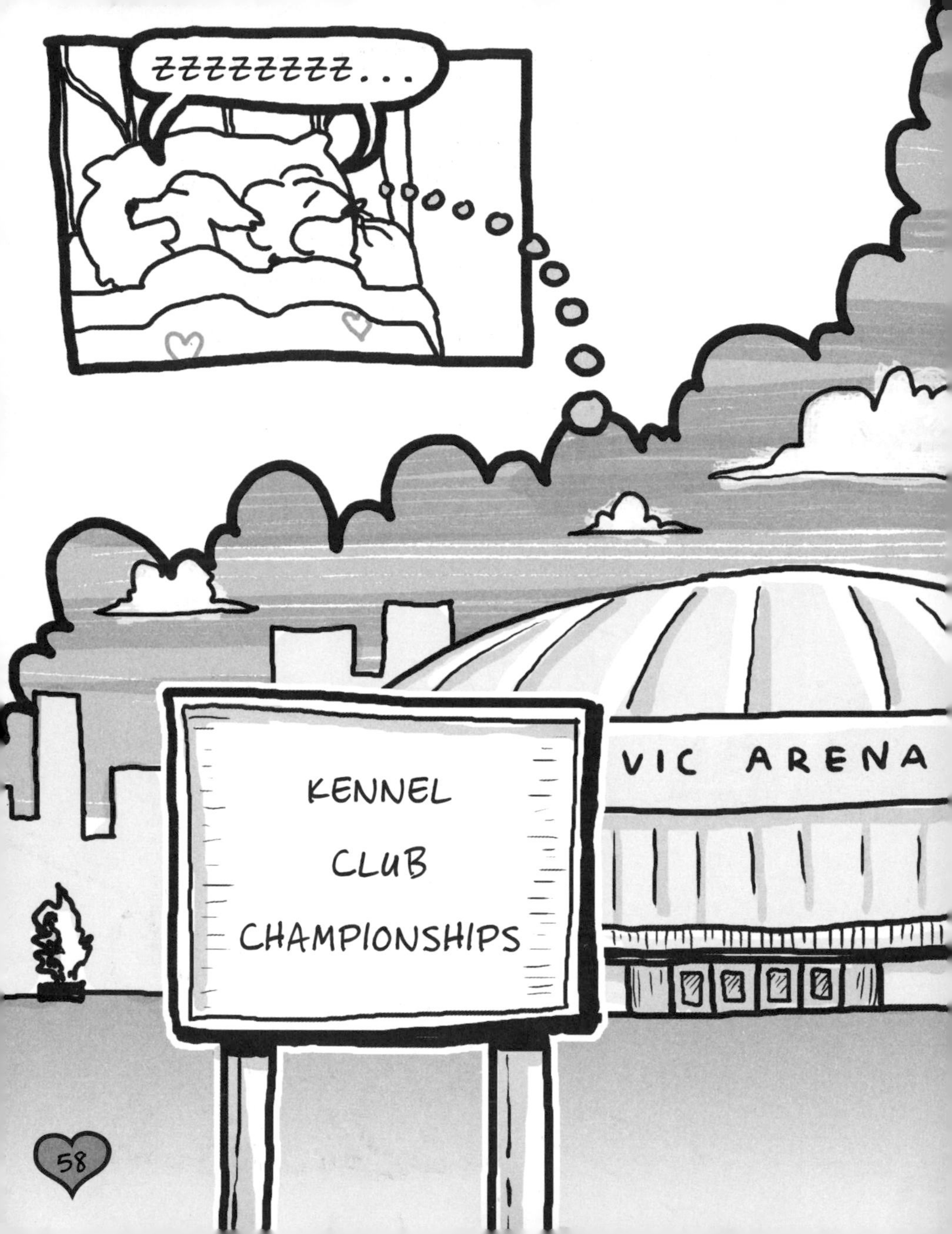
ZZZZZZZZZ...
VIC ARENA
KENNEL
CLUB
CHAMPIONSHIPS

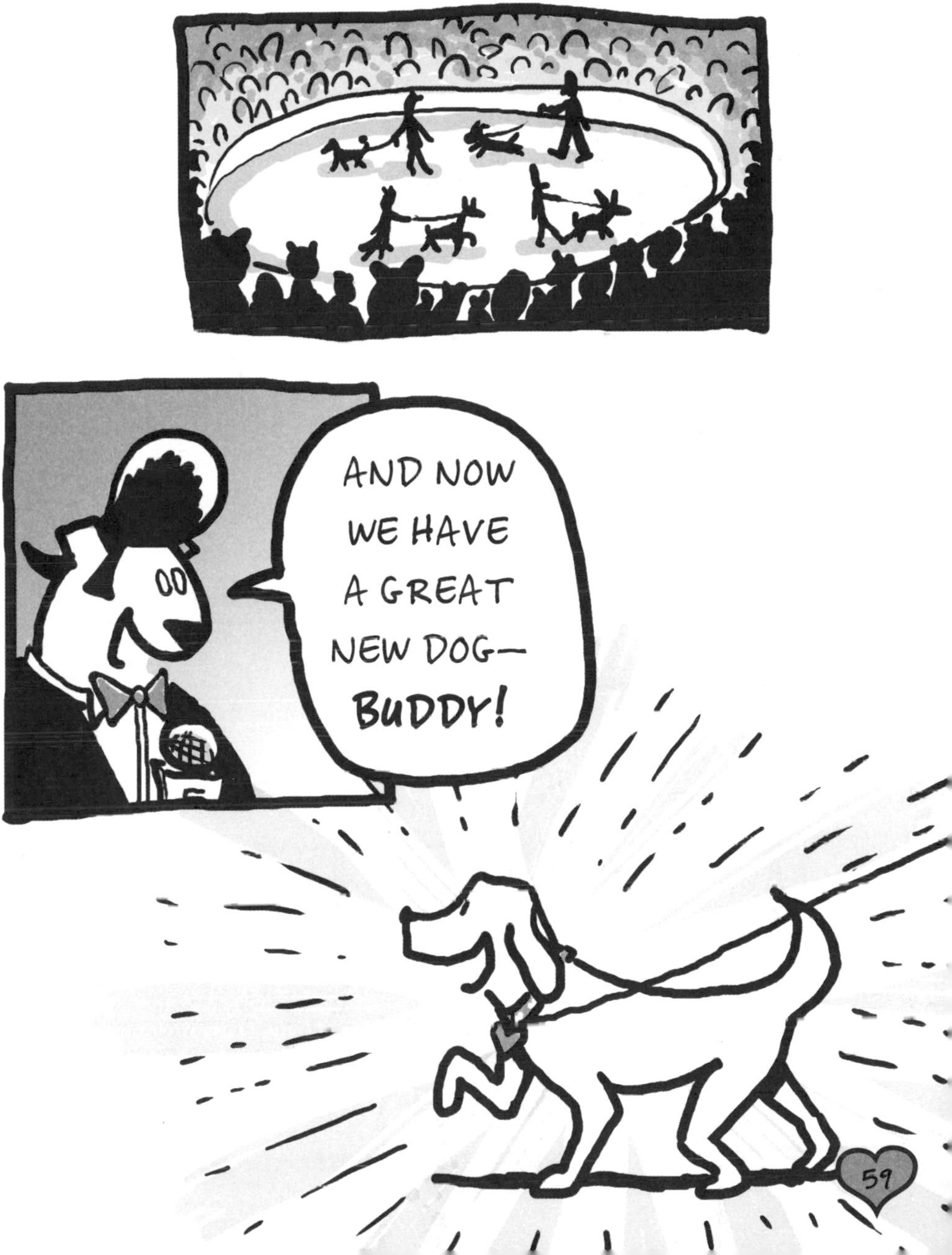
AND NOW WE HAVE A GREAT NEW DOG— BUDDY!

BUDDY IS A PUREBRED LAB-CHOW-TERRIER-HOUND-BULLDOG MIX.

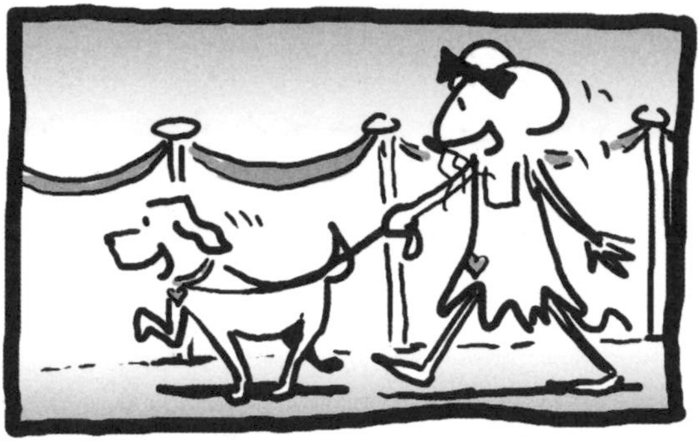

BUDDY'S OWNER, BABYMOUSE, HAS BEEN WORKING WITH HIM FOR SOME TIME NOW.

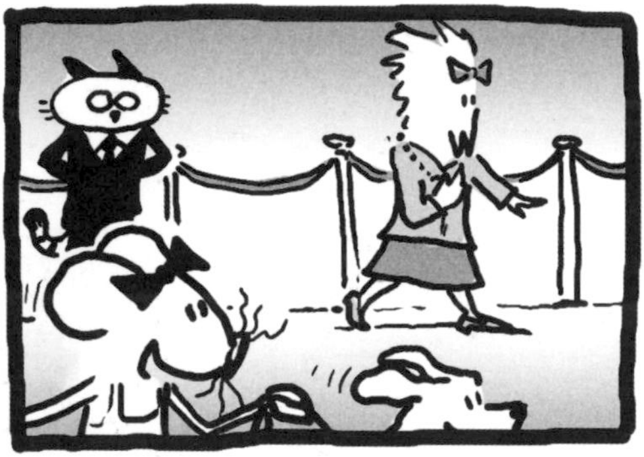

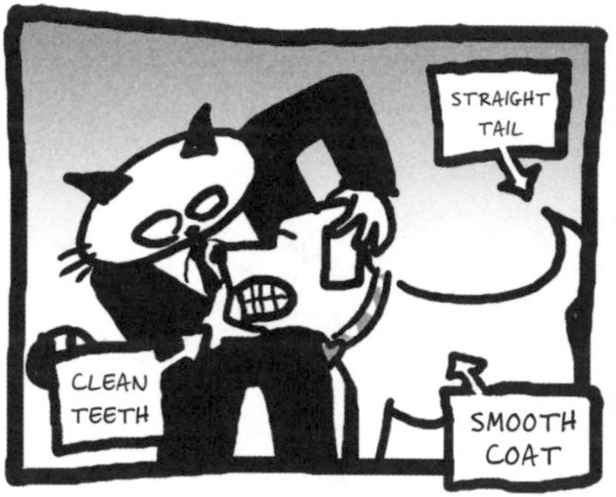
STRAIGHT TAIL
CLEAN TEETH
SMOOTH COAT

LOOKS LIKE THE JUDGES ARE TALLYING THE SCORES...

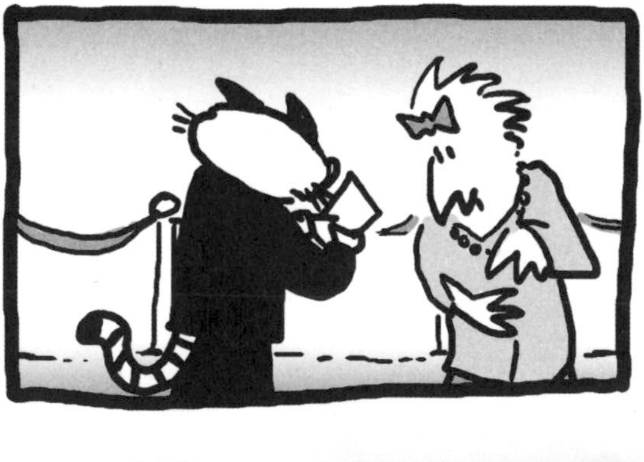

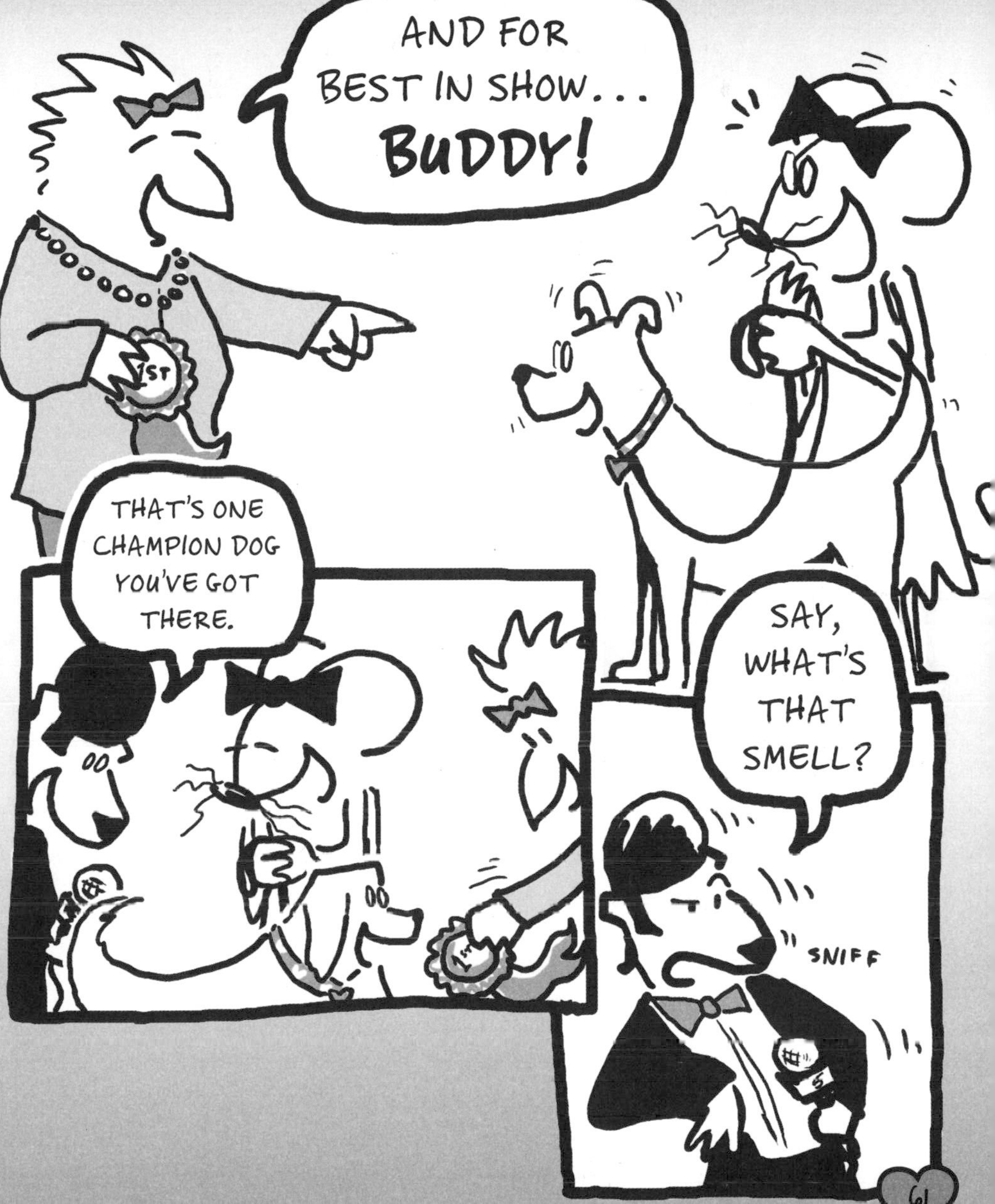
AND FOR BEST IN SHOW... BUDDY!
1ST
THAT'S ONE CHAMPION DOG YOU'VE GOT THERE.
SAY, WHAT'S THAT SMELL?
SNIFF

POP!

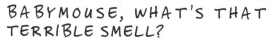

BABYMOUSE, WHAT'S THAT TERRIBLE SMELL?

SNIFF SNIFF

SNIFF

STEP

SQUISH!

EWW!

SOME DREAM, HUH?

MORE LIKE A NIGHTMARE!

SNIFF SNIFF

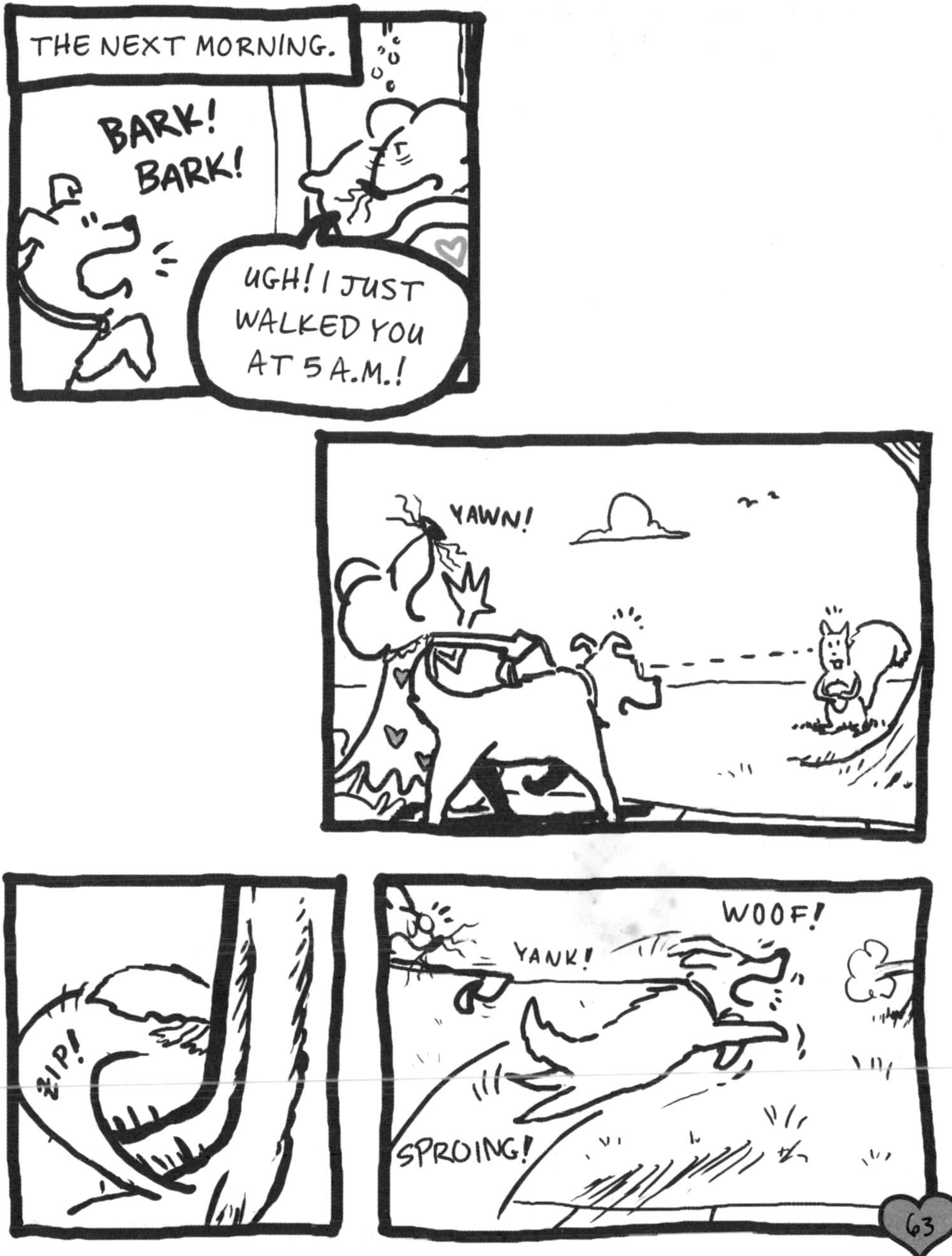
THE NEXT MORNING.
BARK! BARK!
UGH! I JUST WALKED YOU AT 5 A.M.!
YAWN!
ZIP!
WOOF!
YANK!
SPROING!

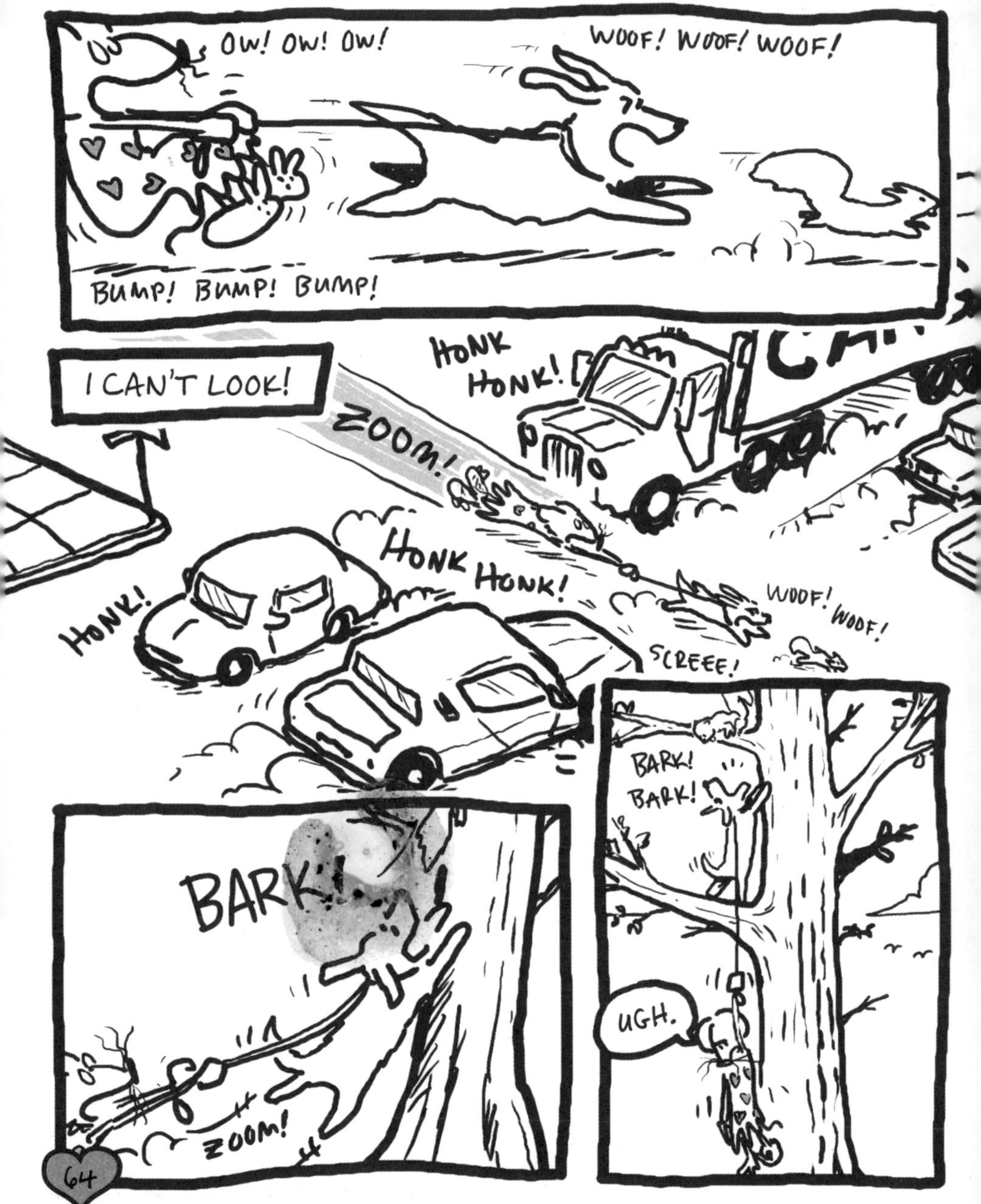
OW! OW! OW!
WOOF! WOOF! WOOF!
BUMP! BUMP! BUMP!
I CAN'T LOOK!
HONK HONK!
ZOOM!
HONK HONK!
HONK!
WOOF! WOOF!
SCREEE!
BARK!
ZOOM!
BARK! BARK!
UGH.

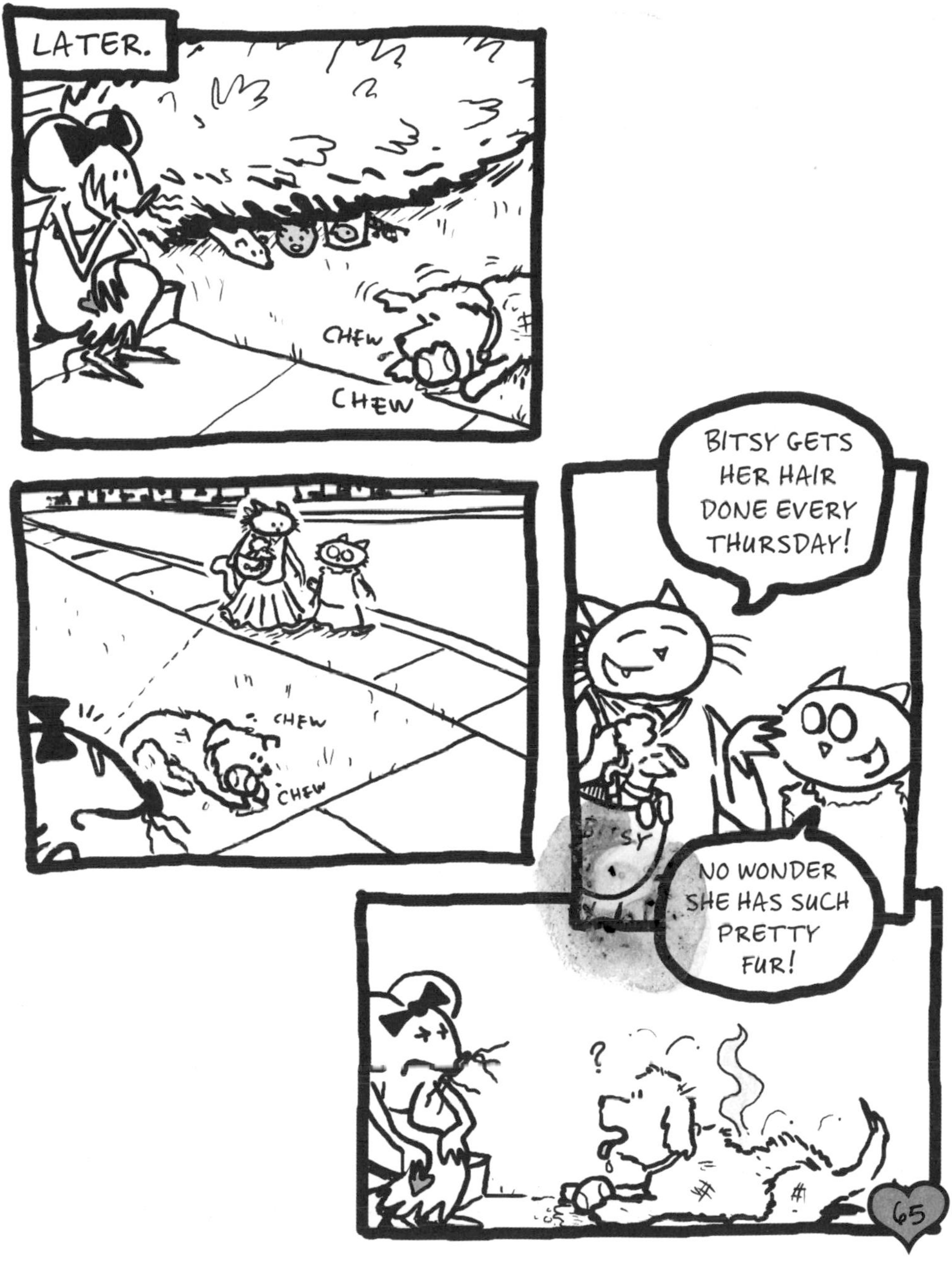
LATER.
CHEW
CHEW
CHEW
CHEW
BITSY GETS HER HAIR DONE EVERY THURSDAY!
NO WONDER SHE HAS SUCH PRETTY FUR!
BITSY

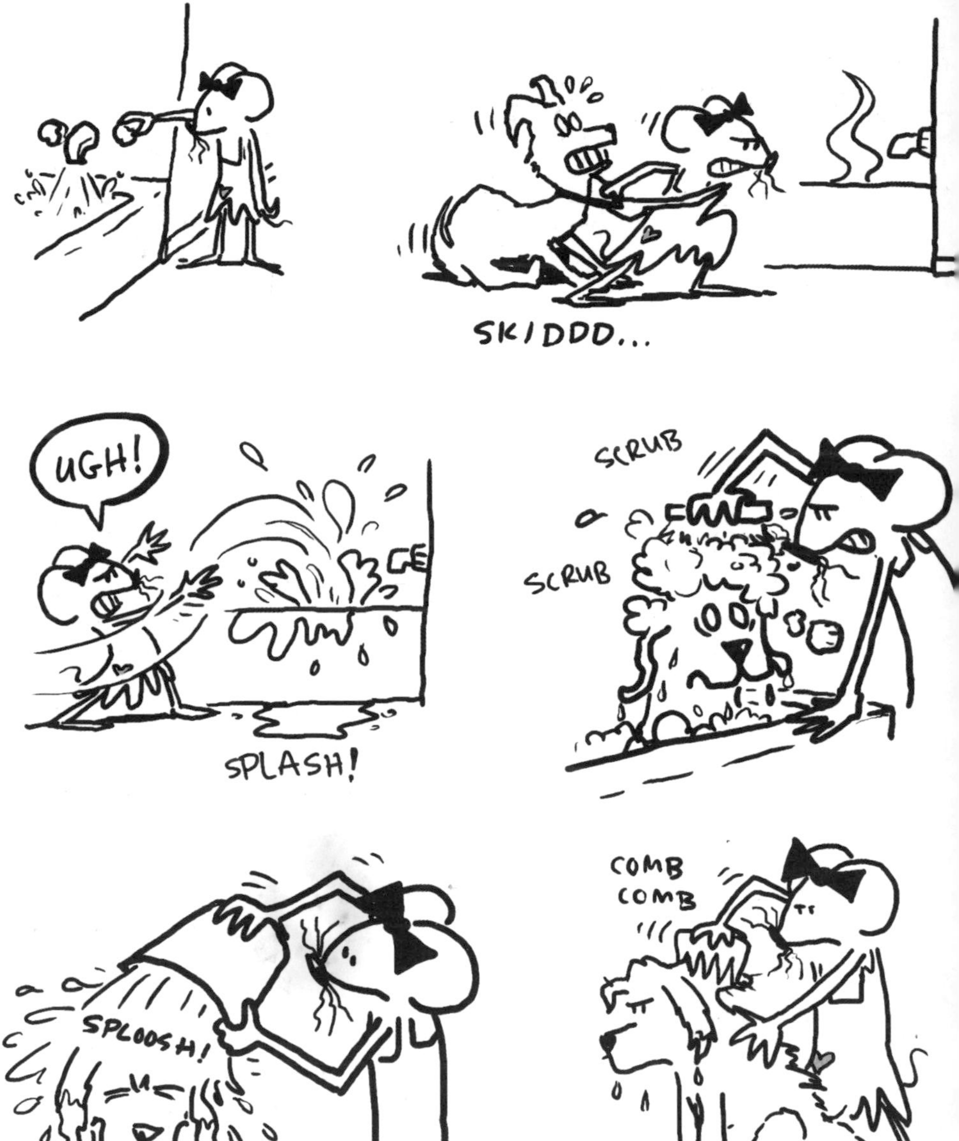
SKIDDD...
UGH!
SPLASH!
SCRUB
SCRUB
SPLOOSH!
COMB
COMB

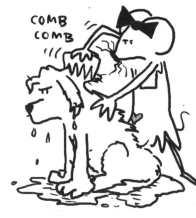

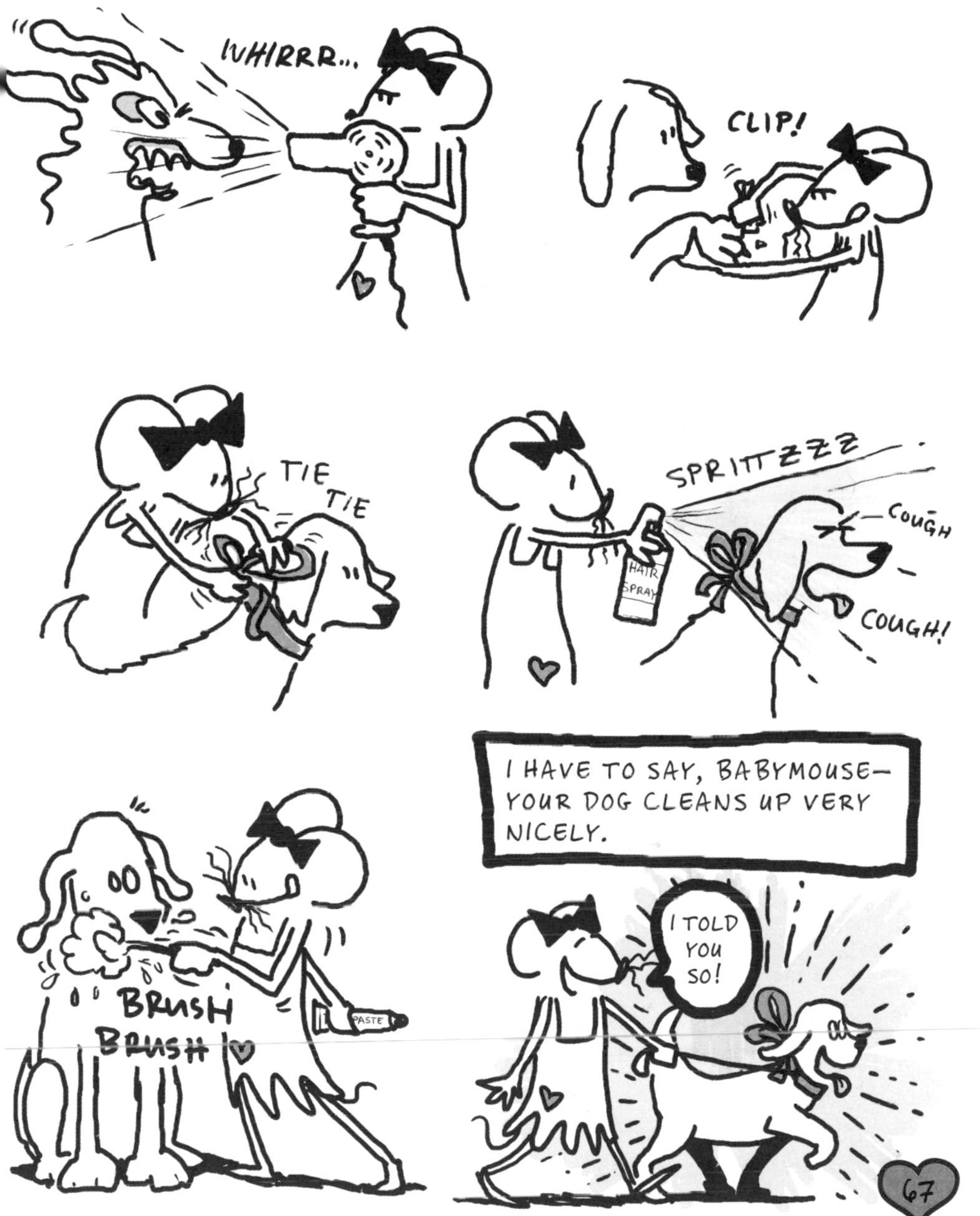
WHIRRR...
CLIP!
TIE TIE
SPRITTZZZ
COUGH
COUGH!
HAIR SPRAY
BRUSH BRUSH
PASTE
I HAVE TO SAY, BABYMOUSE—YOUR DOG CLEANS UP VERY NICELY.
I TOLD YOU SO!

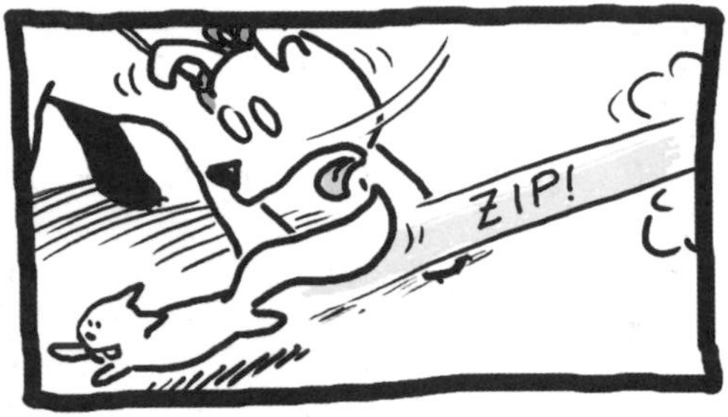
ZIP!

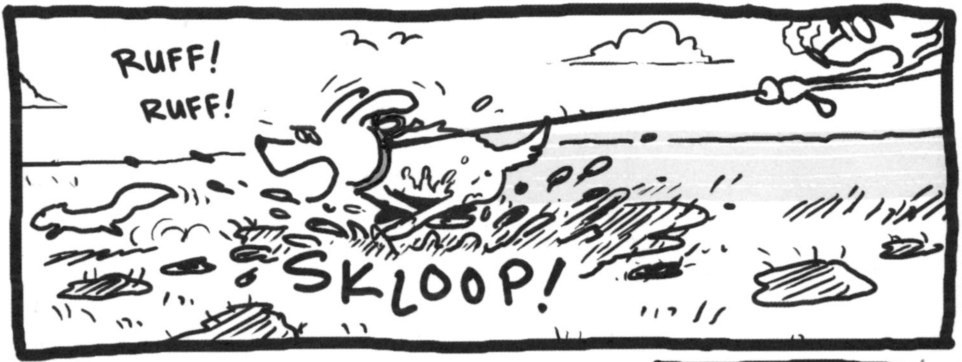
RUFF! RUFF!
SKLOOP!

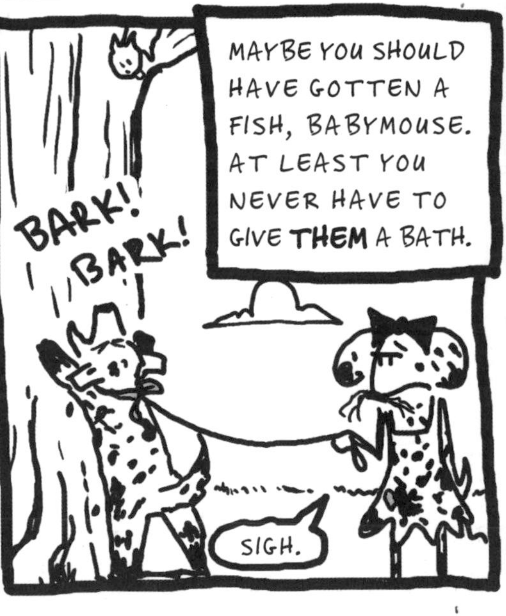
MAYBE YOU SHOULD HAVE GOTTEN A FISH, BABYMOUSE. AT LEAST YOU NEVER HAVE TO GIVE **THEM** A BATH.
BARK! BARK!
SIGH.

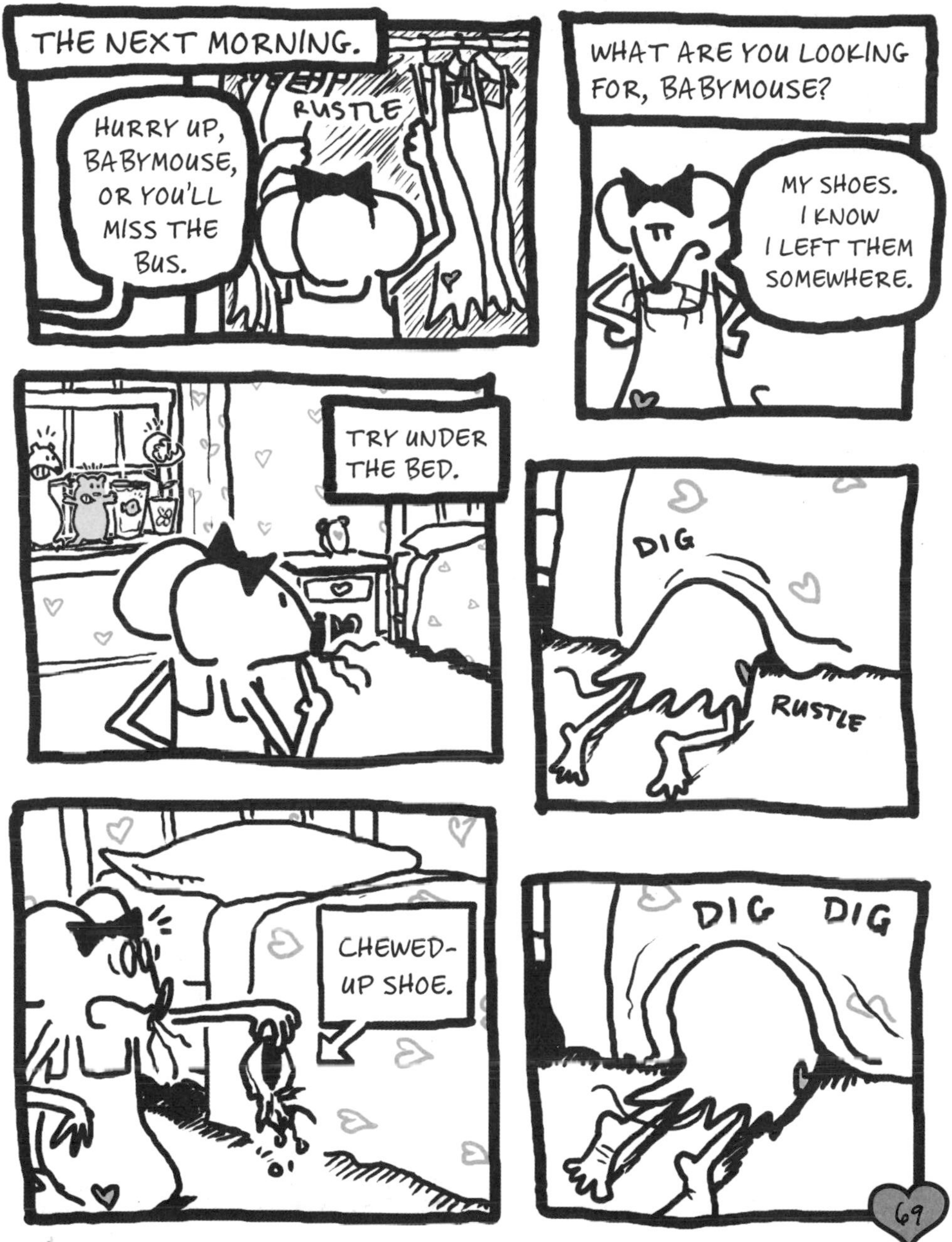
THE NEXT MORNING.
HURRY UP, BABYMOUSE, OR YOU'LL MISS THE BUS.
RUSTLE
WHAT ARE YOU LOOKING FOR, BABYMOUSE?
MY SHOES. I KNOW I LEFT THEM SOMEWHERE.
TRY UNDER THE BED.
DIG
RUSTLE
CHEWED-UP SHOE.
DIG DIG

TOSS

TOSS   TOSS

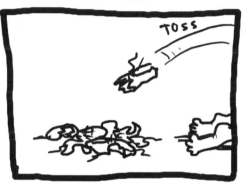

TOSS

DOGS DO LIKE TO CHEW, BABYMOUSE.

NOW WHAT AM I SUPPOSED TO WEAR?

LATER.

BUS

HA HA HA HA HA HA HA HA HA HA HA

SIGH.

70

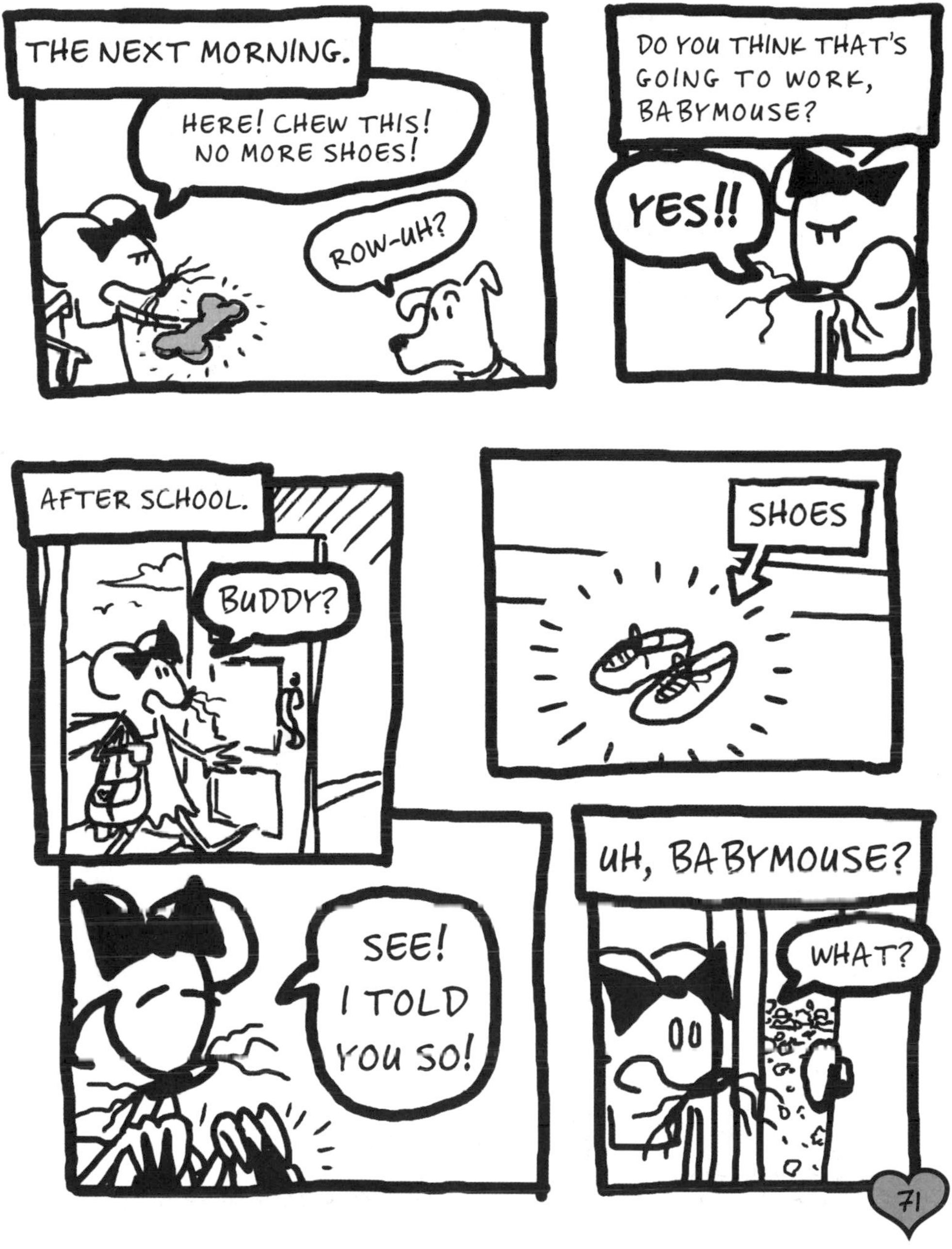

THE NEXT MORNING.
HERE! CHEW THIS! NO MORE SHOES!
ROW-UH?
DO YOU THINK THAT'S GOING TO WORK, BABYMOUSE?
YES!!
AFTER SCHOOL.
BUDDY?
SHOES
SEE! I TOLD YOU SO!
UH, BABYMOUSE?
WHAT?

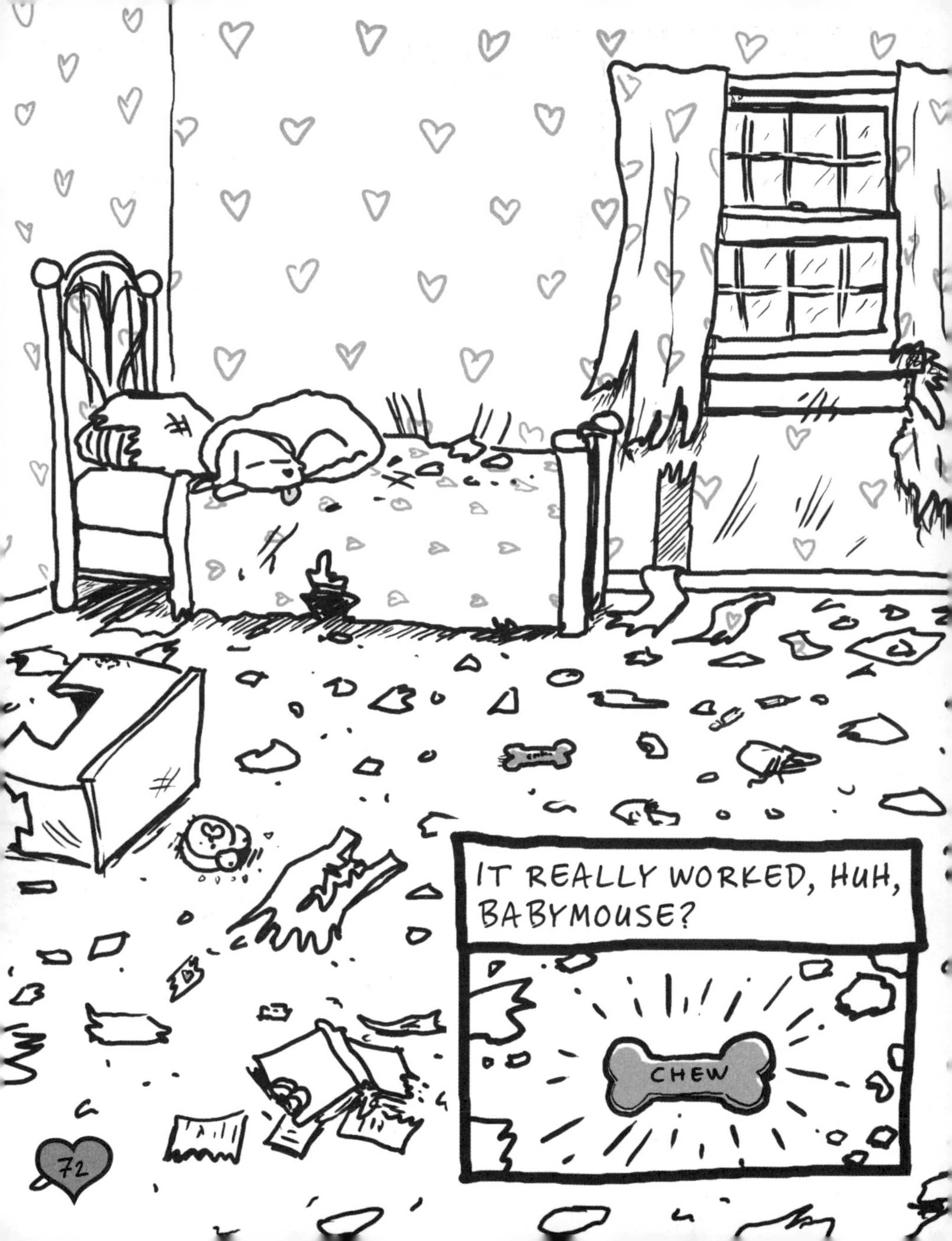
IT REALLY WORKED, HUH, BABYMOUSE?
CHEW

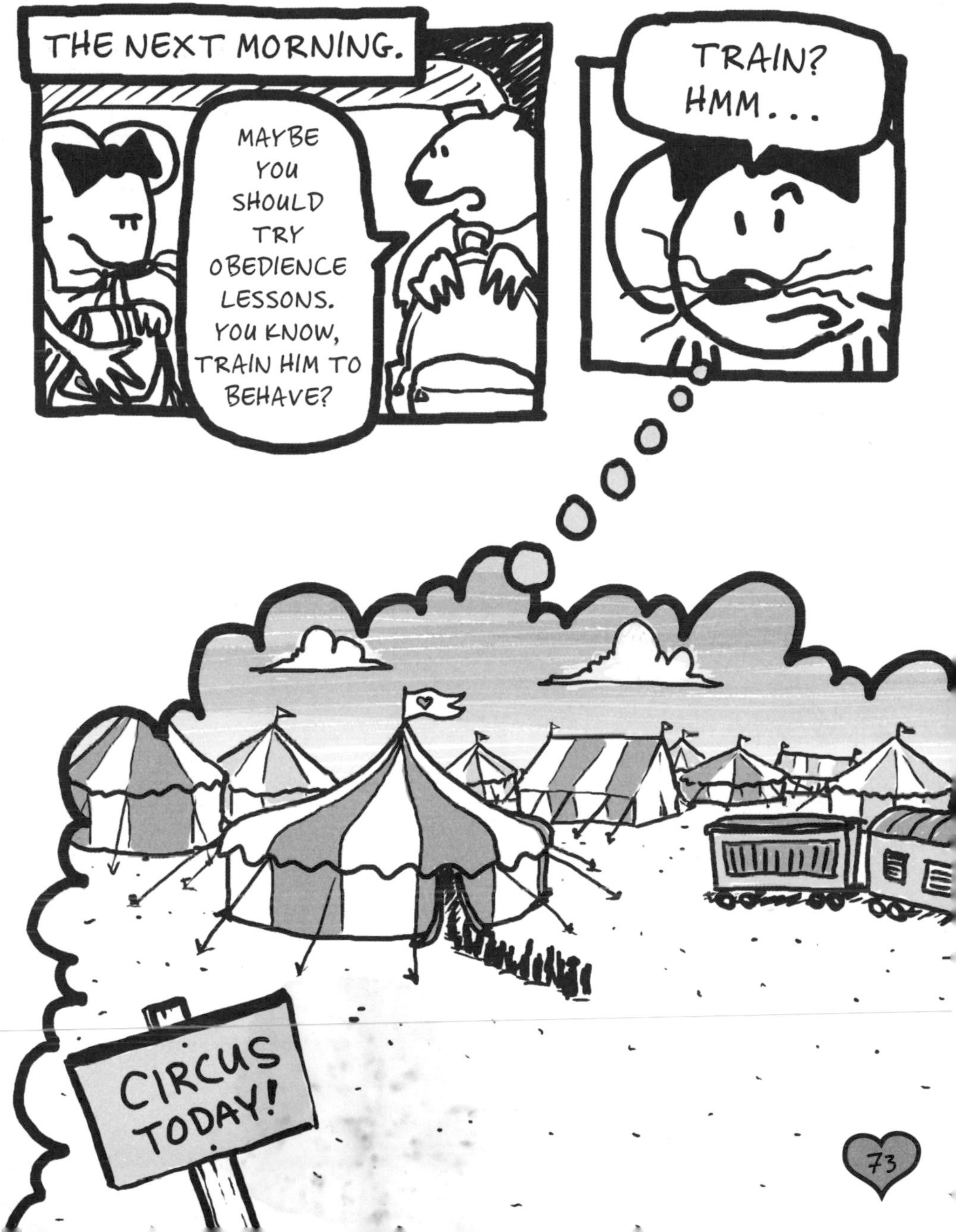
THE NEXT MORNING.
MAYBE YOU SHOULD TRY OBEDIENCE LESSONS. YOU KNOW, TRAIN HIM TO BEHAVE?
TRAIN? HMM...
CIRCUS TODAY!

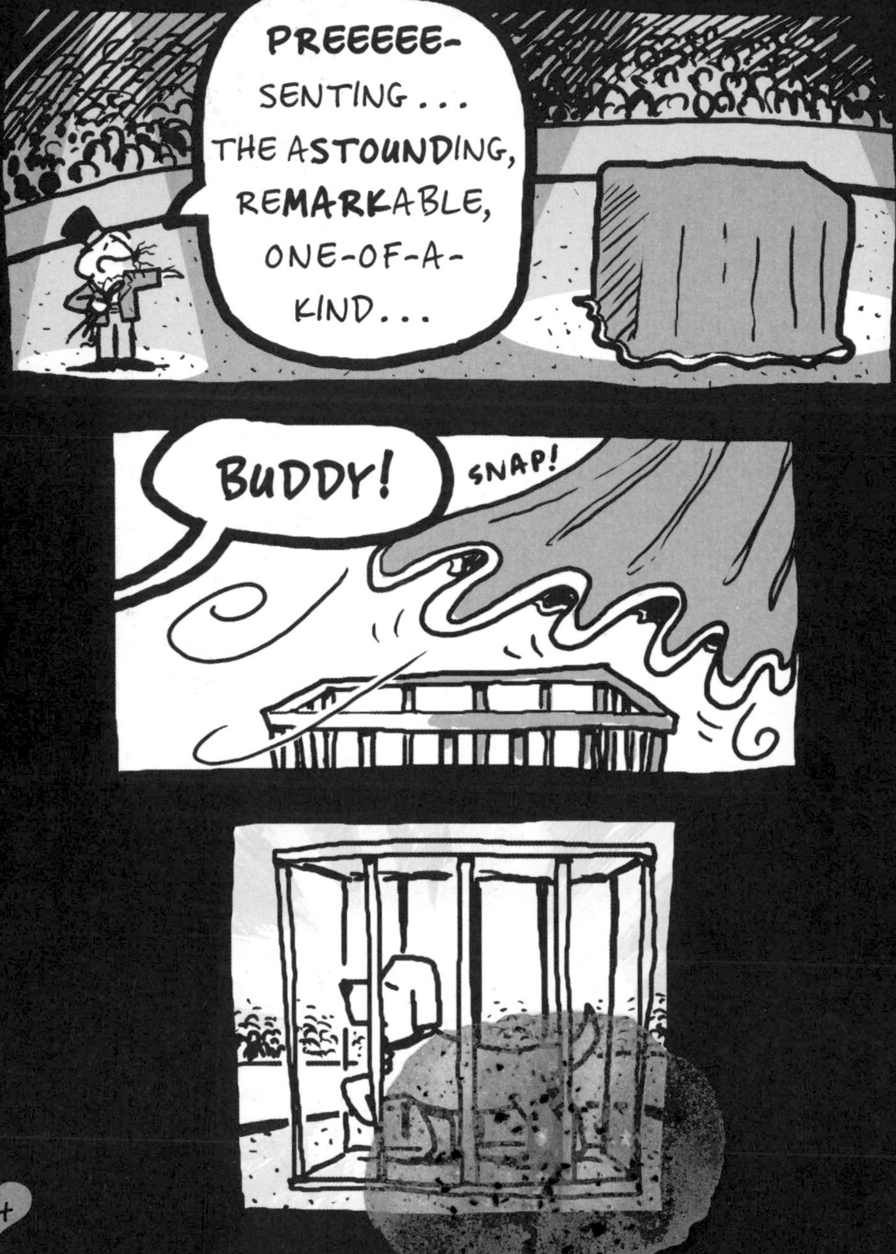
PREEEEE-SENTING . . . THE ASTOUNDING, REMARKABLE, ONE-OF-A-KIND . . .
BUDDY!
SNAP!

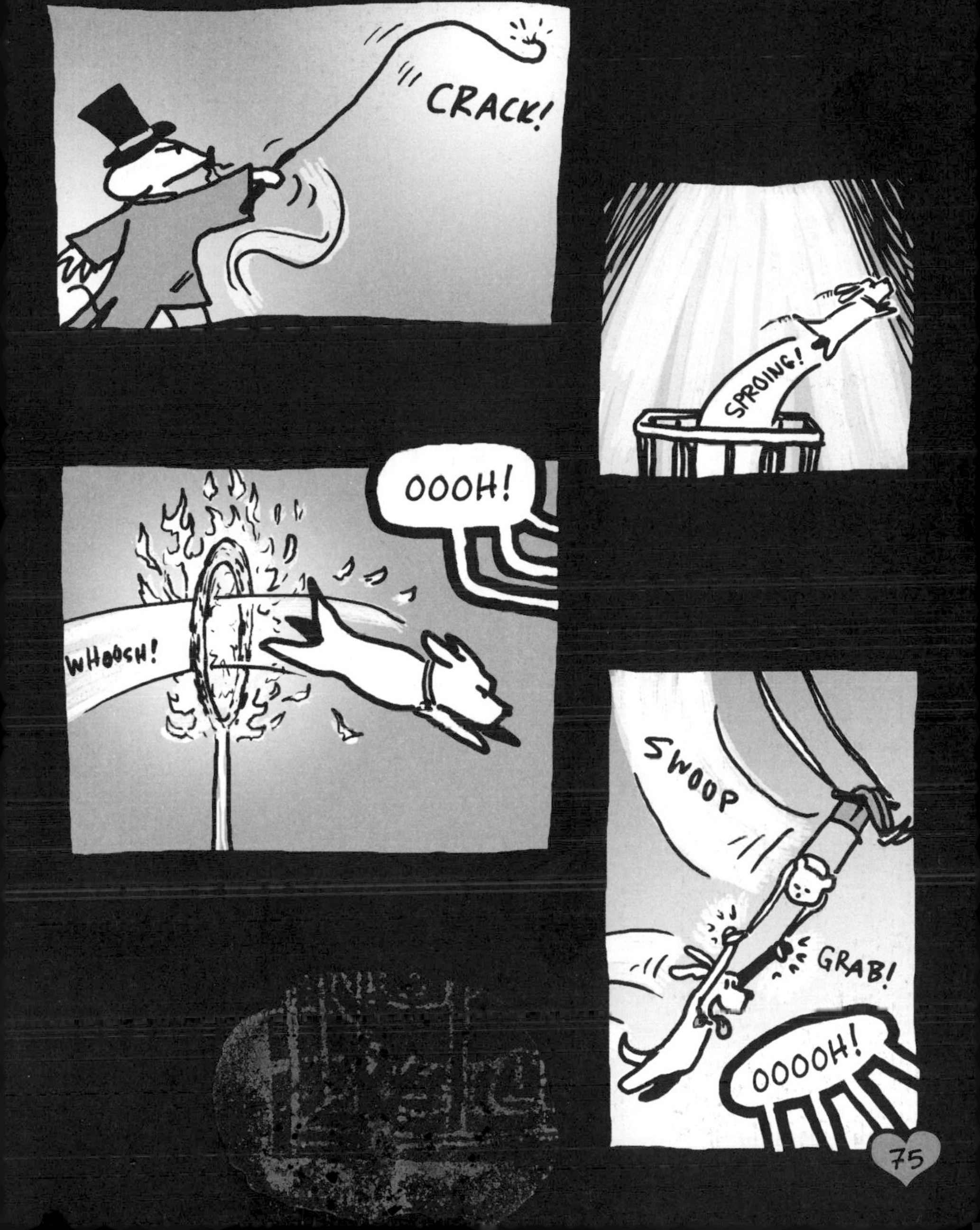
CRACK!
SPROING!
OOOH!
WHOOSH!
SWOOP
GRAB!
OOOOH!

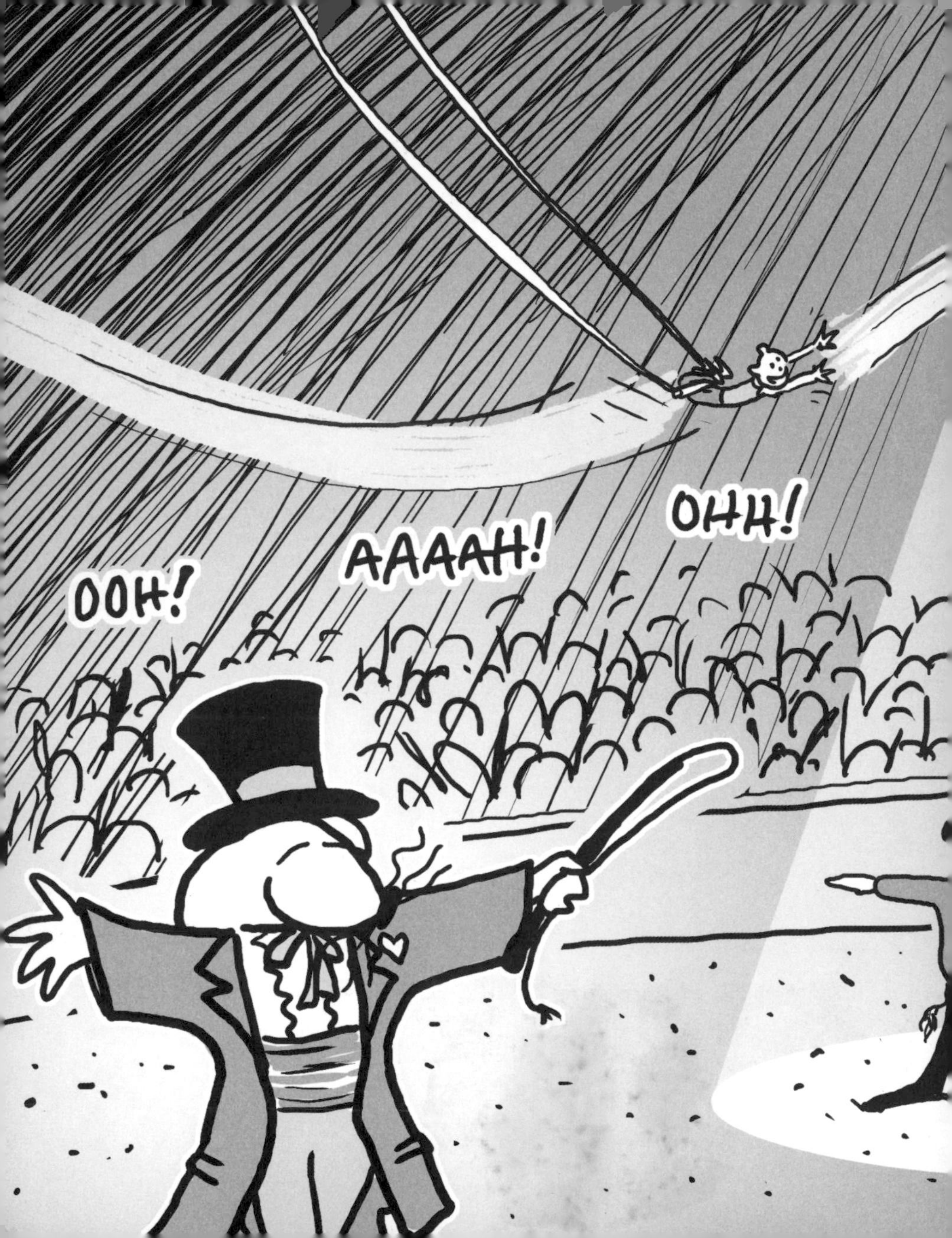
OOH!
AAAAH!
OHH!

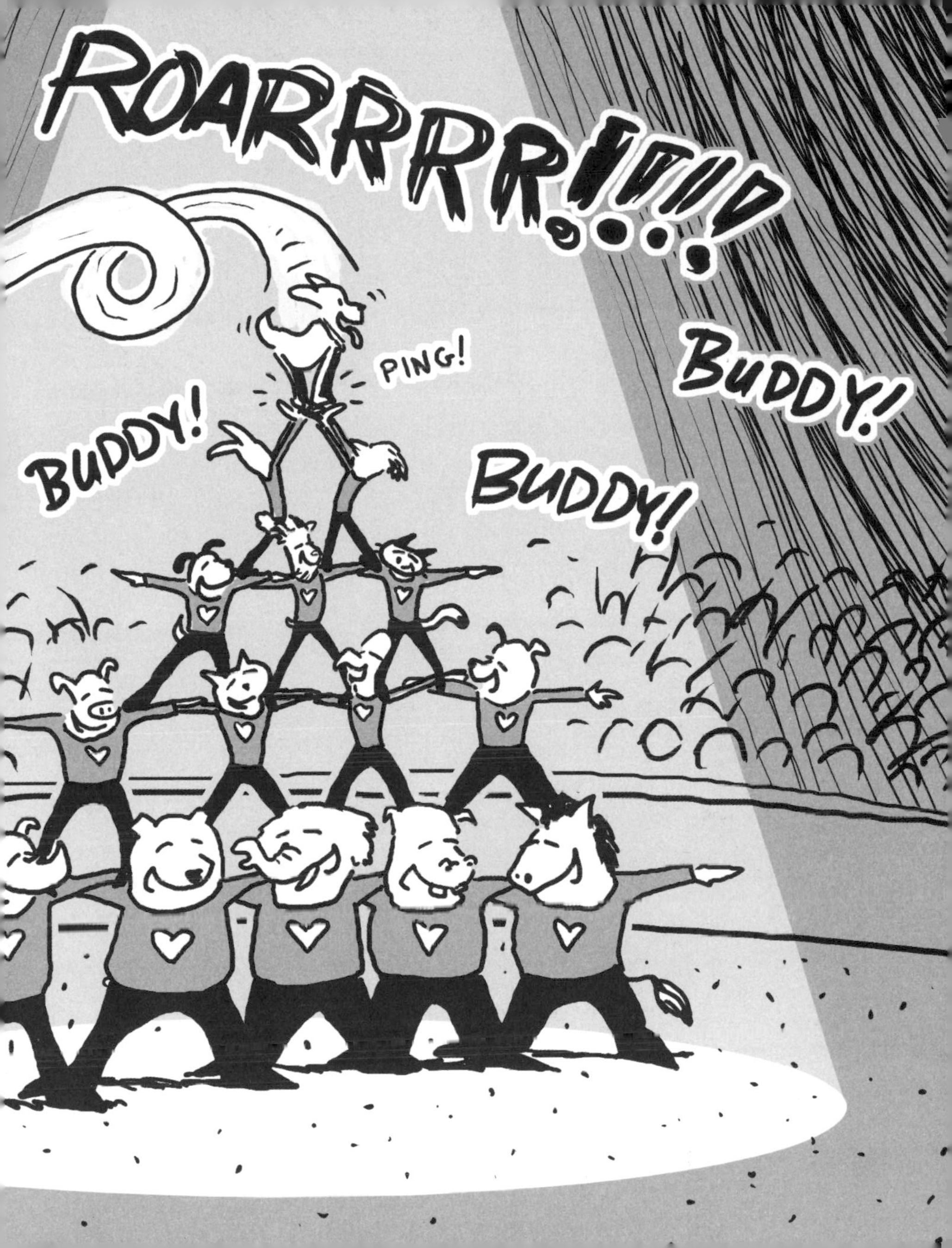
ROARRRRR!!!!!
PING!
BUDDY!
BUDDY!
BUDDY!

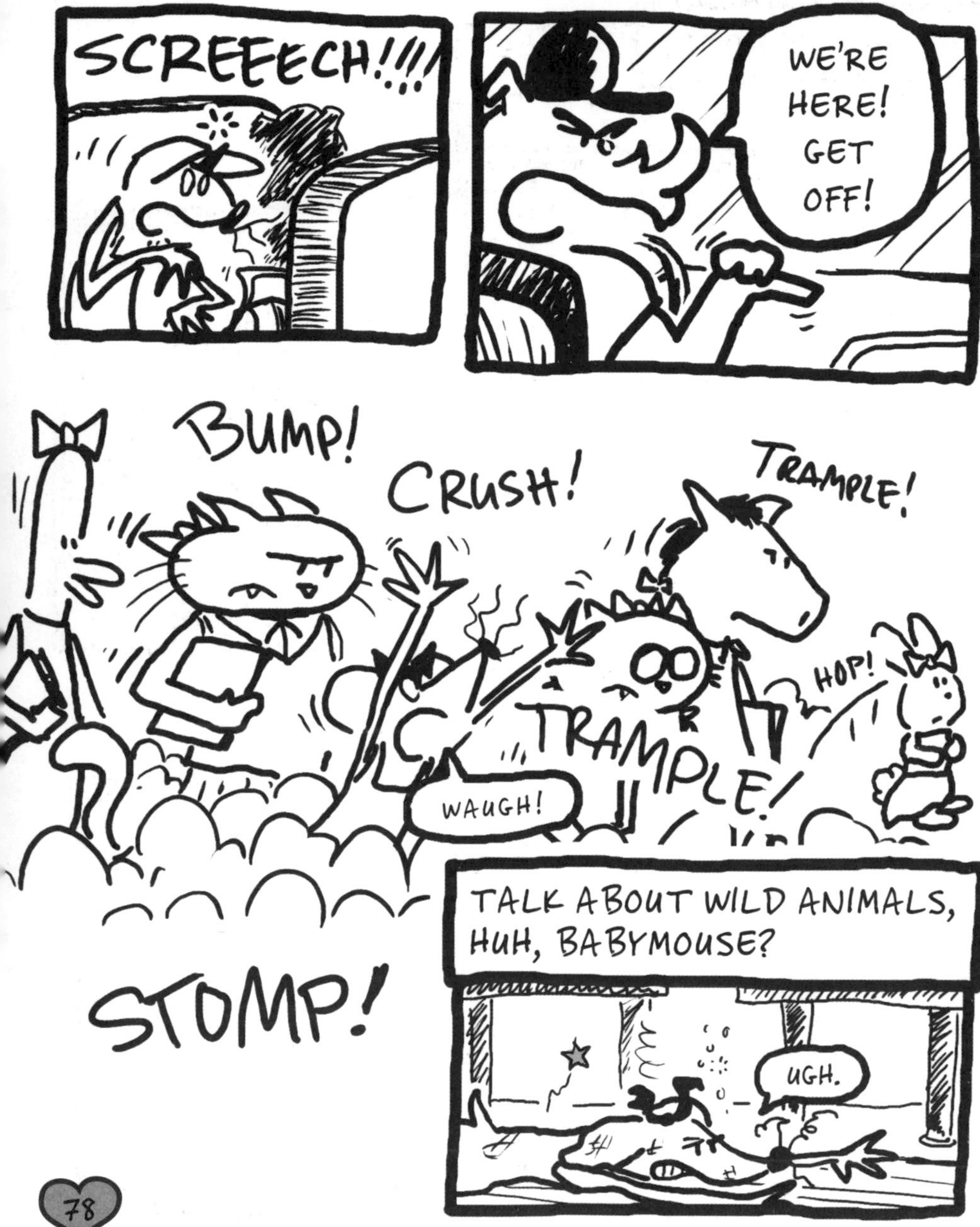
SCREEECH!!!!
WE'RE HERE! GET OFF!
BUMP!
CRUSH!
TRAMPLE!
HOP!
TRAMPLE!
WAUGH!
STOMP!
TALK ABOUT WILD ANIMALS, HUH, BABYMOUSE?
UGH.

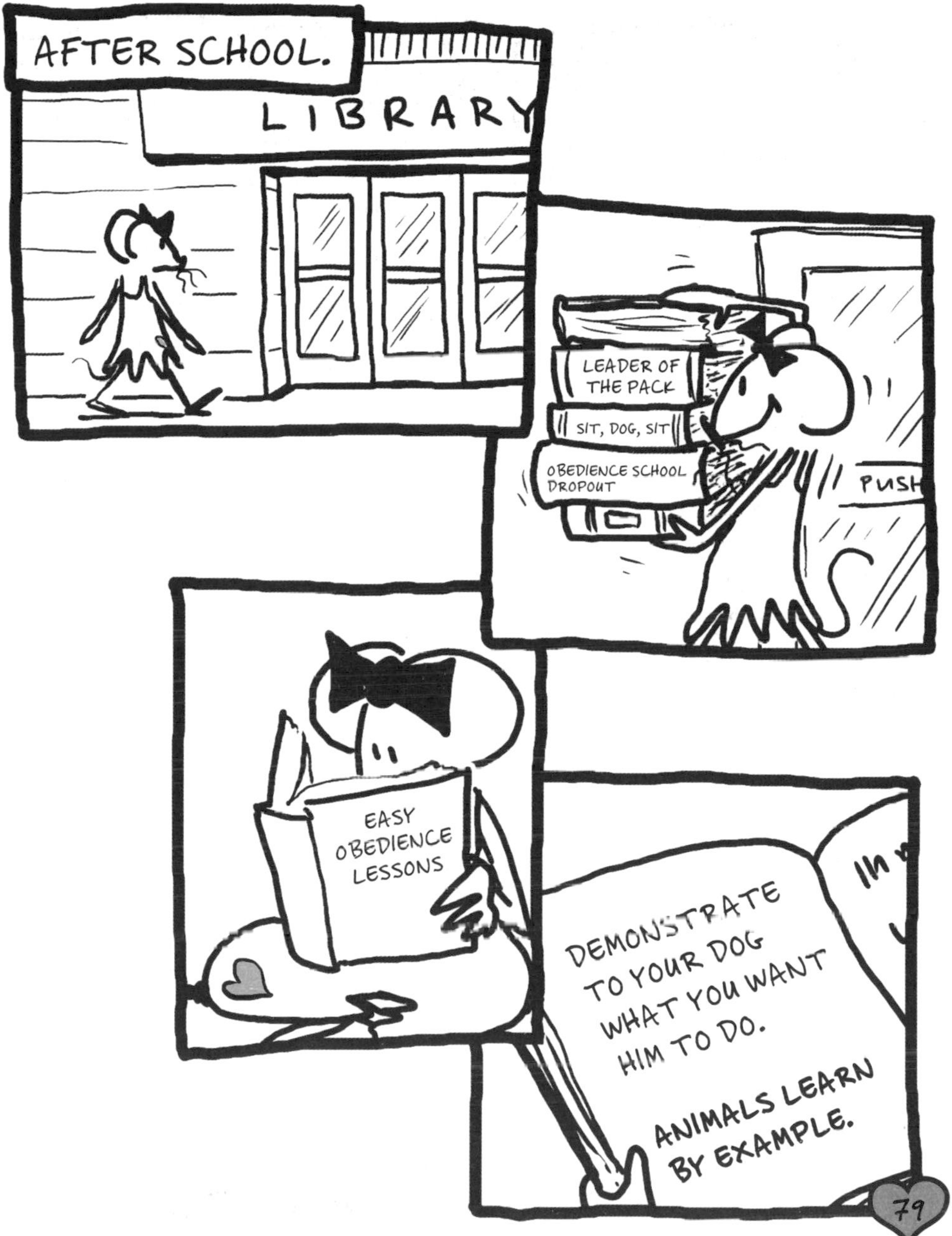
AFTER SCHOOL.
LIBRARY
LEADER OF THE PACK
SIT, DOG, SIT
OBEDIENCE SCHOOL DROPOUT
PUSH
EASY OBEDIENCE LESSONS
DEMONSTRATE TO YOUR DOG WHAT YOU WANT HIM TO DO.
ANIMALS LEARN BY EXAMPLE.

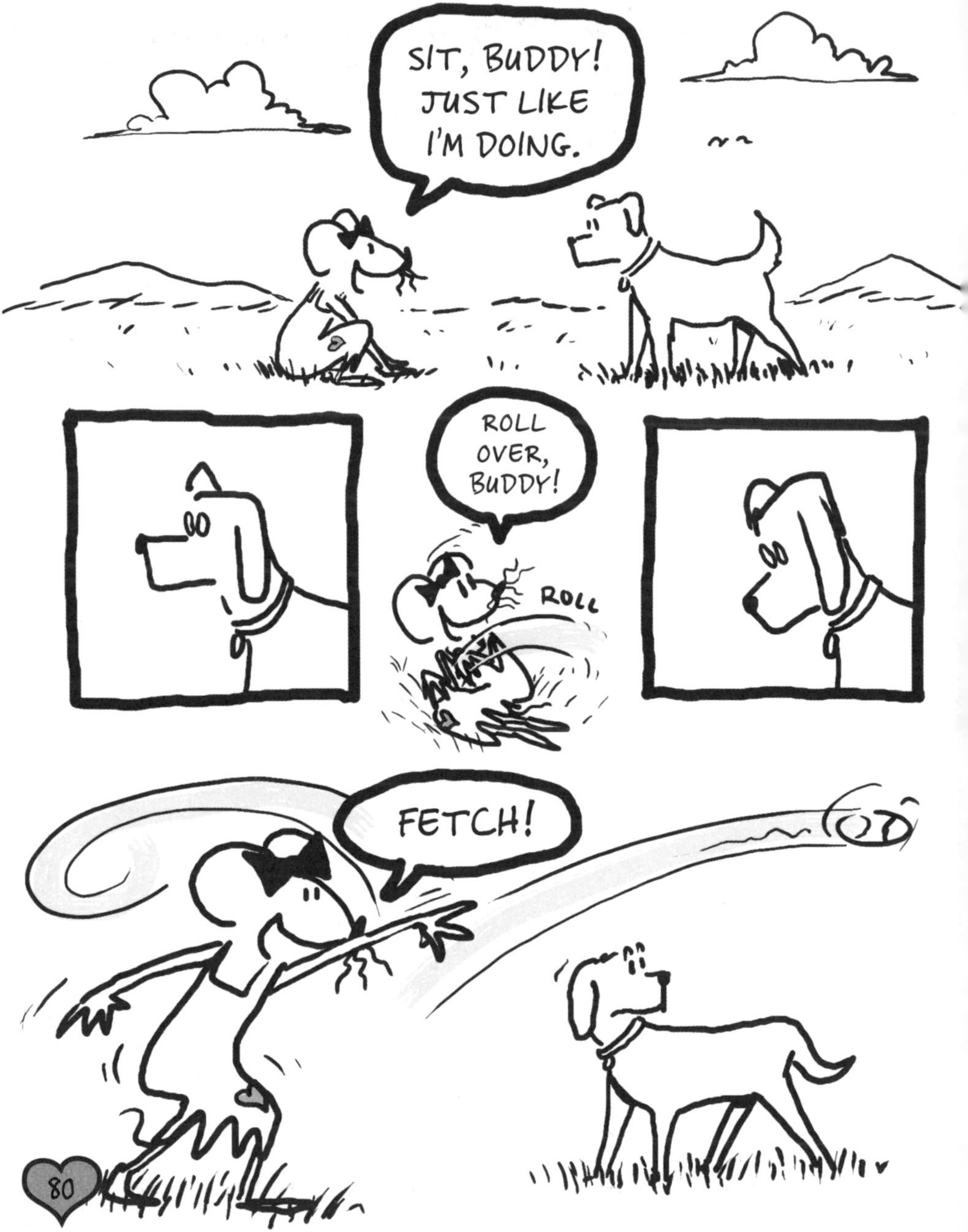
SIT, BUDDY! JUST LIKE I'M DOING.
ROLL OVER, BUDDY!
ROLL
FETCH!

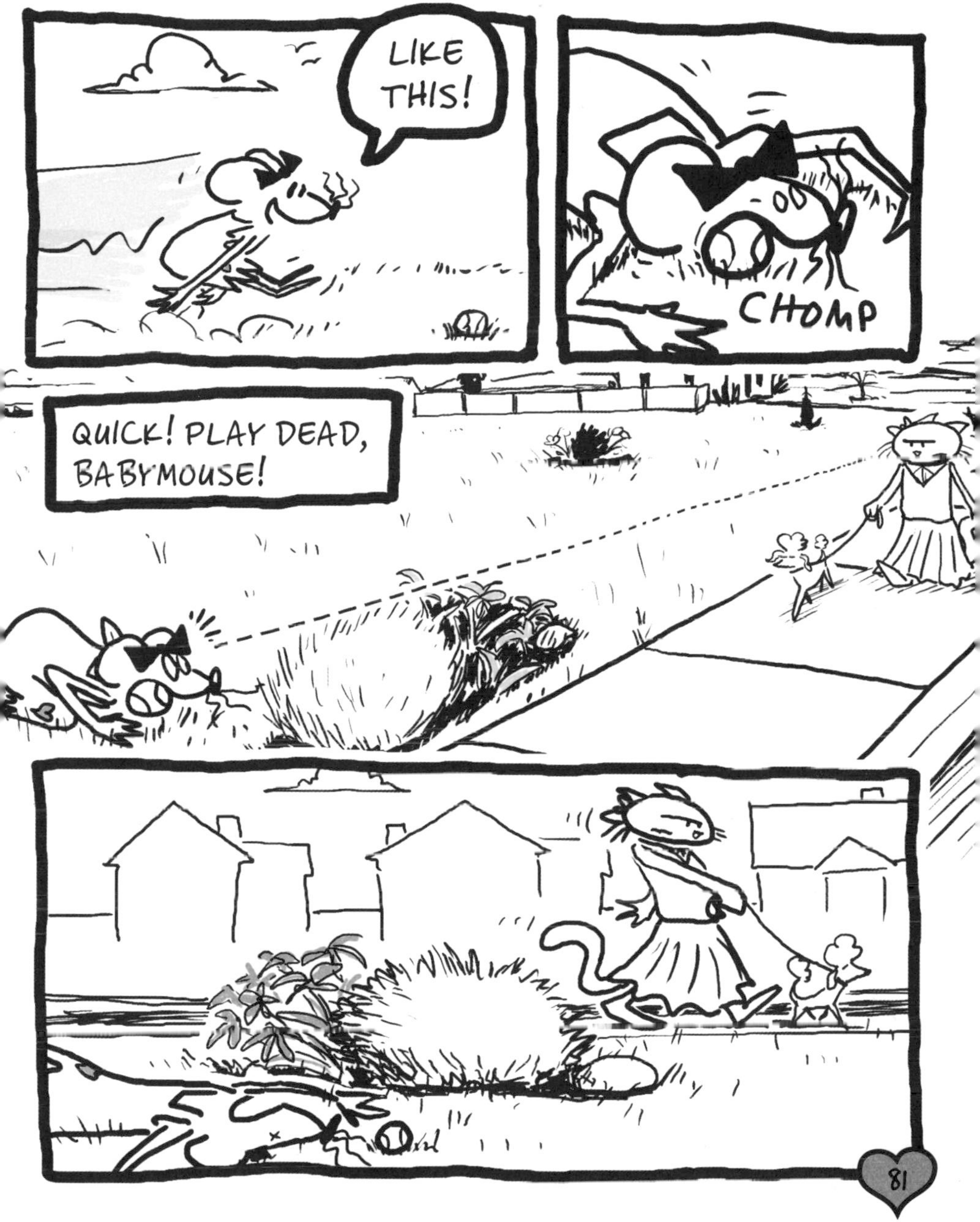

LIKE THIS!
CHOMP
QUICK! PLAY DEAD, BABYMOUSE!

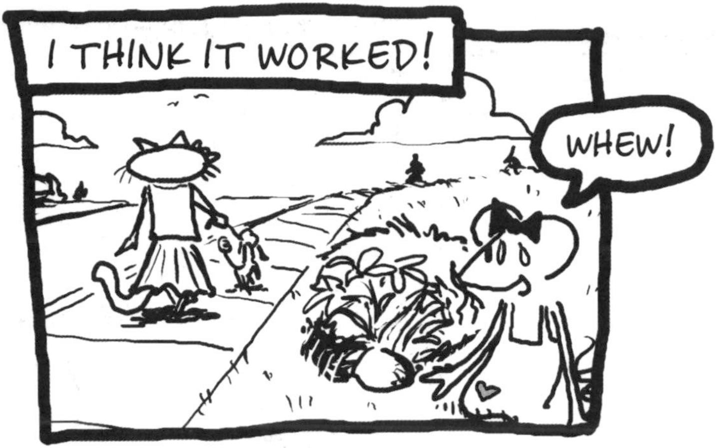
I THINK IT WORKED!
WHEW!

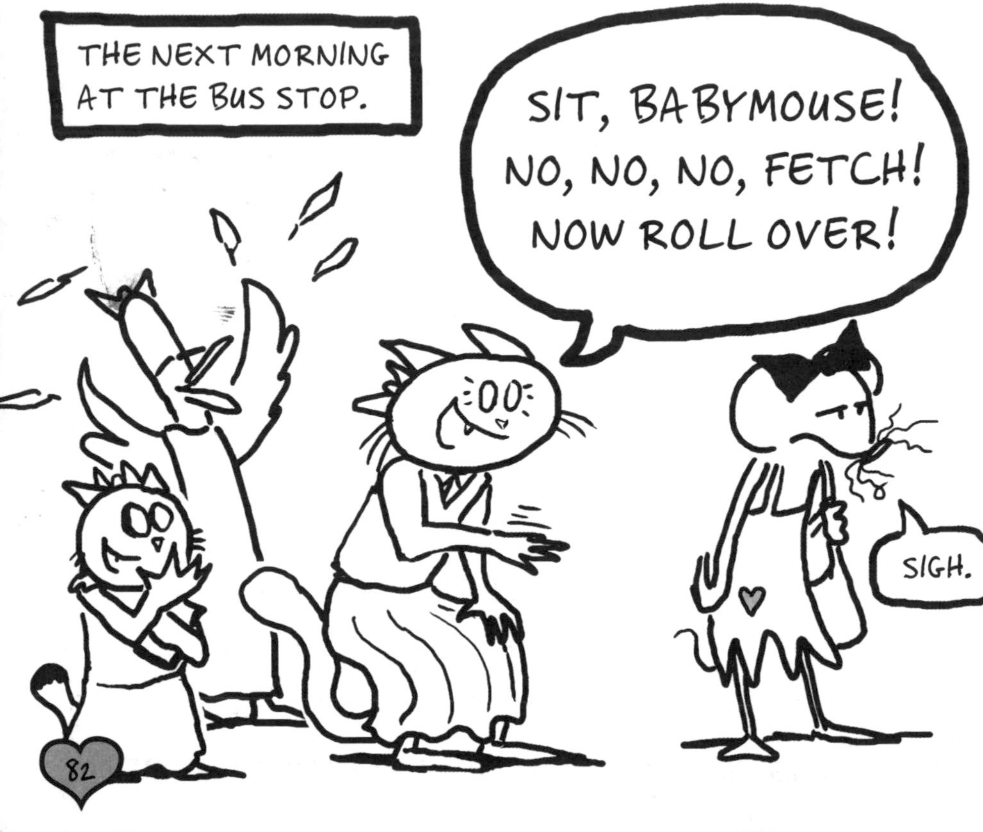
THE NEXT MORNING AT THE BUS STOP.
SIT, BABYMOUSE! NO, NO, NO, FETCH! NOW ROLL OVER!
SIGH.

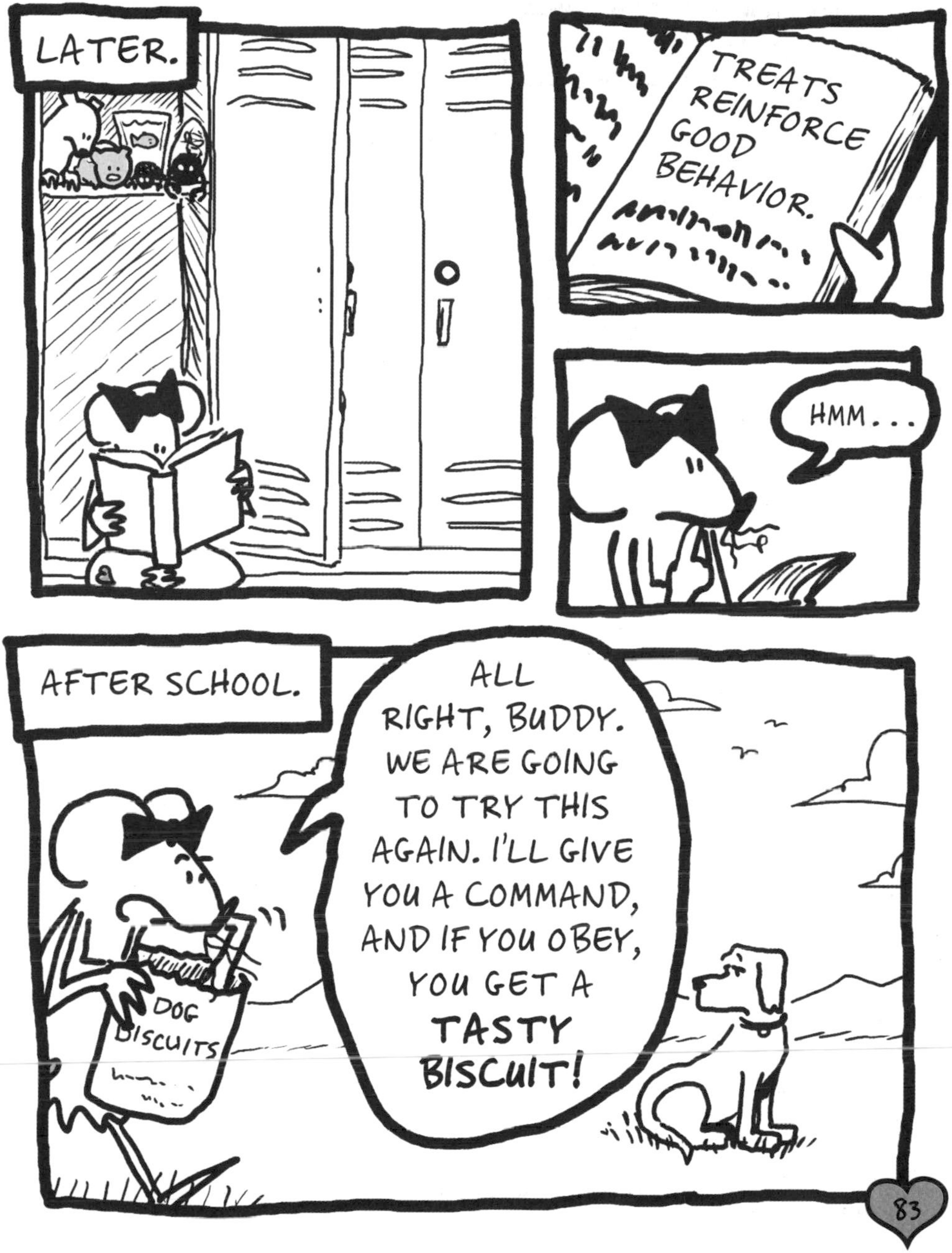

LATER.
TREATS REINFORCE GOOD BEHAVIOR.
HMM...
AFTER SCHOOL.
ALL RIGHT, BUDDY. WE ARE GOING TO TRY THIS AGAIN. I'LL GIVE YOU A COMMAND, AND IF YOU OBEY, YOU GET A **TASTY BISCUIT!**
DOG BISCUITS

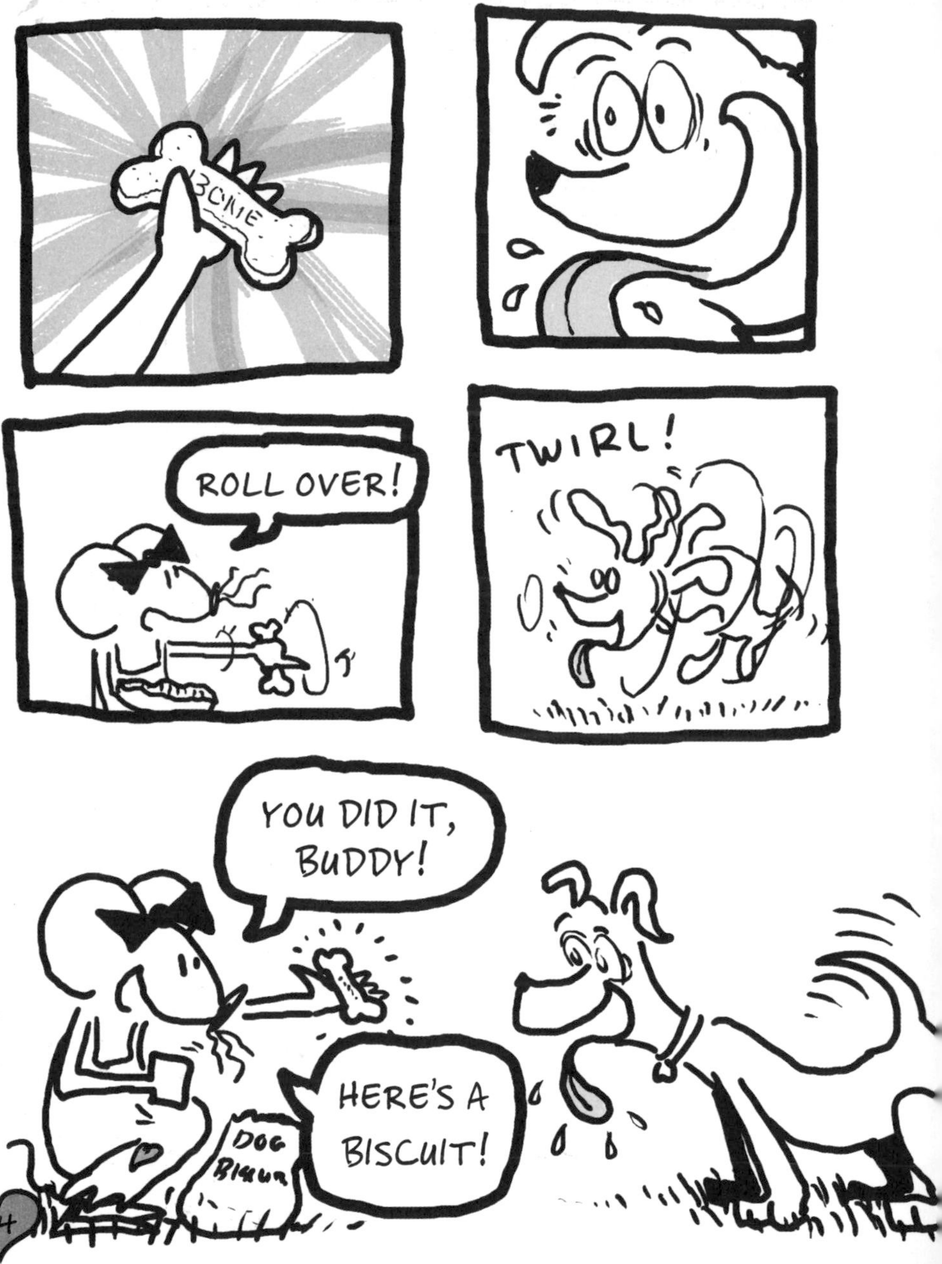
BONE
ROLL OVER!
TWIRL!
YOU DID IT, BUDDY!
HERE'S A BISCUIT!
DOG

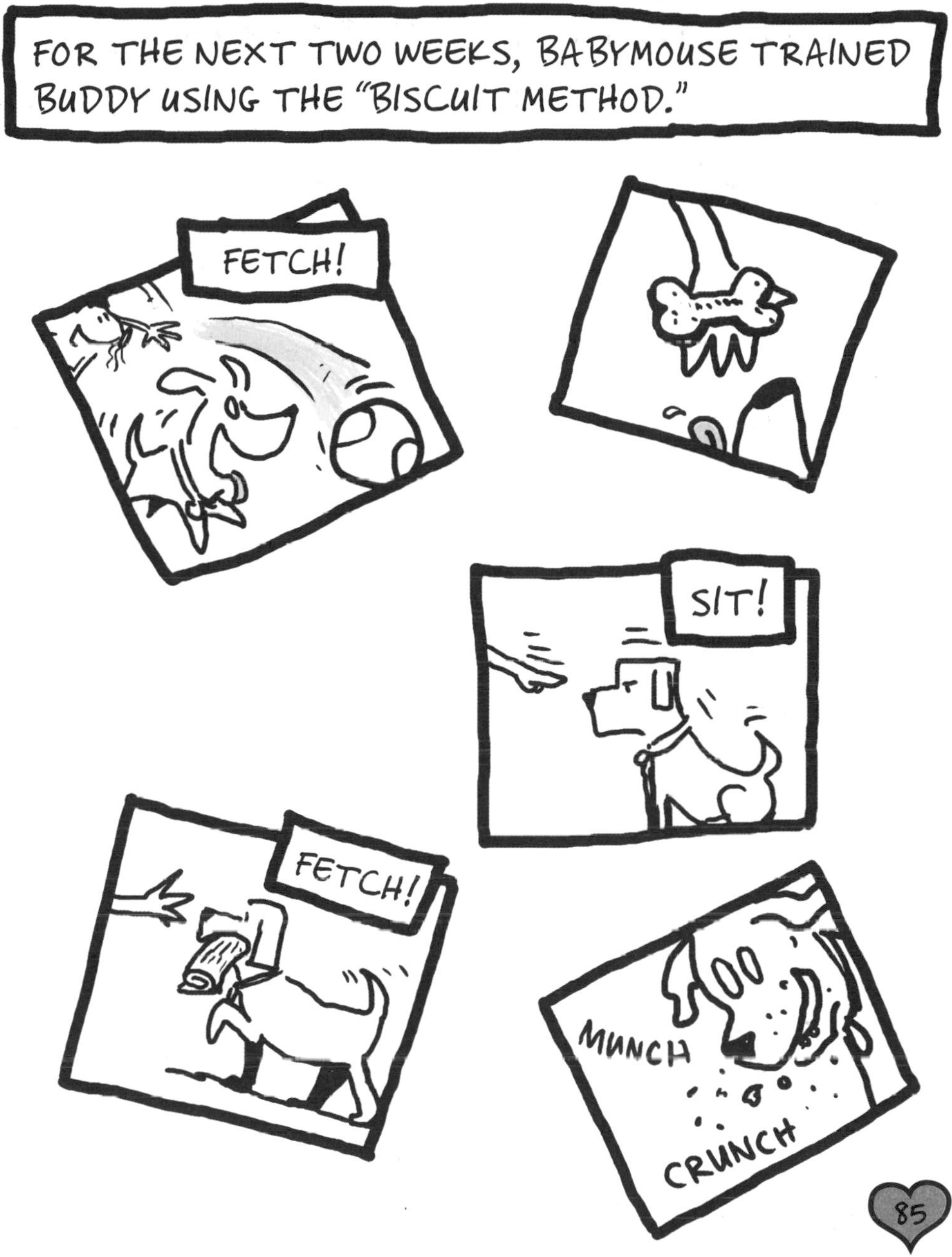
FOR THE NEXT TWO WEEKS, BABYMOUSE TRAINED BUDDY USING THE "BISCUIT METHOD."
FETCH!
SIT!
FETCH!
MUNCH
CRUNCH

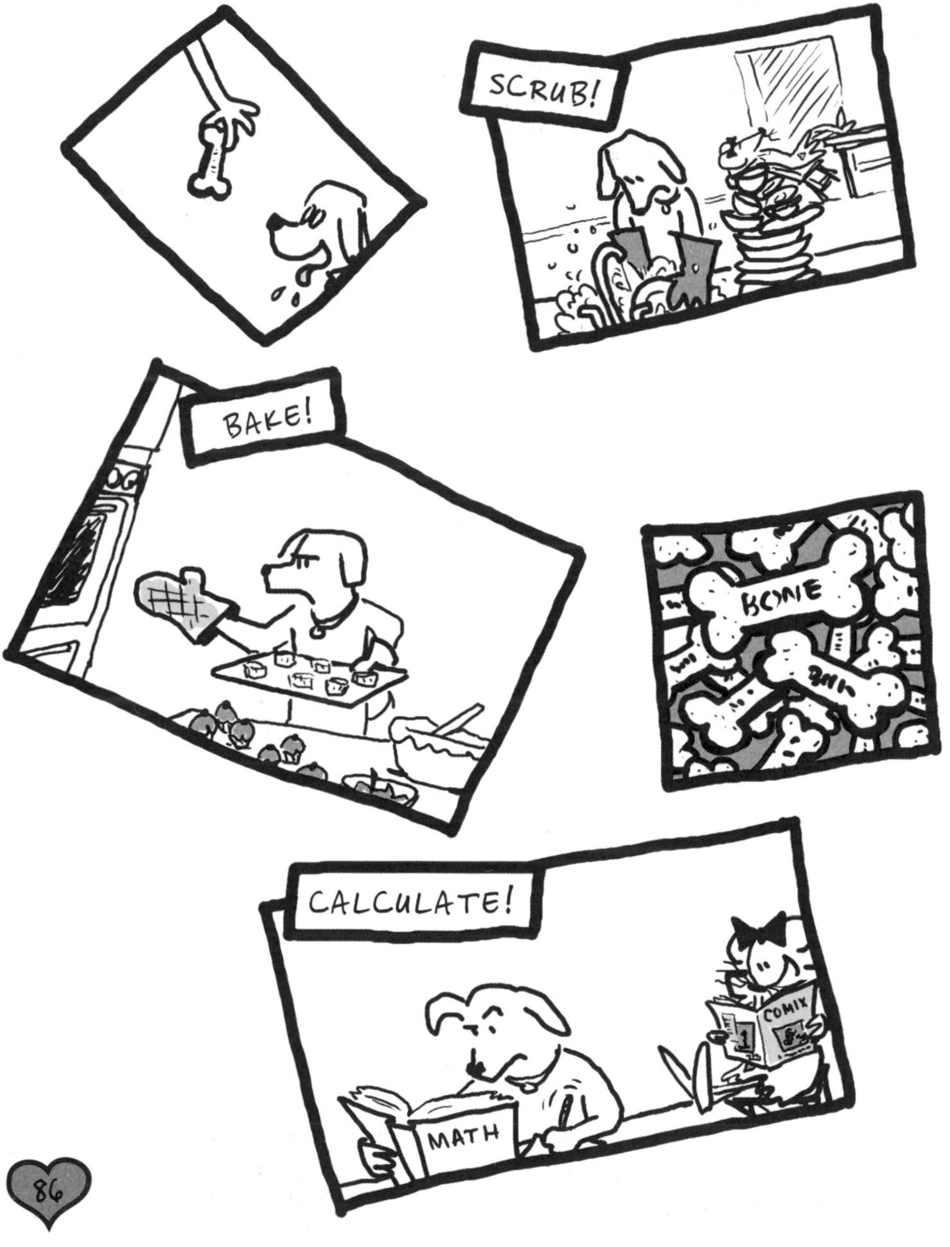
SCRUB!
BAKE!
BONE
CALCULATE!
COMIX
MATH

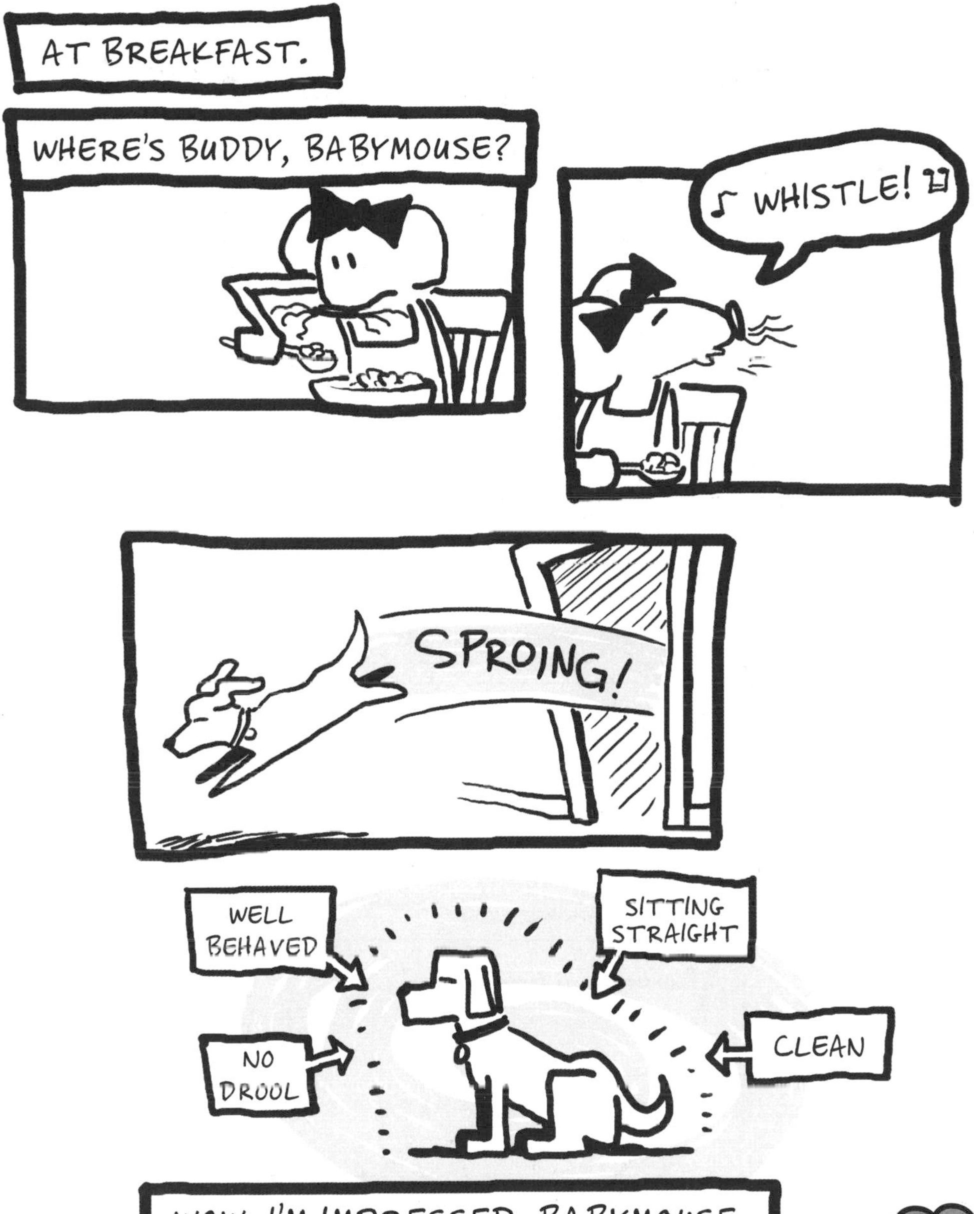
AT BREAKFAST.
WHERE'S BUDDY, BABYMOUSE?
WHISTLE!
SPROING!
WELL BEHAVED
SITTING STRAIGHT
NO DROOL
CLEAN
WOW. I'M IMPRESSED, BABYMOUSE.

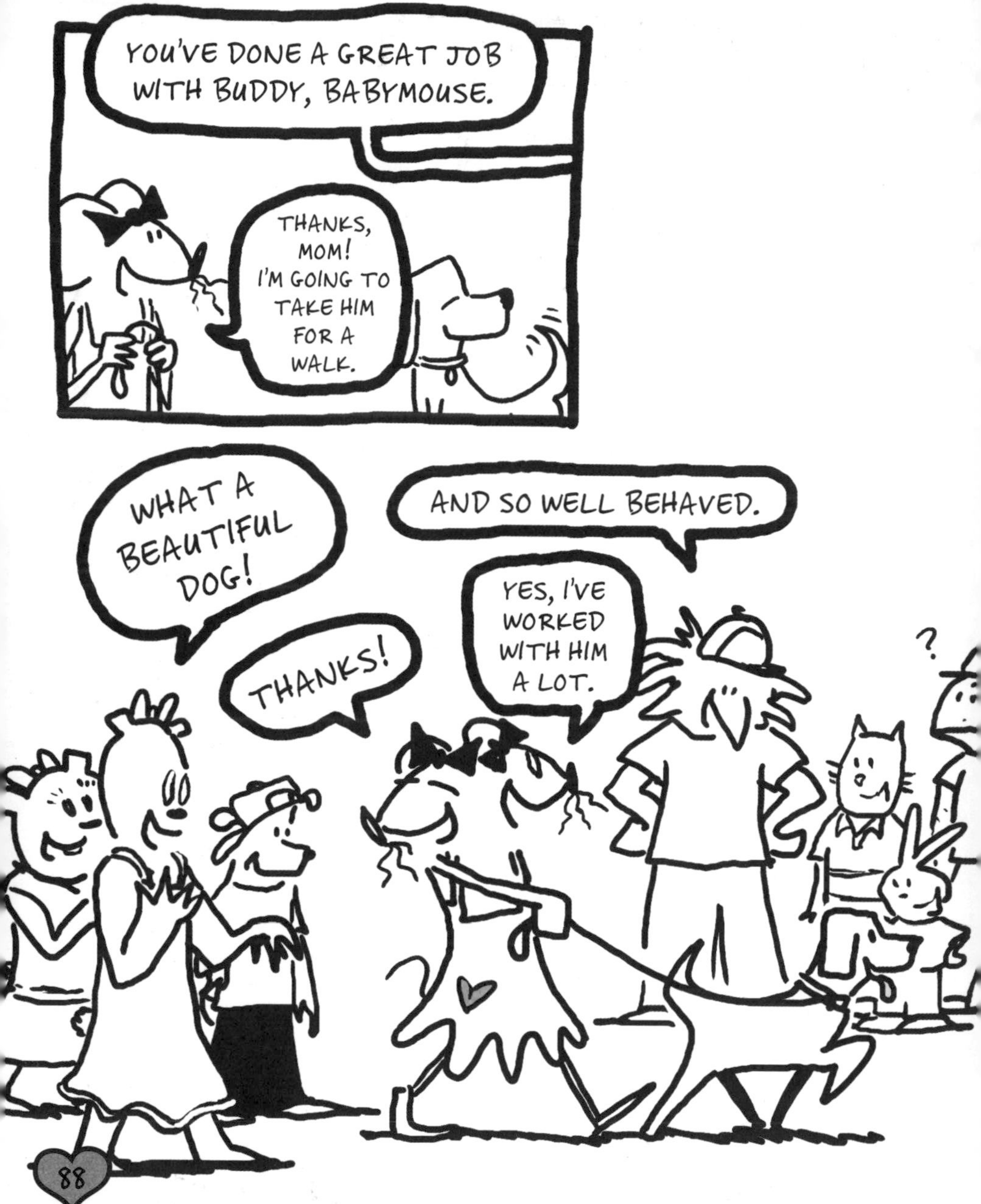
YOU'VE DONE A GREAT JOB WITH BUDDY, BABYMOUSE.
THANKS, MOM! I'M GOING TO TAKE HIM FOR A WALK.
WHAT A BEAUTIFUL DOG!
AND SO WELL BEHAVED.
THANKS!
YES, I'VE WORKED WITH HIM A LOT.
?

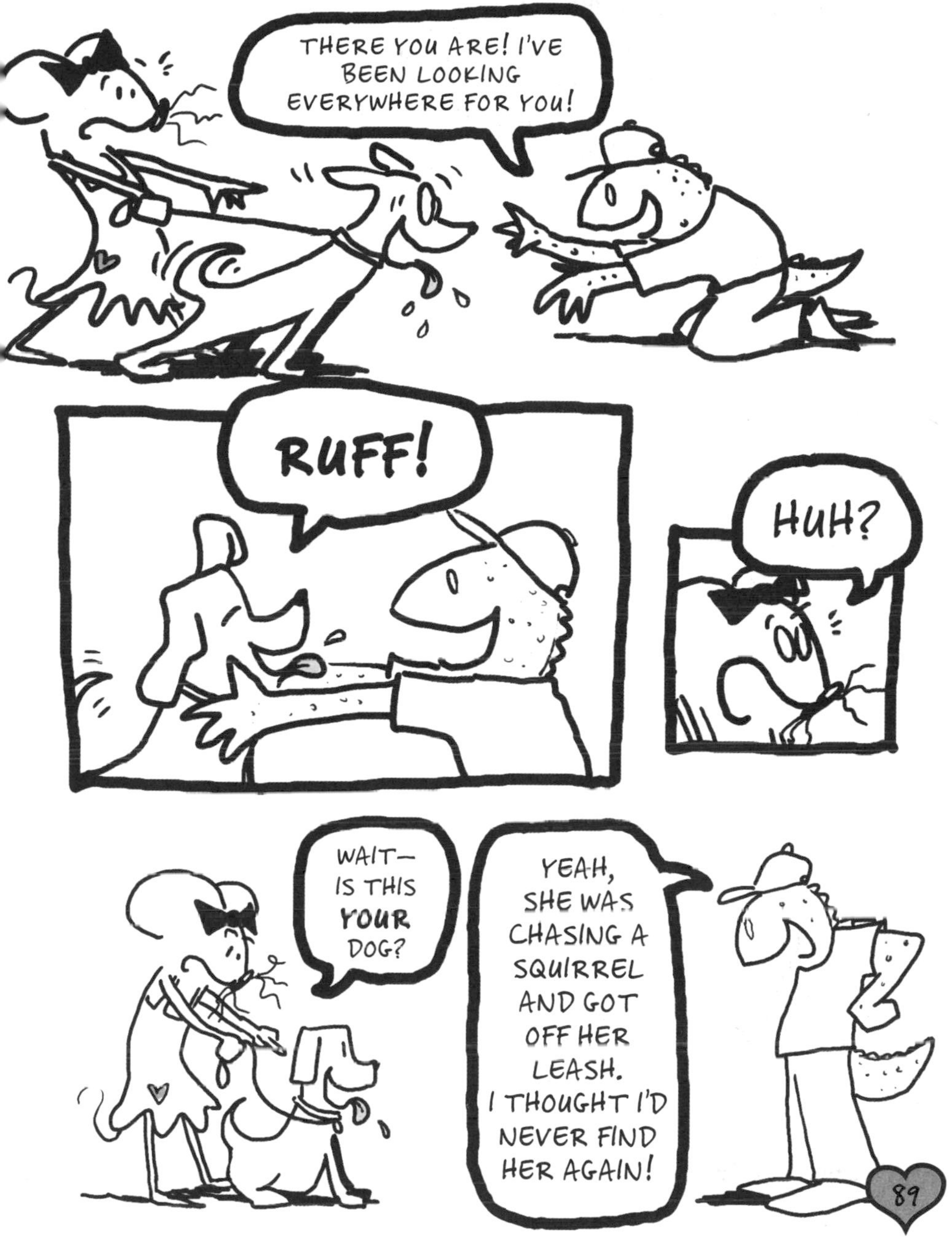
THERE YOU ARE! I'VE BEEN LOOKING EVERYWHERE FOR YOU!
RUFF!
HUH?
WAIT— IS THIS YOUR DOG?
YEAH, SHE WAS CHASING A SQUIRREL AND GOT OFF HER LEASH. I THOUGHT I'D NEVER FIND HER AGAIN!

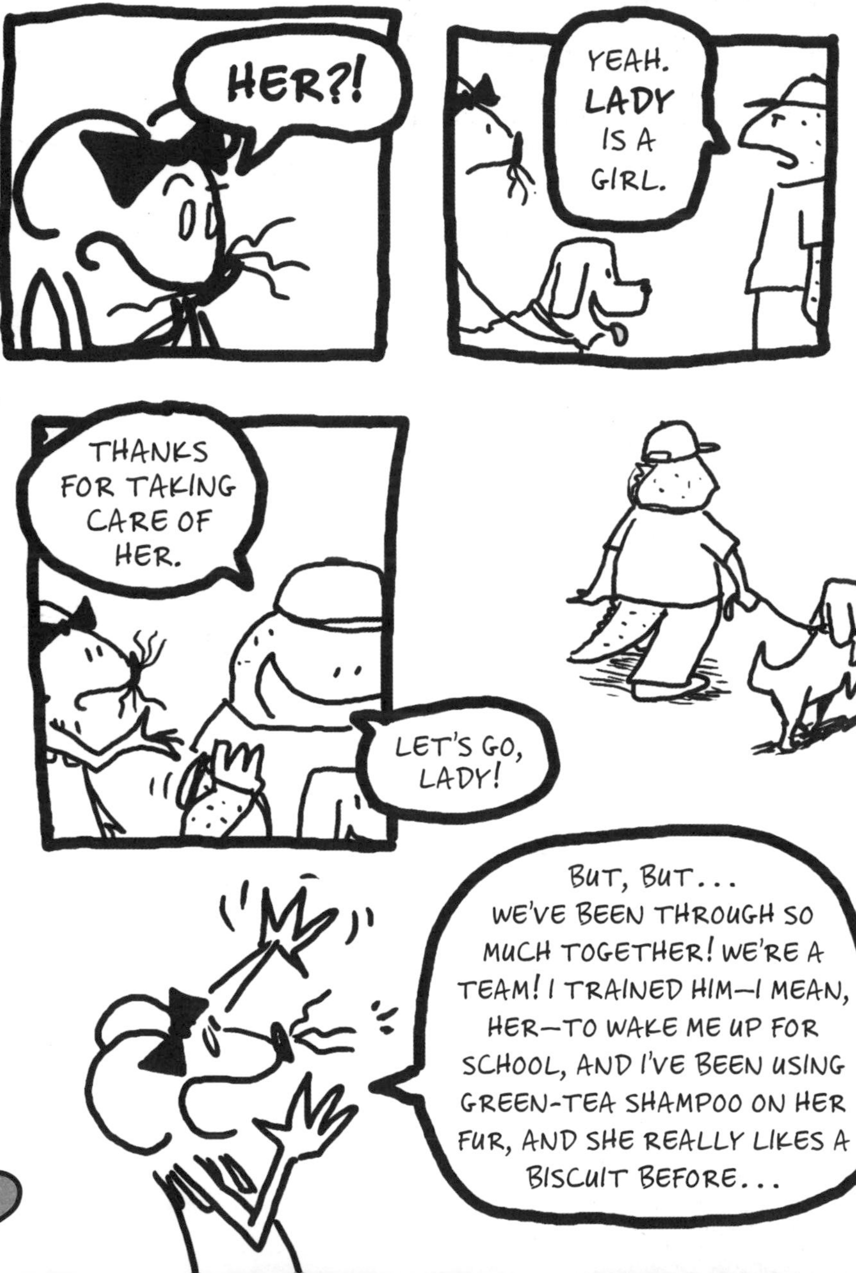
HER?!
YEAH. LADY IS A GIRL.
THANKS FOR TAKING CARE OF HER.
LET'S GO, LADY!
BUT, BUT... WE'VE BEEN THROUGH SO MUCH TOGETHER! WE'RE A TEAM! I TRAINED HIM—I MEAN, HER—TO WAKE ME UP FOR SCHOOL, AND I'VE BEEN USING GREEN-TEA SHAMPOO ON HER FUR, AND SHE REALLY LIKES A BISCUIT BEFORE...

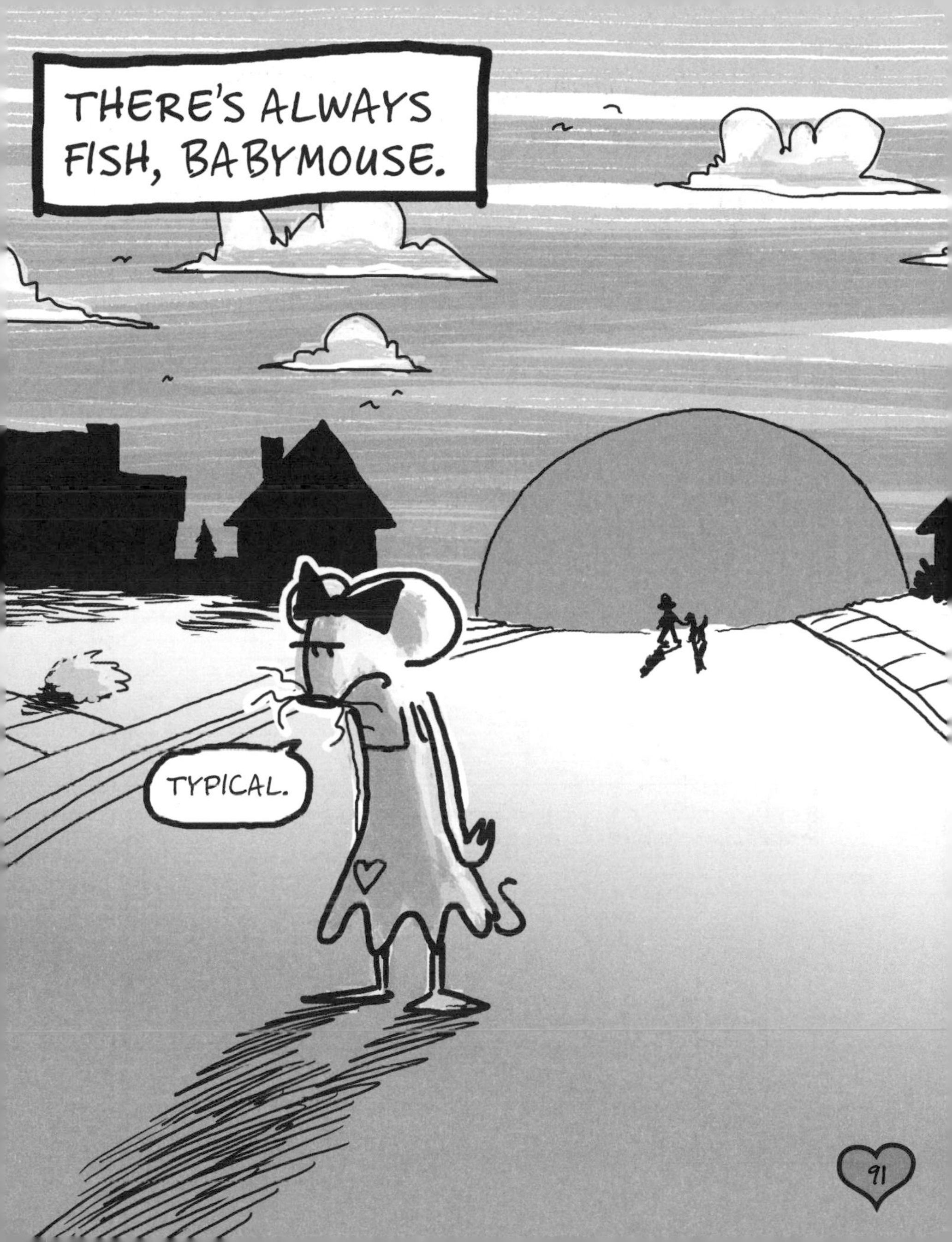
THERE'S ALWAYS FISH, BABYMOUSE.
TYPICAL.

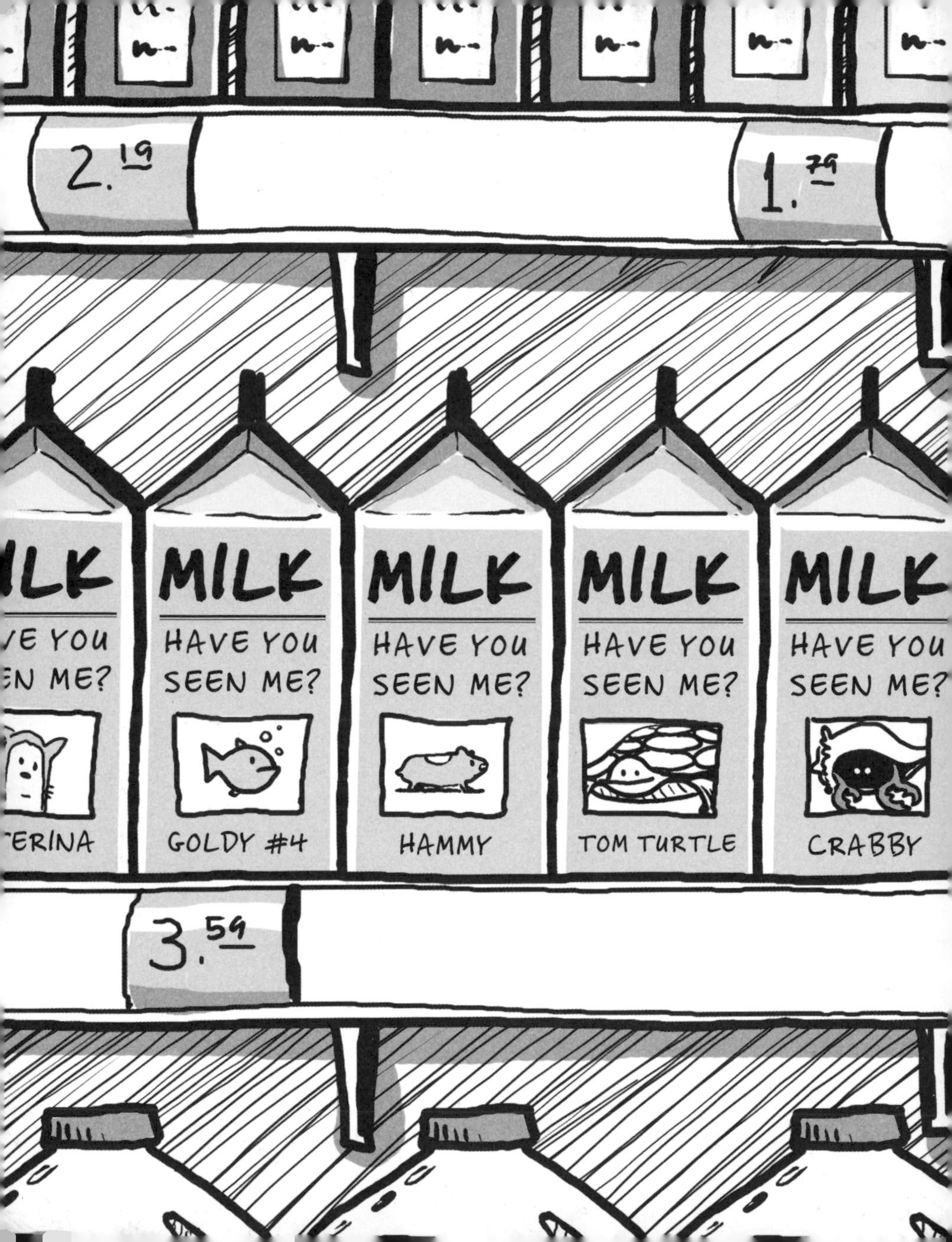
2.19
1.79
ILK
VE YOU
EN ME?
ERINA
MILK
HAVE YOU
SEEN ME?
GOLDY #4
MILK
HAVE YOU
SEEN ME?
HAMMY
MILK
HAVE YOU
SEEN ME?
TOM TURTLE
MILK
HAVE YOU
SEEN ME?
CRABBY
3.59

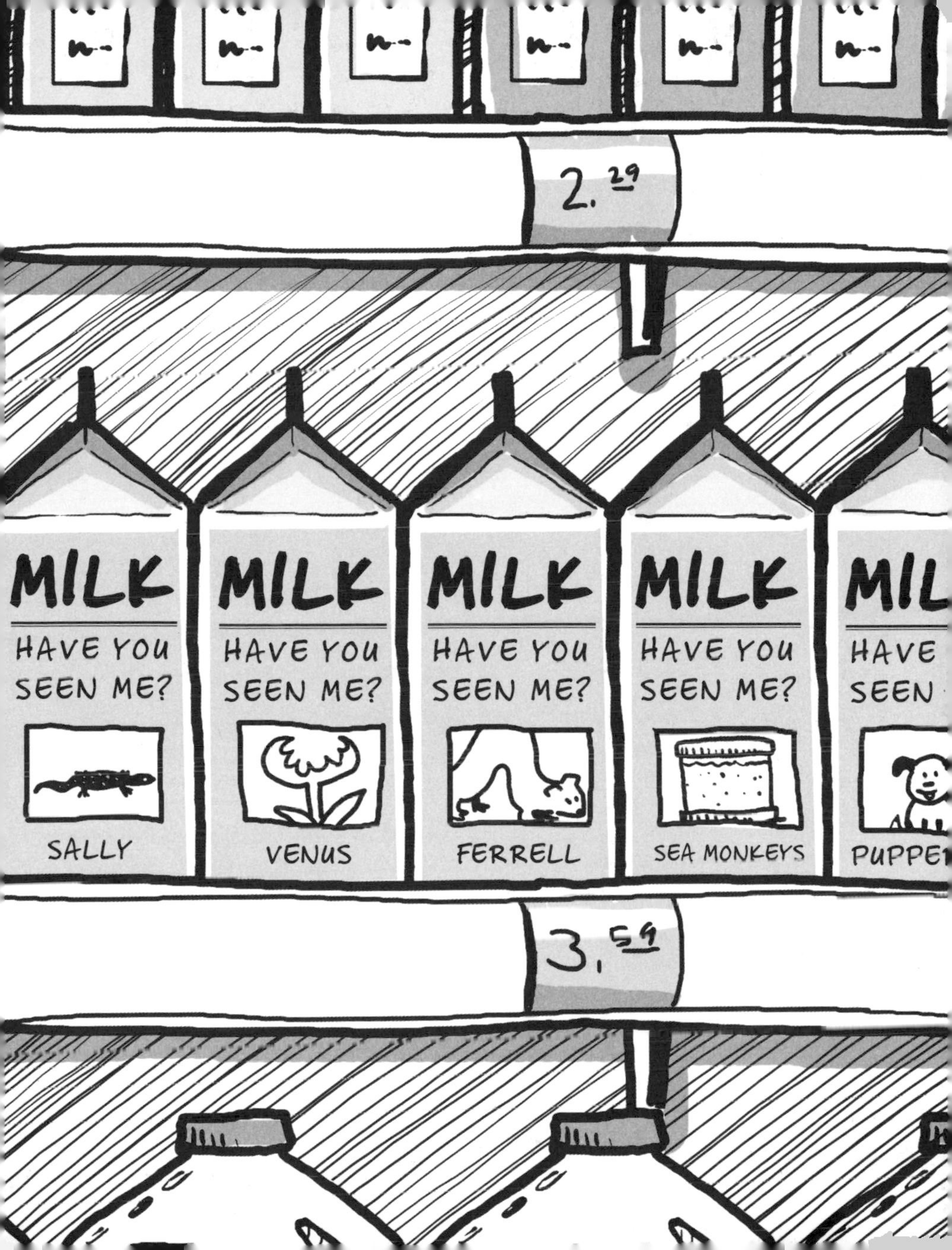
2.29
MILK
HAVE YOU SEEN ME?
SALLY
MILK
HAVE YOU SEEN ME?
VENUS
MILK
HAVE YOU SEEN ME?
FERRELL
MILK
HAVE YOU SEEN ME?
SEA MONKEYS
3.59

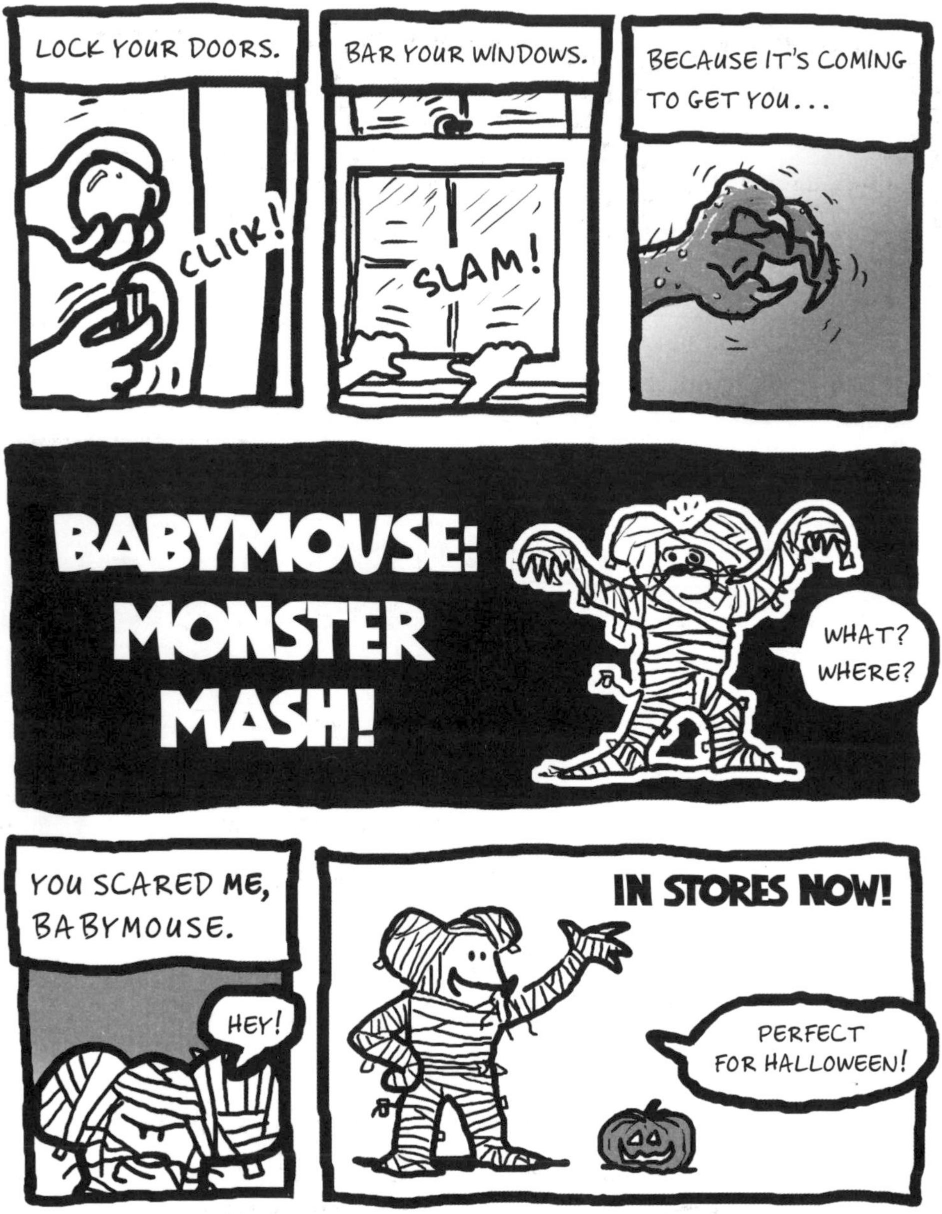

LOCK YOUR DOORS.
CLICK!
BAR YOUR WINDOWS.
SLAM!
BECAUSE IT'S COMING TO GET YOU...
BABYMOUSE: MONSTER MASH!
WHAT? WHERE?
YOU SCARED ME, BABYMOUSE.
HEY!
IN STORES NOW!
PERFECT FOR HALLOWEEN!

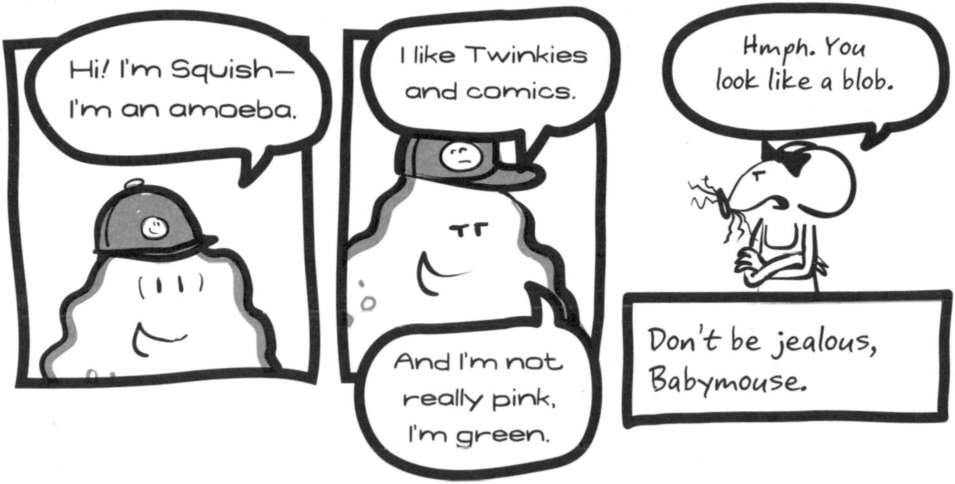
Hi! I'm Squish—
I'm an amoeba.
I like Twinkies
and comics.
And I'm not
really pink,
I'm green.
Hmph. You
look like a blob.
Don't be jealous,
Babymouse.

READ ABOUT SQUISH'S AMAZING ADVENTURES IN:

#1 SQUISH: Super Amoeba

#2 SQUISH: Brave New Pond

#3 SQUISH: The Power of the Parasite

#4 SQUISH: Captain Disaster

#5 SQUISH: Game On!

AND COMING SOON:

#6 SQUISH: Fear the Amoeba

★ "IF EVER A NEW SERIES DESERVED TO GO VIRAL, THIS ONE DOES."
—*KIRKUS REVIEWS*, STARRED

If you like Babymouse,
you'll love these other great books
by Jennifer L. Holm!

THE BOSTON JANE TRILOGY
EIGHTH GRADE IS MAKING ME SICK
MIDDLE SCHOOL IS WORSE THAN MEATLOAF
OUR ONLY MAY AMELIA
PENNY FROM HEAVEN
TURTLE IN PARADISE

THEY'RE REALLY GOOD! TRUST ME!